Press Three for Goodbye

To Rachel,
I hope you enjoy the read.
All the best,
Diane. x.

Diane Need

Diane Need.

Press Three for Goodbye © 2017 by Diane Need.

All rights reserved

No part of this book may be reproduced, stored or introduced in a retrieval system, or transmitted by any means without written permission from the Author. Any person who does any authorised act in relation to this publication may be liable to criminal prosecution and civil claims for damages.

All characters, other than those clearly in the public domain, are fictitious and any resemblance is purely coincidental.

ISBN – 13 978-1545265833
Published by Diane Need
First published April 2017
Printed and bound by Createspace

Acknowledgements

This is my first novel. I've travelled a bumpy road whilst writing it, but it's been an amazing experience that I'd have struggled to get through without the support and encouragement I've been fortunate enough to have received from my family and friends. I'd like to say thank you to a few of them here.

Sincere thanks to my former MS nurse, Jayne Roberts, for her support and belief in me.

Thank you to the Multiple Sclerosis Society, who have supported and encouraged me throughout this venture.

I couldn't have started my writing journey without the support, encouragement and patience of my fabulous and supportive partner, Andy, and my wonderful family; my daughters Amanda and Stephanie, and my son, Christopher.

To my brother, John, a sincere and grateful thank you for everything.

Big hugs and love to my grandson, Oliver and for Stuart, James, and Paige – thanks for putting up with the non-stop "book" chatter!

To my brother, Barry, a big thank you for all the support and great technical help.

To my brother, Mike, thanks for the encouragement and support.

A hug and love to my stepchildren: Melissa and Mark, Natalie and Nathan, Daniel and Russell.

Thank you to Andy Dunn, for his tech guidance.

Thank you and hugs for my dear friend, author Shelly Betts, for her amazing help and support, which has meant so much.

Thank you and hugs for my dear friend, author Doctor Val Wilson, for her inspiration and support, for which I'm really grateful.

Thank you and hugs for my dear friend, Jacqueline Vali, for her support, encouragement and belief in me.

Thanks to fabulous tutors: Alison May, Sue Johnson, Karen King and Janet Gover, for their knowledgeable guidance, advice and patience.

Thank you and a hug for Fiona Lindsay and Christine Shaw, brilliant proof-readers, friends and fellow authors.

Thank you to my friend, author Sue Watson, for her encouragement and advice.

A special mention and love to my sister-in-law and dear friend, Frances Hurst and sisters-in-law Pamela Turbutt & Carole Green.

A special mention and love to Chris Twinberrow, Diane Heffy and my goddaughter, Melissa Perkins, who have always believed in me.

Hello to my family and friends: Uncle Stan and Aunty Olwyn, Joan Stevens, Gemma & Lauren Heffy, Su Smith & Mark Williams, Caen Myles, Sian Maxfield, Kerry Ward, Lynne Matthews, Claire Ibrahem, Debbie Clack, Dawn Buffrey, Sue & Phil Sayer, Shelley Ann, Tracy Newman, Hannah, Phil & Cee, Richard and Tracey.

Last, but by no means least, hello to all my friends, including authors and "sounding boards", Chalmere Davis, Rachel Hodges, Sheena Wilkinson, and all the people I've been fortunate to meet on my writing journey.

Thank you all for your help and for cheering me on all the way.

Press Three for
Goodbye Diane Need
© 2017

"I love this well-written story of love and life told with compassion and humour – it made me laugh and cry." Sue Watson, author of Love, Lies and Lemon Cake.

"A truly wonderful debut novel!
A roller coaster of emotions as we witness Beth pursue a new life as a single woman."
Shelly Betts author of *Let It Go*

Table of Contents

Acknowledgements

Table of Contents

Chapter One: Black Stockings and Beef Lasagne

Chapter Two: Oil on Troubled Birthdays

Chapter Three: Duvet Days and Fireballs

Chapter Four: Worrying for England and Heavy Birds

Chapter Five: Jackie

Chapter Six: Cold Turkey and Embarrassing Dogs

Chapter Seven: Paul

Chapter Eight: Shaken, not Stirred

Chapter Nine: Equity and an Easy Ride

Chapter Ten: Paul

Chapter Eleven: Kleenex and a Sense of Purpose

Chapter Twelve: Jackie

Chapter Thirteen: Brussels Sprouts and Shabby Chic

Chapter Fourteen: CV and a Spare Tyre

Chapter Fifteen: Cocoons and Cat's Pee

Chapter Sixteen: Paul

Chapter Seventeen: Flat Shoes and Cheap Umbrellas

Chapter Eighteen: Sat Navs and Cellulite

Chapter Nineteen: Eastern Europeans and a Splash of Cold Water

Chapter Twenty: Aztec Patterns and Three Witches

Chapter Twenty-One: Quality Time and a Mystery

Chapter Twenty-Two: Fifty Shades of Grey and a Luminous Green Cat

Chapter Twenty-Three: Unexpected Visitors and a Chippy Pong

Chapter Twenty-Four: A Polo and a Manky Mint Imperial

Chapter Twenty-Five: Ideas and Old Tat

Chapter Twenty-Six: Only Fools and Rodney

Chapter Twenty-Seven: Offers and Bargains

Chapter Twenty-Eight: Rolling Days and Bright Ideas

Chapter Twenty-Nine: Oil over Troubled Waters

Chapter Thirty: Roast Beef and Revelations

Chapter Thirty-One: Wise Words and Deaf Ears

Chapter Thirty-Two: Paul

Chapter Thirty-Three: Piccadilly Circus and Verbal Diarrhoea

Chapter Thirty-Four: Red Bull and Prickly Heat

Chapter Thirty-Five: Paul

Chapter Thirty-Six: Friendship and Sleeping Dogs

Chapter Thirty-Seven: Beggars can't be Choosers

Chapter Thirty-Eight: Paul

Chapter Thirty-Nine: Pastures New

Chapter Forty: Ryan

Chapter Forty-One: Misgivings and Worldly Goods

Chapter Forty-Two: Marigolds and Fruitcake

Chapter Forty-Three: Interrogation and a Bird's Nest

Chapter Forty-Four: Ryan

Chapter Forty-Five: Clutter and Dirty Evidence

Chapter Forty-Six: Jackie

Chapter Forty-Seven: All Shook Up

Chapter Forty-Eight: Jackie

Chapter Forty-Nine: A Dog Sitter and a Rural Existence

Chapter Fifty: Unrequited Love and Birthday Treats

Chapter Fifty-One: Regrets and Disappointment

Chapter Fifty-Two: Raindrops and Paradise

Chapter Fifty-Three: Chamomile Tea and Russian Dolls

Chapter Fifty-Four: Paul

Chapter Fifty-Five: Ryan

Chapter Fifty-Six: Agendas and Regrets

Chapter Fifty-Seven: Buses and Edward VIII

Chapter Fifty-Eight: Zumba and Complementary Therapies

Chapter Fifty-Nine: Man Trouble and Awkward Moments

Chapter Sixty: Distress and Revelations

Chapter Sixty-One: Soul Searching and Excitable Humans

Chapter Sixty-Two: Something Money Just Can't Buy

Chapter Sixty-Three: Paul

Chapter Sixty-Four: Made for Sharing

Chapter Sixty-Five: Unwelcome Communication

Chapter Sixty-Six: Karma and Wobbly Eyes

Chapter Sixty-Seven: Padlocks and Commitment

Chapter Sixty-Eight: Ryan

Chapter Sixty-Nine: Good Friends and Pharaohs

Chapter Seventy: The Magic of New Beginnings

Author Bio

Chapter One
Black Stockings and Beef Lasagne

Beth Bishop clipped her silk stockings onto the suspender fastenings of her lacy red basque. God, why was it such a palaver, she wondered, as she struggled not to snag the sheer mesh. After fighting with the wretched things for a few minutes, she padded over to her bedroom mirror.

When Beth married Paul, she'd weighed under eight stone. If only, she thought, sucking in her stomach as hard as she could. The basque did nip in her waist and the well-moulded cups lifted up her slightly sagging cleavage, but she groaned at the thought of wearing the torturous contraption for the entire evening. Goodness only knew how anyone could wear the thing on a daily basis. Imagine trying to do a supermarket shop wearing one of these!

She heaved an impatient sigh. The dratted suspenders had already managed to work themselves loose and the stockings were now sliding down her thighs. She hoisted them up, stretching them over the fiddly fastenings. The last thing she needed was for them to crumple down her legs, making her look like Nora Batty. All the hassle would prove worthwhile, however, if it injected some oomph into her redundant love life.

Slipping her arms into her black silk robe (well, it was nylon from Primark, but at least it looked the part), she attacked her red curls with a brush, wrestling them into submission with a can of hairspray. After carefully applying eyeliner to her emerald eyes, she headed downstairs to check on the beef lasagne. Peering inside the oven, she smiled guilty when she saw that the lasagne, Paul's favourite, was turning a pleasing golden brown on top. Her husband always assumed it was homemade and she'd stuffed the empty packet down inside the wheelie bin.

Rodney, their tan and white terrier cross, sat next to the oven, salivating.

Beth turned down the temperature gauge and shut the door, then knelt and ruffled the dog's ears. 'I'll save you some,' she promised.

The Prosecco was chilling nicely in the fridge and she'd opened a bag of a mixed leaf salad, adding chopped red and yellow peppers, together with slices of tomato, cucumber and beetroot to make the meal more appealing.

She paused for a moment; what else was there? Ah, of course, candles and background music, both essential for a romantic evening! She lit the candles that graced the dining table and selected Adele on her iPod, feeling a ripple of excitement run through her body in anticipation of Paul's arrival.

Paul was a solicitor who dealt with divorce matters. He'd been told he was up for promotion to senior partner at Mortimer's Solicitors. All being well, it would be Mortimer and Bishop soon and Beth thought it had a nice ring to it.

Tonight was all about a cosy celebration for the two of them.

Her heart did a little flip as she wondered what he'd make of his sultry new-look wife. He'd worked so hard these past few months that the two of them barely sat down to eat together, let alone held anything resembling a decent conversation. Even their sex-life, which had already dwindled to once a week, had become non- existent, and, not for the first time, she wondered if her husband still fancied her after twenty-three years.

Still, she reasoned, his job was indeed stressful, his impending promotion even more so. Tonight she hoped they'd catch up properly over the main course, and maybe there would be more than cheesecake to look forward to for afters.

Checking her watch for the umpteenth time, she saw it was eight o'clock. Paul had been due home around seven, so it was a good thing she'd allowed for that. He'd told her from the outset that, if he was being put up for senior partner, he'd have to put in plenty of extra working hours.

Fishing her "Scarlet Woman" lippy from her bag, she smeared her lips with another coat. A tingle of nervous excitement coursed through her body as she smoothed her hands over the soft material of her basque. She tried to imagine her husband's face when he saw her in this sexy get-up rather than her usual jumper and leggings.

*

Paul walked into the kitchen-diner. Without acknowledging Beth, he dropped his leather briefcase on top of the black marble work surface.

Rodney padded over, his tail wagging in greeting. Paul knelt down and distractedly patted the dog's head.

Beth was growing decidedly uneasy at her husband's demeanor and felt her mojo ebbing away. 'Have you had a good day, darling?' she purred, in the hope of resurrecting it.

She willed her tone to sound sexy, but, regrettably, to her own ears it sounded more as if she was coming down with flu.

Paul raked long, slim fingers through his wavy, blond hair as he stood up and faced her. His piercing blue eyes didn't meet hers. 'It's been busy.' He scratched his baby-smooth chin thoughtfully. 'Look, there's something I have to tell –' his mouth dropped open as he stared at her.

Beth stood provocatively with her arm draped around the back of a chair and one leg resting on a footstool, smiling enticingly as she pulled her robe open to flash a glimpse of suspender.

He blinked rapidly, as though trying to clear his vision. 'Why on earth are you dressed up like a tart?' he spluttered.

Withering under his wide-eyed scrutiny, she tugged the robe tightly around her body. She felt ridiculous, now, as if she were the only one wearing fancy dress at a party. 'I wanted to surprise you –' seeing the look of disdain in her husband's eyes, she trailed off.

Paul breathed out a heavy sigh. 'Look –' he paused, struggling to find the right words.

Beth held her breath, wondering what was going through his mind.

Clearing his throat, the words he'd been searching for tumbled out in a rush. 'There's never going to be a right time to tell you this ... so I might as well come straight to the point. It's something I've been putting off for a while, and – well – I'm seeing someone else.'

His words spun round and round on a loop in Beth's brain.

'I really am sorry it's worked out this way,' he continued gravely. 'The thing is – Emily understands me – she really gets me – you know? I'll pack some of my stuff and leave first thing in the morning.'

Beth stood frozen to the spot, her mouth opening and closing like a goldfish on speed.

'Emily? – Emily, your PA?'

He nodded solemnly. 'I'm sorry,' he repeated, in

a monotonous voice.

She felt as though she was listening to some robotic voice on an automated phone line: *press 1 for apology; press 2 for explanation; press 3 for goodbye.* Just like an automated line, she knew she was going to have trouble getting through to an actual explanation.

'We've got no common ground, nothing to talk about,' he added flatly.

The cooker timer pinged in the background, a reminder for Beth to take out the beef lasagne.

Paul threw his hands in the air dramatically. 'What's the point of us carrying on like this? Life's too short. Sometimes you have to take the plunge and grab it with both hands.'

She clenched her fists, her nails digging into her palms. 'Oh, yes,' she replied shakily. 'I can see you're grabbing *it* with both hands alright – and with the senior partner's daughter too – how very convenient!'

Fixing his gaze on the black and white chequered floor tiles, Paul chewed his bottom lip.

As she stared at him in disbelief, Beth's mind raced. She knew things hadn't been all hearts and flowers between them, but surely most marriages were like that after twenty-three years, weren't they?

'*Why now – after all this time? Why her?*' She was conscious that her voice was high pitched and dangerously wobbly. *She did high pitched and wobbly far better than sexy and sultry.*

His lips compressed into a thin line.

They were supposed to be celebrating his success, Beth thought helplessly. The kids had finally flown the nest; this was supposed to be *their* time. After twenty-three years of marriage, how the hell could he stand there and calmly announce that he was seeing someone else?

All thoughts of the basque digging into her flesh were forgotten as she stood in a void of disbelief, grappling with the enormity of what her husband had said.

Rodney skulked away from the delicious beef and cheesy smell wafting from the oven and gazed sheepishly from one to the other, his ears down, his normally wagging tail firmly tucked between his hind legs. Beth knelt down and scooped him up, holding him against her and finding some comfort in the rhythmic beat of his heart and the warmth from his little body.

Paul shook his head, his eyes still downcast. Without uttering another word, he turned and walked out of the room.

Beth heard his footfall on the stairs. After a moment's hesitation, she raced after him and stood on the bottom step. 'I hope you're packing your stuff!' she cried. 'I just want you to go.'

As she returned to the kitchen, the lump inside her throat felt as if it would choke her. After putting Rodney into his basket, she donned the red and white checked oven gloves and pulled the tray of lasagne out of the oven, and then pressing open the pedal bin, she flung the food inside.

Rodney looked up at her with sad chocolate button eyes. With a sigh, she dipped her gloved hand into the bin and gingerly fished out the tray of food, now accessorised with a soggy tea bag. She brushed off the offending bag and placed the lasagne aside to cool. 'Don't worry, boy,' she whispered, 'it's all yours.'

On autopilot, she marched over to the dining table and blew out the candles with the ferocity of a force nine gale. Adele's track, *Someone like You*, played softly in the background. Beth jabbed frantically at the "stop" button of her iPod, cutting Adele off in her prime. On impulse, she grabbed the Prosecco from the fridge and yanked out the cork, putting the bottle to her lips and taking several large gulps.

Out of the corner of her eye, she spotted Paul's prized bottle of Johnnie Walker Blue Label whisky sitting on top of the dresser. It was his favourite tipple, and she knew how expensive it was at over £130 a bottle. Picking it up, she unscrewed the cap and poured it down the sink, feeling a childish sense of satisfaction as the amber liquid gurgled and glugged its way down the drain.

Staring at the empty bottle, tears smarted at the back of her eyes, her satisfaction short-lived as the reality of the situation kicked in with brute force: she was being airbrushed out of her husband's life.

Hot, angry tears squeezed through her lashes and spilled down her cheeks as she crumpled to the floor.

Rodney padded over and tried to lick her face. Pulling him close, she buried her damp face in his soft fur, stroking him with long, rhythmic strokes. She was unsure how long she sat there, but her muscles were stiff and sore when the penny dropped with a resounding clang. As if played out in a film, she recalled with clarity all the "work" meetings Paul had to attend that went on for hours. *"Of course, it would've been rude to refuse a drink afterwards",* he'd said.

Naturally, Beth thought bitterly, as she chewed the skin around her thumbnail; she'd been exactly what was expected of her: the dutiful, understanding wife. Then there had been the myriad of residential courses that all seemed to come out of the blue. Remembering how she'd carefully ironed his shirts, although she hated ironing with a passion, her eyes hardened. She'd even looked out his toiletries and packed his bloody suitcase, for God's sake!

The thoughts snapped away at her brain like hungry piranhas. *How stupid was she to have soaked it all up like a sponge? Why the hell had she been so naive?* All the time she'd believed her husband was putting in extra hours because of an impending promotion, and now she became conscious of how often Paul had mentioned Emily's name: how she'd been an *"integral part of the team".* How he *"couldn't possibly have managed without her".* Her face burned as it dawned on her that he just couldn't manage to keep it in his trousers.

Another thought struck her - why hadn't she heard any signs of him leaving?

Grabbing the worktop for support, she dragged herself to her feet and scraped some of the cooled lasagne into Rodney's bowl. He gobbled it down greedily before she let him out into the garden for his final wee, then he padded back inside. Sensing the strained atmosphere, he curled up in his basket, regarding her with soulful eyes. She knelt down and gave him a last bit of fuss, and then, with her stomach in knots, she climbed the stairs.

All she wanted Paul to do now was to get out; she couldn't bear the thought of being anywhere near him.

Her breath caught in her throat as she pushed open the door to their bedroom. Paul's tousled blond head was poking out from under the duvet. How the hell had he got the nerve to climb into bed and fall asleep like everything was normal? Even worse, he was snoring like a pig in pain. *BASTARD!*

Her eyes alighted on his Louis Vuitton suitcase standing next to their bed. *So he'd managed to pack it himself this time,* she fumed. No doubt it contained his designer shirts and his ridiculous canary yellow Armani boxers. They were so damn tight around his privates she'd secretly nicknamed them his "budgie smugglers".

In hindsight, when she'd discovered all his new flashy designer underwear in his drawer she'd had a hunch something was up *(excuse the pun),* but, when she'd jokingly asked Paul whom he was trying to impress, he'd snapped and told her not to be so ridiculous. She wondered fleetingly if he were going through some kind of male menopause, but he was so moody these days it would be difficult to tell.

Tiptoeing over to the tall sash window, she pulled open the green jacquard curtains and dragged it open as wide as it would go. Holding her breath, she crept over the thick pile carpet to the door, lifted up the heavy case and, using all her might, heaved it up level with the window ledge where she unclasped the metal lock, emptying Paul's designer garments out into the cold night air.

She watched with a weird sense of calm as his flamboyant shirts fluttered to the ground like multi-coloured ghosts. Balled socks, silk ties and lurid pants followed in their wake. She thought the case was empty, but then spotted a rogue pair of Armani boxers snuggled into a corner. She snatched them out with a vengeance. 'Ha, ha – got you!' she shrieked, like a deranged witch, before dangling them out of the window and watching with satisfaction as, carried on a breeze, they drifted down and finally came to rest draped over the thorny rose bush beneath their bedroom window.

Paul's eyes snapped open. He sat up in bed, using his hands to shield them from the light. 'What – what in the blazes are you doing, woman? Have you lost your bloody marbles?'

She nodded manically. 'Yes! Yes, I must have!

I've been married to you for all these years, so I must be truly certifiable! I want you to go – right now.'

He heaved a sigh. 'I've told you – I'll leave first thing in the morning.'

'Oh, no, you won't –'

'Oh, yes, I will –'

'For Christ's sake – we're not in a bloody pantomime! What I'm saying is that you will leave – *right now!*' The venom in her voice took her by surprise, but she'd gone past the point of no return and was unable to control her attack of verbal diarrhoea. With her hands on her hips, she leaned forward. 'Look – just do one, *will you?* I don't want to spend another second with you!'

Paul shrugged. 'But it's my house –'

'You're the one who wants to leave – so go!'

'Come on, Beth. Be reasonable – it's the middle of the night!'

'Me be reasonable? You're un-believable, d'you know that?'

He looked at his, now empty, suitcase and shook his head. 'All my stuff's going to be ruined – '

'Oh, diddums. *How awful*. You poor thing.'

With an irritated sigh, he clambered out of bed, glaring stonily at Beth as he pulled on a pair of beige chinos and a navy mohair sweater.

She heard the thunder of his feet on the stairs and watched from the window as he went into the garden and began gathering up his clothes and stuffing the items back into his case.

His angular profile was taut as he loaded it into the boot of his gleaming, white Audi. Finally, he leapt into the driver's seat, revved up the engine and crunched down the long driveway, scattering gravel in his wake.

Time froze; everything felt surreal, as though Beth was outside of her own physical body observing events as if they were happening to someone else.

It took her several minutes before she could move away from the window.

She tore off the ridiculous basque that was suddenly digging into every spare ounce of flesh and, shivering from head to toe, she climbed into bed and huddled under the duvet, pulling it up under her chin. In the darkness, the space beside her felt vast and empty. Closing her eyes, she rolled over, burying her face in Paul's pillow, and breathed in the fresh, heady smell of his Armani aftershave.

Overcome with anger and disbelief, her tears soaked through the cotton pillowcase.

Tossing and turning, she watched the luminous face of the digital clock as the numbers flipped over, displaying every protracted minute.

At five a.m., she admitted defeat. Throwing off the covers, she scrambled out of bed, shoving her feet into her mules before groggily making her way to the bathroom.

Her hand flew to her chest as she glimpsed her

putty-grey complexion and the dark purple half-moons shadowing her eyes. She hadn't looked this awful, she thought, since she'd been a new parent and had lost count of the number of late night films she'd watched whilst trying to coax the kids to go back to sleep. Way back then, she'd thought she might actually die through sleep deprivation, but that had been nothing compared to the aching hollowness she felt right now.

She splashed her face with cold water and patted it dry with a towel. If it wasn't for having to look after the dog, she'd grab her secret chocolate stash and a bottle of red wine and hide under the duvet all day.

Her head continued to pound with a mixture of tiredness and emotion as she set about attempting to do all the daily "normal" stuff. She let Rodney out into the garden and gathered up a load of washing from the laundry basket, shoving it unceremoniously into the washing machine. A new thought pinged into her exhausted brain: *why the hell should she wash his dirty stuff?* Tugging it out again, she sorted frenziedly through the jumble of clothing, bundling Paul's clothes into a separate pile. She found a black bin bag, into which she shoved his dirty laundry before re-loading her own garments, including the dreaded basque, and set the washing machine to synthetic wash.

It was far too early to take Rodney out for his proper morning walk. He'd already been in the garden to relieve himself, and, if she took him for walkies now, she knew he'd pester her to go out again before lunchtime. She just couldn't bear the thought of facing anyone, and she didn't want to leave the house unless she absolutely had to.

Wandering distractedly over to the dresser, she poured out a large glass of red wine - sod it that it was still early morning. Lifting it to her lips, she took a huge gulp, shuddering as the tepid liquid assaulted her taste buds. Right now, she was unsure what the question was, but hitting the bottle, she concluded, was definitely not the answer.

Chapter Two
Oil on Troubled Birthdays

It was the fifteenth of December, Beth's thirty-ninth birthday. It was also four weeks and three days since Paul had left.

The moment she opened her eyes, her heart sank. She didn't want to get out of bed and dearly longed to wallow and hide away from the world, yet she instantly felt guilty about her train of thought. Her parents were coming over and they were bringing her Aunt Lena with them. They were treating Beth to a birthday lunch at The Swan with Two Nicks, a lovely local pub and restaurant in a Tudor building, set in a pretty cobbled street in Worcester city centre.

Heaving a sigh as she looked at her reflection in the dressing table mirror, she wondered if she'd be able to look as though she was enjoying herself when they'd gone to the trouble of booking up the meal for her.

As was her routine now, she forced herself to get up, then showered and dressed before taking Rodney out for his walk.

*

They made their way over the playing fields at Diglis, walking on as far as the foot and cycle bridge.

Leaning against the metal rails, Beth gazed down at the river, admiring the calmness and serenity of a swan as it glided gracefully along with the flow of the water.

Lifting one of the many padlocks attached to the bridge's steel structure, she read the message engraved into it: Tony and Annette forever.XXX. It was a great tribute, she thought, writing a message on a padlock and locking it onto the bridge to symbolise your love, locked together forever; yet reading it she felt more alone than ever.

Slivers of fragile sunlight filtered through the clouds as they headed across the bridge. Rodney trotted on ahead and Beth had to increase her pace to keep up with him. Before she knew it, they'd walked over half a mile and were standing on the edge of the city centre.

She clipped the dog back onto his lead and continued walking towards the High Street, passing the Commandery, a half-timbered Tudor house which was now a Civil War museum. The next turning led to Paul's office. Beth's heart rate quickened as she tried to hurry past, but Rodney had other ideas and tugged on his lead. She realised that he remembered going to see Paul en route to the vet's. 'No, boy!' she told him firmly, although the thought crossed her mind that she'd be only too happy to call in if she could take Paul to the vet's instead. She could have his bits chopped off.

By the time they'd reached home and she'd drank a couple of mugs of strong, sweet coffee, she felt a bit more optimistic about the day ahead. She hadn't seen her aunt for over a month - Lena had been holidaying with her friend, Olive, on the Greek islands (buy three weeks, get a fourth week free). Lena was her mum's, slightly eccentric and wonderful, older sister.

Brenda and Lena were like chalk and cheese in both their looks and personalities, while everyone who knew both Beth and Lena remarked that Beth took after her aunt.

As she went to pour some biscuits into Rodney's bowl, she heard a rustling noise. It seemed to come from upstairs. Beth froze, clutching the packet to her chest. Rodney's ears had picked up too. 'Woof! Woof!' he barked, darting off to investigate.

What the hell was going on? And why had Rodney stopped barking?

Hardly daring to breath, she crept along the hall and peered up between the stairs rails.

She gasped. Paul stood on the top step clutching two bin liners overflowing with his clothes. 'I've come for the rest of my stuff,' he said matter-of-factly.

She blew out a long, shaky breath. 'You nearly gave me a heart attack! You should've called first –'

Clambering down the first two stairs, he heaved an impatient sigh, the plastic bags rustling as they rubbed against his long, jean-clad legs. 'Like I've said, before, it's my house.'

'But it's no longer your home,' Beth retorted, turning on her heel and retreating to the kitchen.

She flicked on the kettle and watched, her vision blurred; as the water level rose through the transparent gauge. When it boiled and steam escaped from the spout, her temper boiled with it. How dare he come around unannounced and frighten her like that? And how could he forget that today was her birthday after they'd shared twenty-three years together? Or could it be that he remembered, but simply didn't give a damn about her feelings?

A short while later, he stuck his head round the kitchen door. 'Right, I'm off now, but I'll be back. I can't possibly fit all my stuff in my car in one go.'

Without turning to face him, Beth busied herself by spooning instant coffee into her mug.

'Not going to offer me one?' he asked, with mock surprise.

Her grip on the mug handle tightened. She spun around, hurling it at him.

Paul ducked, shielding his face with his hands; the mug missing him by a whisker. It bounced off the wall and smashed into three large pieces as it hit the floor. He shook his head in disbelief. 'What the hell?' 'For God's sake, woman – you could've done some serious damage with that!'

Hysteria bubbled up inside her. 'Guess what? – I don't give a damn!'

*

Beth's eyes prickled with tears as she swept up the broken china. Was it all in her imagination when she'd believed they were ever a happy family? Had she really meant so little to her husband that he'd forgotten her birthday?

After clearing up, she splashed her face with cold water, determined that she wasn't going to look all red and blotchy when her family arrived to pick her up.

As she dried her face, she noticed a mauve envelope poking out from behind the toaster. It was addressed to her in her best friend's handwriting; she'd found it lying on the doormat the previous day. Picking it up, she eased out the card inside. The front read: *You'll always be my dearest friend.* There was a picture of two little girls running along a beach holding hands, one with blonde hair, the other red. She opened it and read: ...y*ou know too much!* She managed a wobbly smile at the joke and continued to read the handwritten message: *To Beth*, my *dearest friend. I hope you have a wonderful day and the wonderful life you deserve. Your friend always, Jackie xxx*

*

Although Beth had thought she wasn't hungry, her mouth watered as a tantalising aroma of coffee and baking emanated from the kitchen at The Swan and Two Nicks. The pub had a cosy atmosphere, its low beamed ceilings adorned with an assortment of beer mats. Convivial chatter flowed from the customers.

A waitress brought their food over and her mum smiled at Beth. 'It's lovely to be eating something I haven't cooked for a change, love.'

Beth returned her smile. It was good to see her mum waited on after all her years of cooking for everyone else. When Beth had lived with her parents, they'd indulged in huge family meals which were always on the table at one o'clock sharp. They'd all sit together and chat about life in general, and, more importantly, they'd laugh together. How simple things had been then, she thought, although it seemed like a lifetime ago.

Aunt Lena gave her arm a gentle squeeze. 'Have you heard anything from Paul, love?'

'He collected his stuff this morning,' she replied, doing her best to keep her tone steady as she speared a chip with her fork.

Her mum overheard her and clicked the roof of her mouth with her tongue. 'He collected his stuff on your birthday?'

Beth simply nodded and concentrated on eating her chip.

'You what?' Dad spluttered across the table, his full cheeks burning, turning his normal ruddy complexion scarlet. 'How dare he? What an absolute – '

Mum touched his arm. 'That'll do, Ted. I'm sure you sounding off won't help.'

Beth held her mum's gaze for a moment, and she gave her a grateful smile. She knew Dad meant well, but if he carried on grumbling about the injustice of it all, she'd probably break down in front of everyone in the pub.

'Don't you worry, love,' Aunt Lena told her. 'You're worth ten of him any day of the week. That trollop's welcome to him!'

She couldn't help but smile; it was comforting to know that her family was always in her corner.

They chatted as they ate, reminiscing about how Beth had loved visiting her aunt when she was young.

'I loved your treasure box!' Beth said, with a fond smile.

'It's a bespoke piece, you know,' Lena said proudly as she folded her napkin. 'Your uncle carved it especially for me.'

Beth had heard the story about Uncle Harry making the box many times, but never tired of it.

'It was a real labour of love,' her aunt continued.

And indeed it had been. The cherry wood had been varnished to a high gloss shine and was inlaid with a crescent moon and stars. The centre of the box concertinaed outwards to house her aunt's vast selection of essential oils. It was finished off with a gold clasp and padlock, reminding Beth of a pirate's treasure chest.

Lena was qualified in carrying out all manner of complementary therapies. Her main passion was aromatherapy. She'd patiently explained the many and surprising uses of essential oils to Beth, teaching her what base oils would complement the individual oils. Under her aunt's eagle-eyed supervision, she'd been allowed to experiment and mix her own blends.

'Do you still use your oils?' Beth asked.

Lena nodded. 'Only for my regulars. They've been coming to me for God knows how many years. But I'm getting a bit too long in the tooth to take on new clients.'

'Of course you're not! You're always so full of life,' Beth told her.

At seventy-six years old, Lena stood just over five feet tall. She was petite with curly red hair and sparkly emerald eyes, just like Beth's. Beth also shared her aunt's caring nature and had fully embraced her interest in complementary therapy.

'Talking of my treasure box, I've got something here for you.' Lena rummaged through her multi-coloured patchwork bag. 'Ah – here it is.' She handed Beth a purple gift bag decorated with silver stars and moons.

Pulling out an amber glass bottle filled with lavender oil, Beth unscrewed the cap and put it to her nostrils, breathing in the fresh, sweet smell, and remembering what her aunt had told her when she'd been nine years old: 'Lavender is the most versatile oil, Bethany,' she'd said knowledgably, as she'd cleaned up a graze on Beth's knee. 'It's relaxing for the mind and body and good for cleansing cuts and bruises.'

She'd given her a bottle of blended oil to take home, and, whenever Beth felt troubled or anxious and had difficulty sleeping, she'd pop a few drops on a tissue as instructed and place it under her pillow.

'I thought it might be useful,' Lena added.

'Thanks, Auntie. It's just what I need right now.'

Her aunt studied her thoughtfully for a moment before speaking. 'I've been thinking, Beth. Why don't you think about going back to college? You used to really enjoy it.'

Beth's keenness to learn about essential oils and their benefits had blossomed over the years. When she'd left school, she'd signed up for a course in complementary therapies, but, once she'd got married and given birth to Ben and Tash, she hadn't found time to pursue it. The years had melted away, and the constant support she'd provided for Paul and their children had overtaken all other aspects of her life.

In fact, she thought wryly, with empty nest syndrome when Ben and Tash had left home, followed by Paul's desertion, what was she supposed to do after all these years of focusing on being a wife and mother?

Chapter Three
Duvet Days and Fireballs

On top of a subdued birthday, Beth endured a bleak build up to Christmas, which, needless to say, she was dreading. There's always so much pressure on everyone to make it a jolly, smiley occasion, she thought gloomily. She was cooking Christmas lunch, and, no matter how wretched she felt on the inside, she was determined to paint on a smile for her family. There was going to be quite a houseful, too, with her mum and dad, Aunt Lena, Tash and her son, Ben, who was bringing Sam, his boyfriend.

Ben was newly qualified as a solicitor and worked with Paul and Emily. This was something of which Paul was extremely proud, a far cry from when Ben had come out and told his parents he was gay. At first, Paul was ominously quiet about it. Secretly, Beth had likened it to waiting for a bomb to explode, and explode it certainly had. Paul had told Ben, in no uncertain terms, that it was a "stupid phase". He insisted Ben should "bloody well hurry up and grow out of it". He also began referring to his son in the past tense: "Ben used to enjoy a good curry" when, in fact, Ben still did. The way his father had behaved had caused Ben to feel that he'd failed him. Beth had lost count of the arguments she'd had with Paul and her mother-in-law, Penelope, who stuck by her son no matter what.

It had been Beth who'd comforted Ben, assuring him that she loved him unconditionally. Tash was also very supportive of her older brother and was furious with her dad.

It was only when Ben had gained his law degree that things had changed for the better.

Paul was still unhappy, but became reluctantly accepting of the situation, provided there were no public displays of affection, otherwise known as PDAs, when he was around.

Beth had been incensed at her husband's attitude, but Ben assured her that he'd rather have it that way than his father completely disowning him. Sam was now one of the family. Even Paul had had to admit that he'd grown quite fond of the gentle young man, who obviously cared a great deal for his son. Of course, Penelope followed suit, finally accepting that Sam was a decent person and gradually thawing towards him.

When Beth had broken the news to Tash and Ben that their dad was leaving, Ben admitted that he'd had his suspicions about his father and Emily for some time. He'd even asked Paul if there was anything going on. Paul had vehemently denied it.

Tash was angry, but naturally broken hearted at the same time. 'How could he do it to you – to us,

Mum?' she'd asked her eyes dangerously bright with tears.

Beth hugged her. 'I don't know, love. But, whatever's happened, he's still your dad and I know he loves you and Ben very much.'

Threading his long, slim fingers, that were so like Paul's, through Sam's, Ben gave a derisive snort. 'If he loves us so much, he wouldn't have buggered off with his PA.'

Beth sighed. 'It's not you and your sister he doesn't love, son. It's me.'

The silence had inflated in the room like a giant balloon until Tash had burst into tears.

Beth put all her hurt and angst on hold to comfort her daughter, but when Tash returned to Uni following compassionate leave, Beth seemed to morph from a fireball of energy, hell bent on recreating herself, to an emotional mess who huddled under the duvet and hoped it would all go away. Yet somehow she summoned up an inner spirit that spurred her on. 'This won't do,' she'd admonished herself whenever the lure of a duvet-day had been tempting. She'd get through this. She had to.

As much as she wasn't looking forward to Christmas, she had to face it. She was determined not to make anyone feel more grotty and miserable than they already did, so she'd planned to do the whole roast turkey thing, have everyone seated round the table and put out the tartan crackers (with mini Christmas trees on the front), which were stashed away at the back of a kitchen cupboard. Like the good sport she was, she'd even wear the paper crown that fell out of hers.

Chapter Four
Worrying for England and Heavy Birds

Beth awoke bright and early on Christmas morning after a decent night's sleep, thanks, in no small part, to the lavender oil from Aunt Lena.

She felt surprisingly calm; the day would be over soon enough. Plus, she reasoned, she'd already worried for England – surely she didn't have the energy left to worry anymore? Worry was a bit like crying, though, she conceded. You think you're all cried out and can't possibly have any more tears left, yet somehow there's always a fresh flow waiting in the wings. How she wished she had an "off" switch to give her brain a rest.

These past few weeks, as well as adjusting to life as a singleton, she'd learnt how to manage the stingy allowance Paul gave her each month and how to set up direct debits for the mountain of household bills. She'd also had to learn how to budget for food and sundries, although, with the exception of the large Christmas food and gift bill, she was mainly living on beans on toast.

Everything felt alien to her; Paul had always

handled the finances and there seemed so much to learn. It hadn't taken her long to realise her allowance wasn't going to be anywhere near enough to enable her to live comfortably.

She drew in a deep, determined breath. Today wasn't the time for worrying about these things; she had her family to think of.

After washing her hands and face, she tied back her hair and pulled on her multi-coloured flowery leggings, and her old Aran jumper (a comfy favourite), and then headed into the kitchen to prep for Christmas lunch. After pre-heating the oven, she heaved the turkey out of the huge, American fridge freezer. She'd certainly been glad of the space inside; the bird weighed over twenty pounds!

She set about making a stuffing mix using sage, breadcrumbs, sausage meat, eggs and chopped onion and duly stuffed the cavernous turkey, then checked the time before man-handling the bird, with great difficulty, into the oven.

Tash was visiting a friend for pressie swapping before coming round, and the others weren't due to arrive until one thirty for pre-dinner drinks and gift opening, so she was glad she had heaps of time to get organised.

She wished Jackie could've joined them, but Jackie had planned to stay with her cousin Lisa on the farm in Wales where she lived with her husband and five year old twins.

Beth smiled wistfully. She'd met Lisa and her family, and knew that Jackie would have a fun and lively time with them. The children were bright and chatty, and, with her husband working on the farm all over Christmas, it was difficult for Lisa to manage with the kids single handed.

She'd have loved to have gone away for Christmas too, but she'd felt too guilty to clear off and leave everyone else to it. She'd decided, instead, that no matter how much she was dreading it, she was going to try to make the best of things.

Chapter Five
Jackie

Jackie Clarke's head snapped up from her pillow as her mobile sprang to life. She blinked, pressing her fingers hard on her pounding temples. How many shots had she consumed the previous night? She didn't even dare think about it! All she could remember was that it had been a riotous Christmas Eve party.

Feeling movement, she groaned inwardly. She rolled over cautiously, her heart plummeting as she saw the spiky dark head of the naked guy lying beside her. What the hell was his name? She fought to remember. *Jim? Or was it John?* It definitely began with a "J" – at least, she thought it did. What did it matter anyway? She wouldn't be seeing him again.

Reaching out, she grabbed her mobile from the bedside table, a pang of guilt sweeping over her as Beth's name flashed up onto the screen. She would've enjoyed spending Christmas day with Beth and her family, who treated her like one of their own, but she always spent Christmas with Lisa and George and Lucy, the twins. She knew they were looking forward to seeing her; her work had been so hectic that it was the only chance she'd had to go and visit them this year.

Jim or John hesitantly raised his head from the pillow, rubbing at his eyes with the back of his hands. 'What time is it?'

She sighed. 'It's time you were gone. I have to leave soon.'

Propping himself up on one elbow he turned to face her. His dark eyes searched her face as his hands began to roam expertly over her naked body. 'You've got time for a proper goodbye, though,' he said, planting feather-light kisses over her neck.

Her breath caught in her throat at the touch of his rough, large hands exploring and stroking her soft, warm skin. His generous lips travelled over her body until they reached her breast. He trailed his tongue in a circular motion around her nipple before sliding on top of her.

She gasped as his hardness pressed into her. Soon she was swept along on a tidal wave of passion that washed away her troubles.

Finally spent, he rolled off her, and, with a thoughtful look in his eyes, he lifted a strand of her long, honey blonde hair, weaving it between his fingers. 'So, when can I see you again?'

Jackie jumped up as though a bucket of cold water had been poured over her. 'I – I'm not sure. Look, you'd better get dressed. I have to go.'

Chapter Six
Cold Turkey and Embarrassing Dogs

Determined to get into the Christmas spirit, Beth poured herself a glass of sherry and sang along to the tunes on the radio. 'I wish it could be Christmas every day,' she trilled, as she peeled spuds, prepared sprouts and chopped up swede and carrots. 'It'll be Lonely this *Christmas,*' Mud crooned over the airwaves. 'No way!' she muttered, thumping the "off" button. She drained her sherry glass and did a quick mental check.

Satisfied she'd done everything she could, she decided it would be a good idea to take Rodney out and get some fresh air before making herself look presentable.

*

Beth huddled into her warm parka. Despite the north wind chill, the sky was streaked with pale blue and a glimmer of weak sunshine filtered through the clouds. Her lips eased into a smile as she watched children out and about, riding around Diglis Park on their pristine new bikes and scooters, anxious parents clinging onto their saddles for dear life, zigzagging along behind them. She remembered fondly when she'd done the same for Ben, then one day she'd let go and, sure enough, he was riding the bike by himself. A proud smile had lit up his face when he'd left her several feet behind.

Stopping for a few moments to take a breather, she stood entranced, watching as some of the older kids performed stunts on their home-constructed skateboard ramps. *'Wow,'* she mouthed, as a tall, dark haired lad of around fourteen leapt off a high ramp and skilfully spun the board around. She'd never been that agile in her life!

Rodney gave her an annoyed look, as if to say, *'Hurry up, where's my ball?'*

Throwing the dog an apologetic smile, she pulled the well-chewed rubber ball from her coat pocket and launched it into the air. It sailed off, landing in a patch of long grass, and Rodney bounded away in pursuit. Stuffing her hands deep into her pockets, she followed him. At least he was enjoying himself, she thought. With a jolt, she realised that she was quite enjoying herself, too.

As Rodney approached the grassy area of the park, he veered off to the right where a tarmac pathway cut through. A couple of teenage girls, one blonde, the other with grey hair *(yes, grey – Tash had informed Beth that it was very current)*, jogged along the path, followed by a lolloping black dog with a curly-coat. Rodney galloped over to them and leapt up at the grey-haired girl excitedly.

Beth snatched up his ball and hurried over,

calling his name. As she drew level, she made a grab for his collar, but, thinking it was a game, Rodney was too quick for her and darted out of reach.

'That bloody dog's out of control!' the grey-haired girl snapped, brushing down her paw-muddied tracksuit.

Catching her breath, Beth threw her palms upwards. 'I'm so sorry!'

Grey-Haired Girl's pale eyes narrowed. She looked Beth up and down. 'I do so love your flowery leggings,' she sniped.

Her blonde friend sniggered. 'Where did you get those?'

(Beth was wearing her Primark buy two for a fiver). 'Oh, they're Primarnie, actually,' she replied breezily, momentarily enjoying the confusion spreading over their smug faces.

Blonde-Girl's eyes widened. 'Shit!' she cried.

Beth did a double take. She hadn't expected her to be that shocked.

She soon realised Blonde-Girl wasn't actually looking at her anymore; she was looking beyond her. Spinning around, she witnessed Rodney trying to hump the black dog. Before she could react, a little girl riding a red scooter stopped in front of them and tugged at a woman's sleeve. 'Look, Mummy! That doggy wants a piggy back!'

Beth cringed inwardly. The poor woman looked as mortified as she felt.

Finally, she managed to drag a very reluctant Rodney away. 'I'm so sorry,' she spluttered repeatedly to everyone within the vicinity. 'I don't know what came over him.'

Grey-Haired Girl stuck her pierced nose in the air and thrust out her chest, her ample boobs straining against the fabric of her red Adidas jacket.

In a bid to save face, Beth opted for diversionary tactics. Kneeling down, she ruffled the dog's head. 'She's a lovely dog. What breed is she?'

'*His* name's Jeremy and he's a cockapoo. Not that your dog seems fussy what sex he is,' Grey- Haired Girl huffed.

Beth gritted her teeth. *Why were these girls so rude?*

A tall, sandy-haired guy, whom she guessed to be in his late twenties, strolled towards them. He was dressed casually in dark blue Levis and a black leather jacket, his hair flopping over one eye. He reminded her of an older, muscular Ed Sheeran. He was holding a tan and white Staffordshire bull terrier on an extendable lead. Judging by his mile-wide grin, he must've witnessed the fiasco. She glared at him indignantly. 'I don't know what you're smirking at!'

The Ed lookalike raised his eyebrows. 'Sorry –' he trailed off, his blue-grey eyes widening as Rodney lunged towards him, sniffing excitedly at his crotch.

The two girls clutched one another, guffawing, as

Beth twisted Rodney's lead tighter around her hand and heaved him away. 'Sorry,' she mumbled, blushing furiously.

Ed raised his hand and flicked his hair away from his eyes. He smiled a warm and genuine smile. 'Don't worry about it,' he said pleasantly.

She felt ashamed that she'd had a go at this guy with his soft voice, kind eyes and just a hint of a Midlands accent. Clipping Rodney safely back onto his lead, she flashed him an apologetic smile before turning away and striding purposefully towards the exit, the girls' laughter still ringing in her ears.

In retrospect, Beth acknowledged that she'd have probably laughed, too, if she'd witnessed that spectacle. She risked a backward glance and watched Ed, lean and muscular, striding away in the opposite direction, the staffie trotting obediently alongside him.

*

Letting herself back into the house she quickly shut the door, leaned the weight of her body against it and breathed a relieved sigh. Rodney sloped off into his basket, sensing that he was, quite literally, in the dog house.

Beth's face was still burning with embarrassment as she headed upstairs to take a shower.

Fine needles of hot water danced on her skin, and, as she lathered herself with exotic lotus flower scented gel, she felt the tension begin to leave her body. She'd never seen the girls at the park before, or Ed, come to that, and she'd probably never see them again. Yet somehow the thought of never seeing Ed again made her feel a little disappointed.

After stepping out of the steamy shower cubicle, she wrapped herself in a fluffy cream bath towel, warm from the radiator, and sat at the end of the bed to dry her hair. Pulling the dryer from her bedside drawer, she was about to plug it in, but froze as her hand neared the socket. Her heart plummeted as it dawned on her there was no tantalising whiff of roasting meat!

Taking the stairs two at a time, she yanked open the oven door, gasping in dismay when she saw that the power light was no longer glowing red. The temperature was barely lukewarm; even the turkey had goose-bumps.

She began fiddling with the control gauge, but to no avail. She flicked on the switch for the kitchen light, but nothing happened. 'The electric's gone off!' she cried to a confused Rodney. He turned away and nonchalantly padded back to his basket.

The back door burst open and Tash tumbled in, heaving two bags of brightly wrapped Christmas presents. 'Merry Christmas, Mum!'

Beth pointed an accusing finger at the oven. 'The electric's gone off! God only knows how I'm going to cook our Christmas lunch now.'

Kneeling down beside her, Tash peered at the raw turkey. Her lips began to twitch. She glanced up at Beth.

'It's not funny!' Beth scolded.

Tash couldn't hold back any longer and erupted with laughter. It was infectious, and, despite her panic over Christmas lunch, Beth couldn't help joining in. Soon they were both clutching their sides, tears of mirth rolling down their cheeks. Gripping onto one another, they scrambled to their feet. Beth was unsure if her bout of hysterics was down to humour or nerves, but whatever was responsible for their convulsive state, it was a great stress-buster.

When everyone else had arrived and she'd explained what had happened, Dad did what she realised she should've done in the first place and flicked the trip switch. Normal service was resumed instantly.

Tash helped her to make endless rounds of bacon sandwiches and poured everyone a glass of sherry to keep them all going while they opened their gifts.

'Grilled bacon isn't what I thought we'd be eating for Christmas lunch,' Beth said apologetically.

Dad grinned. 'Don't you worry about it, love – worse things happen at sea! And you know me - I love a good old bacon sarnie with lashings of brown sauce!'

There were so many presents to unwrap between them that it took well over an hour. Beth loved all her Christmas gifts: a tan leather handbag and purse from Ben and Sam; a selection of crime novels and a pretty pink and white dressing gown with matching furry slippers from her mum and dad. Tash surprised and delighted her with a portrait of Rodney which she'd painted from a photo taken during her last visit home. Beth was also thrilled to open a diary for her handbag and gorgeous gold leaf earrings from Jackie. Aunt Lena gave her a beautifully illustrated book on the uses of essential oils.

At last the turkey was cooked and Dad was summoned to carve the now golden skinned and delicious smelling bird. He loved to do things the old fashioned way - no electric knife for him. He sharpened the carving knife on the block he'd brought round especially for the occasion, and set about the task with relish while Mum made gravy; she was in her element in the kitchen.

The family sat around the festively decorated dining table to eat Christmas "lunch" at seven o'clock in the evening.

After that charade, Beth thought things could only get better, but they plunged to new depths on New Year's Eve. Mum and Dad insisted they all link arms and sing Auld Lang Syne. God, Beth thought, it was awful. Why did people (well, her anyway), get it into their heads that the New Year was going to be different from the old one? That something great was going to happen and things would somehow be sparkly and new? Of course, that was a great philosophy, but this particular New Year she felt pressured into "pulling herself together" and looking forward to a bright future. All her imagination could muster, however, was a huge blank canvas and she didn't know how she was going to fill it.

When she heard Big Ben strike twelve on TV, her heart lurched. As everyone exchanged hugs and good wishes, she wondered, for the millionth time, how Paul could erase their marriage. Although their time together certainly hadn't been easy - and what marriage was, Beth pondered, they'd somehow ticked along over the years and she had really loved him.

She recalled what a good father he'd been when Tash and Ben were children.

As soon as he'd arrived home from work, he'd scoop them up and throw them over his shoulders, running around the garden and making them giggle helplessly. He'd ensured they always had an annual family holiday and they'd all enjoyed spending time together, going down to the beach and playing in the sand, or a trip to the amusement park where they'd eat hotdogs and candy floss.

Paul had changed beyond recognition once Ben and Tash left grammar school, and Beth realised that his change in attitude had coincided with the time he'd joined Charles Mortimer's firm; his ambitious and materialistic nature had come to the fore, turning everything on its head.

'It must be scary,' Mum commented as she and Beth washed up the dishes after their New Year's Eve buffet. 'You've been with Paul for so long, you're bound to feel jittery. But just remember you're not on your own, love.'

Beth sighed as she reached up to put a clean plate back into the cupboard. 'Men are from another planet, Mum,' she remarked dully. 'You can't trust any of them... well, except Dad, of course. You're so lucky to have been happy together for all these years.'

Mum fell silent for a few moments. 'Before I met your dad I'd had my fair share of heartache,' she said quietly.

Beth spun round to face her. Never before had she heard her mum mention any pre-Dad romances. 'I thought Dad was your first love – didn't you meet when you were still at college like me and Paul?'

Mum busied herself wiping the taps with her dish cloth. 'Yes, we did, but –'

'Any chance of a cuppa?' Dad called from the sitting room.

Mum flicked on the kettle. 'Yes – it won't be long,' she called back. 'As I was saying; I did meet your dad at college, but we didn't start dating until I was twenty. I'd had my share of boyfriends before then.'

Beth felt herself blush. It was embarrassing to think of your parents being romantic, let alone her mum being a bit of a "goer" back in the day.

'The first boy I fell for was called Tom,' Mum said, a faraway look in her hazel eyes, 'and he came from a traveller family.'

Beth's eyes widened. She was no snob, but she

thought her mother was – well, a bit of a snob, anyway. Not in her mother-in-law's league by any stretch of the imagination, but still a bit of a snob.

'Go on,' Beth urged.

'Your Grandma Joyce and Grandpa Joe didn't like it one bit. Tom got all dressed up in a suit and tie and had his hair cut. He knocked on our door to ask if he could take me to the village dance. Grandma was really rude to him. She told him, "Over my dead body. No daughter of mine is going out with a traveller!".'

'You must've been so upset.'

Mum chewed her lip thoughtfully for a moment. 'What's that word Tash uses when someone's really upset? That's it – *gutted*. I was totally gutted. I really loved Tom.'

'And what happened then?'

'Well, I didn't dare go against my parents' wishes. You just didn't in those days. So I had to look into his gentle brown eyes and tell him not to call at my house again.'

'You did see him again, though?'

Mum nodded. 'We met in secret for a while. We'd meet at the back of an empty pub out in the country, well away from the main road and prying eyes. It'd been empty for years. But in the end Tom wanted more than furtive meetings – he wanted us to be a proper couple, not having to skulk around like we were doing something wrong, so he asked me to run away with him.'

Beth's eyes were like saucers. 'What did you say?'

'I told him I would run away with him, and, at the time, I meant it. I'd had enough of being told what to do and who I could go out with. So I packed a bag and planned to creep out and meet him at the pub after midnight, only, when it came to it, I was too scared to go through with it. I was worried about what we'd do for money as neither of us had any savings, but even more than that I knew what it would do to your Grandma and Grandpa.' Mum dropped three tea bags into mugs and poured on boiling water. 'Tom didn't want anything to do with me after that,' she added. 'And who can blame him? I often think of him waiting outside that pub for me to show up, and, of course, I never did.'

Her mum's revelation had both shocked and intrigued Beth in equal measure. 'Where's Tom now? Did he meet anyone else?'

Mum nodded. 'He met someone else eventually. She was from a traveller family, too. They got married and had children – three, I think it was. And then he got himself killed in a road accident.'

Beth expelled a long breath. 'That's so sad.'

Mum mashed the teabags vigorously against the side of the mugs with a teaspoon. 'The reason I'm telling you this is because I want you to know you're not alone with your heartache. People only show you the side of themselves they want you to see, sometimes even your old mum.'

A jumble of thoughts filled Beth's head. She'd always known her Mum as a homely figure who offered her help and support and loved her unconditionally. She'd never realised how passionate and vulnerable Mum had been as a young woman. What a terrible shame Mum hadn't had that same support when she'd needed it.

She also knew her mum was right: she certainly wasn't alone. It was just; she deliberated, that when you're going through bad stuff yourself, life can seem so unfair. And then you realise no one's life is perfect. Whoever really knows what others are going through and how people feel on the inside?

'Does Dad know about Tom?'

'He knows Tom was my first love, but he's never asked me much about him.'

Beth could imagine her Dad not wanting to pry too deeply; he was sensitive like that. Plus, like a lot of men, he didn't do emotional stuff; things were far better if they were kept simple.

She felt sad for her Mum not being allowed to be with the man she'd loved, and worried for Dad as she wondered if Mum often thought about Tom and the "what ifs".

As though she could read her mind, Mum looked at her thoughtfully. 'Sometimes life just doesn't go according to plan, love. But that doesn't mean it doesn't turn out just fine. Look at me and your dad – we're very happy and we've been together for over forty years now. I wouldn't swap him for the world.'

*

Determined to lift her post-Christmas spirits on a grey January day, Beth took Rodney out for his morning constitutional. Although they lived close to Worcester city centre, in addition to the park there was also Cherry Orchard nature reserve to explore. It was home to a variety of wildlife, including rabbits and foxes and a host of wild flowers. Her favourites were the sunshine yellow wild orchids that spread over the untamed ground like a thick, golden blanket.

Ducks and swans frequently graced the tranquil waters of the River Severn, and brightly painted houseboats bobbed about gently from their moorings at Diglis Basin. There was a riverboat café where you could enjoy a tasty scone and jam or a slice of home-made cake with a nice pot of tea during the holiday season. And even if it was a massive effort to go out for a walk in the first place, Beth found it therapeutic and felt better for the fresh air and exercise – but not today. The river looked murky and dismal. An icy blast of wind sliced through her and gun metal grey clouds loomed overhead, adding an extra-large dollop of misery.

She trudged through rain soaked grass in search of Rodney's ball. The wind whipped her curls into her eyes, causing red strands to stick to her cold lips. Her nose was dripping like a leaky tap, the skin around it flaky and sore where she constantly had to wipe it. Worse still, her feet were cold and soaking wet.

Rodney sat up in a begging pose waiting for her to throw his ball for him. Shoving her hair behind her ears, she hurled the ball high into the air. Rodney trotted half-heartedly after it, but soon lost interest and wandered off in the opposite direction.

Cursing under her breath, she plodded over to look for it, her feet squelching in her cold rubber wellies. When Beth eventually found it, she also spotted Rodney out of the corner of her eye, squatting down ready to do his business.

Ramming the ball back into her coat pocket, she pulled out a dog poo collector bag from the other pocket and ran towards him. Rodney turned his head and gave her a disgruntled look as if to say, 'I want some privacy, woman!' Abandoning his efforts, he trotted away even further before squatting down once more.

Beth heaved a frustrated sigh. Rodney looked around suspiciously to check she wasn't in pursuit. Blimey, she thought, irritated. Most dogs do their business, and then their owner clears it up – simple. *Why did he have to be so blooming awkward*?

She hung back deliberately, casting her eyes downwards so Rodney wouldn't see her watching him and would finish what he'd started.

An elderly lady bundled up in a grey duffle coat ambled by with a Daz white poodle trussed up in a tartan coat. She cast Beth a stony glare.

'It's OK – I'm getting it!' Beth waved the poo bag frantically to prove she was a responsible dog owner.

The old lady cast her eyes skywards and hurried off, the poodle breaking into a trot to keep pace.

Beth's feet were numb with cold as she knelt down to scoop the poop. Holding the bag at arm's length, she wavered around, lifting each foot in turn to examine the soles of her wellies. Just as she suspected, splits had appeared in each one.

Rodney eyed her curiously as she wriggled her toes in an effort to prevent frostbite. Although her hands were encased in woollen gloves, her fingers were stiff and awkward as she struggled to clip him back onto his lead. She finally managed to attach it to his collar and made to leave the park, but her feet defied gravity. The sodden boots sucked her into the muddy ground as she picked her way laboriously towards the exit.

Miss Pink Lycra Pants was jogging towards them as she did most mornings. She was wearing her Dr Dre headphones, her platinum blonde ponytail swishing from side to side as if in time to her music. As she drew level with them, Beth smelt a whiff of Chanel No. 5. If she went jogging (fat chance), she was sure she wouldn't look and smell all glam. She'd probably end up with sweat patches like puddles and a face you could fry an egg on.

As Miss Pink Lycra Pants overtook her, Beth eyed her retreating, wobble-free "Kylie" bum enviously. She did look like a right stuck up mare – but she'd kill for that bum, though.

She was relieved to reach the "poop scoop" bin so she could lob away the stinky bag she'd carried for the last five minutes. A sign stuck on the bin read: "There's no such thing as the dog poo fairy. Bin it!" *Jeez.* She let out a sigh. Owning a dog is so glamorous.

Fifteen minutes later, Beth feeling bedraggled and exhausted, they arrived home. Clutching Rodney's lead, she balanced precariously on one leg and then the other to try to pull off her wellies. Not wanting to drag the gloopy mud that had squeezed into their grooves through the house, she wobbled around desperately trying to pull the wretched thing off her left foot. With Rodney's lead still wound around her right hand, she wrestled furiously with a soggy sock, yanking and twisting at the toe part while Rodney weaved between her legs, impatient to escape. Giving an extra tug at the grey sodden sock, Beth toppled backwards, landing unceremoniously on the hard gravel drive. Rodney seized his chance and did a Houdini type escape from his collar. As she frantically scrambled to her feet, she sensed someone was behind her.

'Are you OK?' asked a familiar male voice.

Her heart sank as she saw Paul and the Munter staring down at her – "Munter" was Tash's name for Emily.

Emily looked smart and stylish as always in an expensive looking navy trouser suit, her dark elfin crop glossy and immaculate.

'I'm fine,' Beth blustered, furiously brushing mud off her backside.

Paul skimmed his hand half-heartedly over her muddy posterior. Although Emily was still unable to conceal a smirk, it gave Beth a degree of satisfaction that she'd seen Paul's hand on her bum. Sadly, humiliation won over that small triumph.

'I'm fine.' Beth huffed, struggling like mad to untwist the lead that was now wound so tightly around her wrist it felt like her blood supply had been cut off. She glanced around her. 'Where's Rodney?'

Emily's smirk widened. 'He ran into the house.'

For God's sake, Beth seethed. If that bloody woman didn't alter her stupid expression in a minute, she'd be tempted to alter it for her.

Trying desperately hard not to hobble, she clambered through the door in time to catch a flash of Rodney's tan and white fur as he lunged through the door to the sitting room, leaving a trail of muddy paw prints all over the cream carpet. His finale involved frantically rubbing his damp furry bonce all over the sheepskin rug.

'Bloody hell, Rodney!' Beth cried.

Paul rolled his eyes and Emily snorted.

Rodney looked up at Beth with innocent eyes, his fur sticking out at all angles and his tail wagging nineteen to the dozen. Despite her humiliation, coupled with the pain of a bruised bum, she struggled to suppress a grin; he looked like Gnasher from Dennis the Menace.

Bundling the dog out of the lounge, Beth shut the door firmly. Turning to face Paul and Emily, she used a tone which she hoped was cool and nonchalant: 'So, what can I do for you?'

'Well,' Paul scrutinised the paw prints and cleared his throat before continuing. 'I'm –' he blustered, looking to Emily as if for support. 'Well, the thing is – *we're* here about Rodney; we think he should come and live with us. I paid for him, after all – and it's obvious you can't cope with him.'

Anger descended over Beth like a red mist – of all the blooming cheek! They didn't have the decency to care about the effect their actions had had on her and the kids, but Rodney - the dog Tash had begged Paul to let them have from the Dogs Trust, was a different matter. She remembered it like it was yesterday:

'Why would we choose a Heinz 57 that no one else wants when I can easily afford a pedigree from a proper breeder?' Paul had said, genuinely mystified.

Fortunately, Tash had managed to persuade her father it made him a "better person" if he helped a less fortunate animal, so eventually he'd agreed, albeit begrudgingly.

'I don't care *who* paid for him; Rodney stays here!' Beth cried. 'He loves being with me –'

'Well, I think –' Emily interrupted.

Beth's head spun round like the girl possessed by the devil in the film *The Exorcist*. 'What the hell's it got to do with you? God knows why *you're* even here!'

Right on cue, Rodney pawed at the door. Expecting him to demonstrate his love for her by jumping up, Beth pulled it open. He darted past her, something bright pink dangling from his mouth, and headed once more for the sheepskin rug.

Beth clapped a hand over her mouth. *OMG – it was a pair of her old knickers – her "Bridget Jones's"!* To her total horror, Rodney held the material between his front paws and gleefully began tearing the gusset apart.

Paul and Emily stood aghast as she dived to retrieve her tatty pants.

Panting like a madwoman, she finally managed to wrestle them free from the dog's jaws.

Paul shook his head and Emily gave a loud snort.

'Why don't the pair of you just piss off?' Beth yelled. 'And you're not having the bloody dog – he stays with me. *RIGHT?*'

They left without saying another word.

Chapter Seven
Paul

Paul cut into his fillet steak, medium rare, just how he liked it.

Emily topped up his glass from a bottle of Pinot Grigio. 'Have you read the e-mail from the Russell-Smythes today?'

He pursed his lips, nodding vaguely in response. All he wanted after a hectic day at the office was some peace and quiet. It was OK for Emily; she'd had the day off – a perk of being the boss's daughter.

Unperturbed by his lack of enthusiasm, she continued, 'We need to discuss the menu ... and we also need to discuss the dog.' Her tone was insistent now. 'Have you spoken to Bethany again?'

Taking a sip of wine, Paul swilled it around inside his mouth, taking his time as he savoured the rich full-bodied flavour before lowering his glass. 'Not yet, but I will.'

'Well, make sure she knows you mean business,' Emily said tetchily. 'After her theatrical antics with your clothes and the dog episode don't go all soft on her. You need to put her straight.'

His grip tightened around the stem of the glass.

They ate the meal in silence, and Paul found himself thinking about his wife.

Beth had changed over the years, and not for the better in his book. She'd been a good wife in many ways, he acknowledged. He'd had clean clothes each morning and a meal on the table every evening. And, although she'd got a bit plumper than he'd have preferred, she was very easy on the eye. But what she lacked was any get up and go. They'd had nothing in common and very little to talk about since Tash and Ben had left home.

Paul was like his mother; ambition was in his blood.

Ironically, though, he thought his wife had too much to say for herself of late and she'd certainly been too opinionated.

He wiped his mouth on the white linen table napkin.

Emily's feline, kohl flicked eyes widened; she really must get him more housetrained.

Paul pulled out his chair and rose from the table. He strolled through the double French doors and out onto the spacious balcony of Emily's plush apartment overlooking Diglis Basin. Chinks of light were visible from the majestic Worcester Cathedral, and, as he rested his forearms on the cold steel rail, he gazed down at the River Severn. Lights from the apartments opposite cast a golden reflection on the dark, still water.

Curling his hand around a cigar, he puffed hard as

he lit it, and then blew a trail of smoke rings into the star studded night.

Celine, Emily's cat, weaved between his legs. Paul gritted his teeth as his fur clung to his Ralph Lauren trousers like Velcro. For Christ's sake! They'd end up looking as if they'd been made from black cat hair instead of virgin wool! He'd dearly love to shove the wretched moggy out of the way with his foot, but he knew Emily would be angry; the big, hairy lump (who was a male with a female name) was undeniably her "baby". He'd choose a canine over a feline any day. He hadn't been happy about housing a Heinz 57 from the Dogs Trust, but he'd grown very fond of Rodney and believed a house didn't feel like home without a dog.

Emily clattered around in the kitchen, flinging dishes into her new silver Bosch dish washer. It sounded like a night out at a Greek restaurant.

'Are you coming back in, dahling?' she trilled, when she'd finished her crockery flinging.

He cast his gaze skywards. *Couldn't a man have a minute's peace?* 'I'll just finish my cigar,' he replied flatly.

'Well, don't be too long,' Emily huffed. 'We've got to discuss our dinner party with the Russell-Smythes.'

Paul exhaled a long breath. Why the hell did she have to keep on about that pompous prick from accounts? He suffered enough of that boring chap in the office. Mind you, Jules Russell-Smythe was a bit of hot totty. But his thoughts were stopped in their tracks – Emily would watch him like a hawk if he so much as glanced in Jules' direction.

Ah, well, his social standing brought power, so it would all be worth it in the end. After being forced by his parents into a marriage he was far too young for, he was determined to use that power to his advantage. He'd worked hard all his life; he reckoned it was time to play hard, too. A yacht in France was on the top of his bucket list, together with as many far flung holidays as he could fit in, and, well – who knew what else?

Why should he feel guilty for wanting the good things in life? Ben and Natasha were adults now, with lives of their own. Ben worked for Paul and would have opportunities most young men could only dream about; Tash was fiercely independent, and Beth had her family.

Emily hovered in the doorway, her hands on her slender hips. 'Dahling, I really do think you should come in now and close the doors. It's turning chilly – look, I've got goose bumps.'

Paul clicked the roof of his mouth with his tongue impatiently. 'I told you – I'm just finishing my cigar.'

With an exasperated sigh, Emily disappeared back inside. Paul threw his cigar to the floor, grinding it out with his foot. Maybe he'd sounded a teensy bit sharp, he decided, but the last thing he wanted to do was discuss dinner with the Russell-Smythes. There again, he supposed he couldn't afford to upset the daughter of his potential new business partner. 'Sorry, sweet cheeks, I didn't mean to snap,' he called.

Sucking in a long breath, Emily poured herself another glass of Pinot and sank down into the plush white recliner, pressing the automatic button to raise her slim legs up to a comfortable position. It really wasn't on, Paul snapping at her like that. He ought to watch his Ps and Qs if he wanted to stay in Daddy's good books.

She took bird-like sips of Pinot and waited a couple more minutes before downing the remainder in one gulp. She pressed the button to lower her chair and walked out to join Paul, who appeared to be in a world of his own and was now gazing up at the stars. Scooping Celine into her arms, Emily nuzzled her head into the crook of his neck. Paul glanced down at her cute elfin cropped head and gave a half smile. Sensing resistance, Emily trailed pearl-tipped nails down the length of his arm. '*Do* come in now, dahling,' she coaxed. 'We really must go through the menu - and I want to model my new outfit for you.'

He swallowed hard at the thought of the huge walk-in wardrobe crammed with Emily's tailored work suits and her abundance of designer outfits. He raised a quizzical brow. '*Another* new outfit?'

Emily pouted prettily. 'I told you, sweetie, I don't want to look under-dressed.'

Paul knew there was absolutely no chance of that happening. He also knew that Emily's father and his prospective co-partner, the ailing Charles Mortimer, should be retiring sooner rather than later. His lips curved into a smile. He thought the name Bishop and Bishop had a nice ring to it.

Chapter Eight
Shaken, not Stirred

Running warm water into a bowl, Beth added washing up liquid, and swished it around with her hand to lather it up before vigorously scrubbing at the dirty paw marks on the cream carpet - Paul's choice, of course.

'We're having neutral; it's subtle and sophisticated,' he'd said.

She'd have preferred real oak flooring and some brightly coloured rugs any day, but as Paul's mother, Penelope, constantly reminded her: 'It *is* Paul's money that pays for everything, dear, and, of course, he follows me; he does have such classy taste.' She'd never dared argue with a woman whose house was the size of Downton Abbey.

She remembered when she'd painted Tash's old room when her daughter had gone to live in the halls at Birmingham University. She'd chosen a glorious sunshine yellow and she'd hung pale lemon and white cottage-style checked curtains.

'Jesus – it looks like a custard pie!' That wasn't exactly the reaction Beth had been hoping for from Paul. She'd thought he could use the room for his office, but he'd opted for Ben's old room, which was decorated in masculine black and grey. The custard pie room, as it was now known, had become her sanctuary.

*

Beth and Paul had first met when Mum had cleaned for Paul's parents. They'd been short staffed at "Downton" one day, and, as Beth had the day off college, she'd offered to lend a hand. The house was situated in the village of Leigh Sinton on the outskirts of Worcester. It was a large six- bed roomed house with an acre of land and a huge swimming pool.

She remembered back to when Paul had been charm personified, and she'd fallen for him hook, line and sinker.

Of course, Mum and Dad were over the moon; they thought that coming from such a privileged background made Paul a "proper gent" and Mum had a smile on her face for days when they'd become an item – it was as though Beth had won the lottery.

Mum and Dad lived in a two-up, two-down semi on a large estate. It was a decent area to live, and Mum kept their humble home like a palace, although she couldn't help being in awe of Penelope's posh house and lifestyle.

'It's like something out of one of those glossy Home and Garden magazines, Ted,' she told Beth's dad. 'It's even got four toilets!'

Dad shook his head. 'You can only use one at a time,' he'd remarked, as he continued to read his Daily

Mirror.

Dad loved Mum dearly and knew her inside out. He was all too familiar with her aspirations of grandeur, but he was more than happy with his lot. He loved their home; it was within easy reach of Worcester Rugby Club where he'd go to support his local team and he often enjoyed a day at the horse races at Pitchcroft. He was proud of their long back garden, humming with bees as they pollinated his wild flower patch and thought it made Downton soulless in comparison.

To say that Penelope wasn't happy about Paul and Bethany's relationship could be described as the understatement of the century. When Beth had fallen pregnant with Ben, Penelope was truly horrified. Her downtrodden husband, Clive, although not exactly delighted, was nevertheless far more calm and accepting. 'It's happened, and we must do what we can to help them,' he'd told his wife.

The one thing both sets of parents agreed on was that their son and daughter should "do the right thing".

Beth had felt scared; events were tumbling out of her control, gathering pace. However, she'd been besotted with Paul, although, in her heart, she'd never truly believed that he felt the same way.

As her dad had linked his arm through hers and they'd walked into the registry office, there'd been a seed of doubt in her mind, but she'd reasoned it was wedding nerves. After all, she was young, she was pregnant, and what bride wasn't nervous on her wedding day?

Throughout her pregnancy, she worried that Paul was growing further away from her. He didn't hold her hand when they were out together and was always too busy if she asked him to go with her to her ante-natal classes. Fortunately, Mum had been only too keen to oblige.

The bigger Beth's bump grew, the more detached Paul seemed to become. The charm he'd originally shown was gradually being replaced by an arrogant indifference.

To her relief, when Ben was born, followed a couple of years later by Tash, things had improved and she'd felt a kind of contentment. It wasn't the life she'd actually planned, at least not then. Yes, she'd wanted to be a mother and a wife one day, but she'd put her own hopes and dreams on hold to ensure that Tash and Ben had a happy upbringing like she'd been fortunate enough to have. She'd kept house and looked after the kids while Paul worked his way up the legal ladder. And, she realised now, with each rung he climbed, although he loved his son and daughter, he was climbing further away from her.

Dragging herself back to the present, she flicked on the kettle to make a coffee and grabbed a couple of paracetamol for her bruised bum. It was a pity, she thought, she couldn't take something for her bruised pride too.

She poured boiling water over Nescafe instant

coffee granules and opened the fridge door. The carton of milk felt suspiciously light as she took it from the shelf. She gave it a futile shake. *Empty*. Unable to face going out again, she drank her coffee black. In the great scheme of things, she knew this wasn't important, but to her it was the last straw and she was unable to stop hot, fat tears spilling down her cheeks.

Throwing her third snotty tissue into the bin, she drained the last dregs of black coffee and perched the mug precariously on top of a mountain of dirty crockery in the bowl. She knew all she had to do was load the dishwasher, but it needed emptying first and she couldn't even muster the energy to do that.

The house seemed to be closing in on her, and, desperate to escape, she put Rodney on his lead once again and grabbed her jacket as she headed out of the back door.

*

Beth strode towards the town centre with Rodney, who was buoyed up with enthusiasm at his impromptu outing.

They cut through Diglis Park and its surrounding playing field, and passed Diglis Basin. Soon, they were standing outside the apartment block where Emily lived.

Paul certainly had dumped on his own doorstep, she thought angrily. She felt a sudden urge to hurl a stone at Emily's window, but, realising this was futile as she didn't know which apartment she lived in, she marched past, trying to concentrate on the horde of colourful houseboats moored there. She'd always fancied living on a houseboat and being able to sail off to wherever the mood took her. Today, though, under a leaden sky, it didn't seem quite so appealing.

Walking on, she headed towards The Anchor pub. The sound of chatter and laughter was spilled out into the street before she'd reached the door. She paused, taking a deep breath to gather herself; she'd never ventured into a pub alone. Before she could think herself out of it, she pulled open the door and walked inside.

A handful of customers looked round at her, but simply nodded in welcome or continued drinking. It wasn't as daunting as she'd feared it might be. She squeezed past people who were standing next to the bar until she found a vacant barstool. Removing her jacket, she placed it over her handbag and sat down, trying to blend in with the crowd.

After observing their new surroundings, Rodney seemed content and settled down at her feet. A pretty young barmaid, wearing a name badge with "Annie" printed on it, smiled at her and asked her what she'd like to drink. Beth thought about being theatrical and making it a double scotch on the rocks, or a martini, shaken but not stirred, but settled on a simple glass of red.

She was on her second glass when Annie came from behind the bar to collect the empties. She knelt down and stroked Rodney's head. Rodney opened one eye, and then closed it again. 'Aww, he's lovely,' she said.

Beth smiled at her. 'Thanks.' She looked at her thoughtfully for a moment. 'D'you know – this is the first time I've ever been into a pub on my own?'

Annie shook her head, but smiled politely.

'Yep,' Beth re-affirmed, more to herself than to Annie. 'I'm drinking alone in the middle of the day!'

Unsure how to respond, Annie gave her a half-smile and nodded before collecting up the empties.

'You alright, love?' asked an elderly guy seated on the next stool. He had a bushy white beard and a glint in his eye, reminding Beth of Captain Birdseye.

'I'm drinking on my own in the middle of the day,' she repeated.

'And why not?' he said wholeheartedly. 'It doesn't hurt to let your hair down sometimes. We're a friendly bunch in here.'

Beth raised a toast to that and, as soon as her second glass was finished, he ordered her a third. She followed this with a fourth, making small talk with Captain Birdseye as the mellowing effect of the alcohol enveloped her into a warm fuzziness.

As she drained her fourth glass, Rodney grew restless. He stood up and gave her a hard stare. Peering hazily at her watch, she was surprised to find they'd been in the pub for over an hour.

She clambered down off her stool, her body

lurching forward, and made a grab at a nearby table in order to steady herself.

'Are you OK?' Annie asked anxiously, from behind the bar.

Beth nodded. 'I think so.'

Captain Birdseye put his arm around her shoulders. 'I can see you home, love,' he said, 'It would be my pleasure.'

Even in her tipsy state, the inflection in his tone set off alarm bells. 'Nooo, thank you. My husband will be coming to meet me any minute,' she told him hurriedly.

Leaving a crest-fallen Captain Birdseye, she clutched Rodney's lead and weaved her way out of the pub and set off home on wobbly legs.

*

Fumbling around with the front door key, Beth made several attempts to insert it in the lock before she managed to let herself in. By now she felt really dizzy and decided she'd better go and have a lie down. She clutched onto the stair rail as she climbed the stairs and then tumbled into her bedroom and slung her bag onto the bed. As she lurched over to the window to lower the blind, she heard the crunch of gravel and the purr of a car's engine. Opening the blind a fraction, she peered out between the slats. Her heart did a triple nose-dive; Penelope was climbing out of her BMW convertible, "PEN 1"

Clutching onto the hand rail; she hurried back

downstairs. Her befogged mind was in a dazed whirl of panic. She realised it was going to be an impossible task to empty and reload the dishwasher before the doorbell rang.

Grabbing the overflowing bowl out of the sink, she shoved it into the pantry, just managing to slam the door as the bell chimed.

Penelope swooped in on a cloud of Prada, her high heeled Louboutins click-clacking on the tiled hallway. Her dark hair was pulled back from her high forehead with a pink chiffon scarf. She wore a tailored cerise two piece, and a slash of matching pink lipstick stained her thin lips. Beth marvelled at how her mother-in-law always looked so dignified and glamorous.

'What brings you here?' Beth asked, hoping she sounded coherent.

'Well, dear -' Penelope paused, her eyes narrowing as she stared at Beth. 'Have you been drinking?'

Beth steadied herself by holding onto the door frame. 'What business is it of yours if I have?'

Penelope shook her head and emitted a loud tut. 'I must say I'm surprised at you, Bethany.'

Penelope's husband, Clive, climbed out of the BMW and walked over to join them.

'She's drunk, Clive!' Penelope hissed. 'I can smell the alcohol on her breath.'

Beth shook her head defiantly. 'I am soooo **not!**'

Clive, who towered above his wife in stature,

reached out and placed his hand on Beth's shoulder. 'Don't be too hard on the girl. She's had a lot to cope with.'

Penelope glared at her husband, but he ignored her and continued to speak to Beth. 'I'm sorry how things have turned out, Bethany, and, if you want my honest opinion, I think my son's gone quite mad.' He ran his fingers through his silver hair, which, despite his age, remained thick and wavy like Paul's.

Beth smiled her gratitude.

Penelope focused her attention on a stray cobweb attached to the corner of the windowsill. 'Paul thought you'd need an extra pair of hands to help you pack,' she said brusquely. 'There's an awful lot of work to do when you're moving out.'

Chapter Nine
Equity and an Easy Ride

Paul's Audi skidded to a halt next to his mother's BMW. He could do with this like a second backside, he thought.

Beth was sitting in the living room with her in-laws. She stared, wide-eyed, at Paul as he sauntered in. Penelope rose from the sofa to greet her son, while Clive remained seated.

'I'm only doing what you asked, dear,' Penelope wheedled, her tone brimming with faux hurt. She pointed a finger towards an antique bookcase that housed all of Paul's leather-bound law books. 'I know these have to be packed in a specific way, and I'm only too happy to help Bethany to organise things and make the move go as smoothly as possible.'

Shock had caused the mellowed-out wine effect to disappear. Beth now felt stone cold sober. She simmered with rage. 'I'm quite capable of sorting a few books into alphabetical order or whatever! That's not the issue –'

Ignoring her, Paul placated his mother, who awarded Beth with a self-satisfied smile. Clive caught Beth's gaze and cast his eyes upwards.

'I don't understand what's going on,' Beth persisted. 'I'm not moving anywhere –'

Looking sheepish, Paul drew a deep breath. 'I'm afraid the house has to go on the market as soon as possible.'

'Why? You can't just throw me out on a whim!'

'I have debts to pay,' he replied, in his monotonous voice.

'There's zero equity in this house, Bethany,' Penelope cut in, 'and these debts must be cleared.'

Beth shook her head, trying to take it all in. Her husband stood before her, his eyes now cast downwards, like a naughty schoolboy.

She stared at him in disbelief. 'How could you let this happen?'

He looked at her, his eyes narrowing to slits. 'Don't take the moral high ground with me! I'll continue to provide you with an allowance, but you'll just have to find yourself a job – you can't carry on expecting a free ride all your life!'

Beth felt as though she'd been slapped. She rose from the sofa. 'A free ride? You pig! You absolute –' she broke off, unable to continue, and flopped down once more in a daze.

Penelope decided to change tactics and sat down next to her. 'I understand this must have come as a shock to you dear,' she said, tentatively placing a hand on Beth's shoulder, '...but I implore you to reasonable. You don't have to provide a home for Natasha and

Benjamin anymore, and you certainly don't need to rattle around in this big house alone.'

As Beth met her mother-in-law's steady gaze, her face burned with humiliation and anger.

Paul nodded. 'That's true,' he agreed, 'but what I'm asking is, please don't make this any more difficult than it already is. You can, of course, go through the courts, but just think about it. Do you really want to go through all that? It'll be a protracted and stressful affair if you do. And you can check with Ben if you doubt what I'm saying, but the simple fact is I have debts to settle, the house is in my name and I'm giving you reasonable notice to quit. If you, in turn, are reasonable, I'll make sure you're OK for money when I'm senior partner.'

The room, together with Paul's words, spun around in Beth's head. She sat motionless, desperately trying to make sense of it all.

He breathed a heavy sigh. 'Do you really want Tash and Ben to see any more animosity between us? Look, just think it through and I'll call you tomorrow. Surely we can sort this out like adults.'

Penelope rose from the sofa and linked her arm through Paul's. Clive cast his daughter-in-law a sympathetic look as he trailed out behind his wife and son.

Chapter Ten
Paul

Penelope hung onto Paul's arm. 'I'm sure Bethany will see sense, dear,' she soothed.

Clive remained tight-lipped as he climbed into the passenger seat. His son and his wife were so damn well alike, he thought. Penelope had spoilt their only child something rotten, although, after several failed attempts to conceive, followed by a harrowing miscarriage, he understood why she indulged him. Paul, however, was never satisfied and always wanted more. Now the stupid fellow had managed to get himself into debt and it was their daughter-in-law who had to suffer. Still, he'd said all he had to say on the matter. Whatever he did say usually fell on deaf ears anyway.

*

Paul blew out a steady stream of air as he steered the car down the familiar drive. As long as he lived, he'd never understand women. He'd always tried to be reasonable, but lately even his mother had been in his ear, nagging him about being frivolous with money. *Frivolous!* What a bloody joke that was. He was expected to fund Emily's lifestyle as well as his own.

Emily squirreled away the money she earned, together with her hand-outs from her father, and he had no doubt she was gaining maximum interest on her investments. There was no way she was going to let anyone near her stash. It was no wonder he was running up debts left, right and centre.

He did feel rather guilty about Beth. He knew she didn't deserve to lose her home on top of everything else, but sometimes in life one had to be ruthless. He'd come so far; success was now in sniffing distance, and, although it was proving more difficult than he'd imagined to claw to the top, he couldn't let go of the reigns.

He steered his Audi into the nearest garage and pulled a wad of well abused credit cards from his leather wallet. He'd maxed out on most of them, but there was still some credit left on his Platinum card. He shoved the redundant cards back into his wallet, jumped out of the car and started filling the engine.

Paul hadn't actually envisaged things being this way. Charles Mortimer should've already stepped down, allowing him total control. But oh, no - the old bastard was still hanging on in there by his fingernails. It was Charles's daughter who was spending Paul's money as if it was going out of fashion - a Michelin starred restaurant in the capital on bloody Christmas day, for example! Of course, they'd had to invite her parents too. But no one had picked up the tab, had they? Oh, no, he thought bitterly, he'd had to see to that, just like he was the one paying out for Emily's fine jewellery and designer clothes. His girlfriend's idea of slumming it was buying a dress off a rack at the House of Fraser. As for face creams and the like, don't even get him started! Where had Bethany shopped, he wondered. He was damn sure that Simple stuff on her dressing table cost nowhere near as much as Emily's

Crème de la Mer. And what the devil was that face stuff with caviar in it all about? Why on earth would anyone want to smother their face with bloody fish eggs?

He sucked in his bottom lip as he filled up his engine with petrol, trying hard to convince himself that everything would be alright once the house was sold and his partnership secured.

Chapter Eleven
Kleenex and a Sense of Purpose

With a sigh, Beth put her mug down on the kitchen worktop. 'I never thought for one second Paul was in so much debt,' she said. 'And, as if that isn't enough, Penelope's delighting in telling me all about the wonderful Emily: every excruciating detail. Apparently she's incredibly intelligent. In fact, according to Penelope, she's "Paul's intellectual equal" and she "hosts the most amazing dinner parties, dear". Honestly, is there nothing that woman can't do? She probably nips into a phone box and comes out with her knickers over her tights ready to save the day! I haven't been a bad wife and mum - and I'm not that useless, am I?' She dabbed at her nose with a soggy piece of tissue. Kleenex sales must have gone up a hundredfold these last few weeks, she thought.

Jackie shook her head. 'You're talking out of your backside! Stop being so stupid and beating yourself up - it's only been a few weeks. Anyway,' she continued, 'it's not you, it's prat-face – he's a right dickhead!' And, although she'd told Beth this during most of their conversations, it still made her smile. 'What you need,' Jackie added earnestly, 'is a job. It would give you a sense of purpose and put some money in your purse. But let's take first things first. Have you asked Ben for some legal advice?'

Beth nodded solemnly. 'He says if Paul's given me reasonable notice to quit it's going to be difficult to fight it. Although to be honest, Jacks, it feels really weird living there now – like I'm some sort of squatter. I'm not sure I want to stay there anymore. I'm thinking of asking Mum and Dad if me and Rodney can stay with them until I can afford to rent somewhere.'

Jackie frowned. 'Promise me you won't do anything rash; just make sure it's definitely what you want – but, if you're determined to leave, I've got a spare room – you and Rodney are welcome to stay with me if the house is sold.'

'I couldn't ask you to do that –'

'You're not asking. I'm offering. And, for goodness' sake, just ignore the silly old trout! She'll run out of steam eventually.'

'I doubt that,' Beth said dubiously. 'But thanks so much, Jacks, I really appreciate it. I'd only stay for a few weeks, until I could get a flat or something.'

'As far as I'm concerned, you can stay as long as you like. I'll enjoy having the company. In fact, you'll be doing me a favour. There's one condition, though –'

'What's that?'

'You've got to stop worrying about what everyone thinks and get on with your life. You've got a hell of a lot of life to live, missus!'

'I promise I'll do my best. But I can't imagine being able to get a job; I've got no qualifications or experience. What have I got to offer a prospective employer?'

Chapter Twelve
Jackie

Walking back to her flat, Jackie heaved a frustrated sigh. She couldn't understand why Beth hadn't left Paul a long time ago. He was so self-centred, so arrogant and full of his own importance. It wasn't as if she couldn't find someone else either. Beth had a heart of gold. Jackie had always thought she was far too good for him and his materialistic ego. But, in her heart, she knew it was simple: Beth loved him, warts and all, and her priority had always been to do right by her children.

How many other women felt like that, she wondered? It wouldn't ever happen to her, she'd make sure of that. A husband and kids were definitely not on her agenda. She was happy with the way things were, free of hurt and complications.

She'd noticed the subtle way Paul had developed of putting Beth down in front of others, like the time she'd been round there enjoying a cuppa and a natter with Beth and Paul arrived home early. 'Oh, so this is what you do while I'm out grafting,' he'd said, indicating the cups of tea and cakes on the table. 'It's nice to see my money's being put to good use.'

Beth had coloured up and Jackie knew his comment wasn't made as a joke; his tone had been laced with a hint of sarcasm. And that was just one of many examples she'd observed.

She knew from experience that there were far worse men than Paul in the world. Yet throughout the time Jackie had known her, Beth had seemed to live in his shadow, always trying to please him but rarely succeeding.

Jackie felt it was about time her friend recognised herself for the worthwhile person she was.

Her thoughts flicked back to her own childhood, to her mum and dad in their large, well-tended garden. She smiled at the memory; her dad chasing her around and making her shriek with delight. She'd serve him tea and biscuits from her white china tea-set, the tiny cups and saucers emblazoned with fairies, and she'd line up all her dolls and teddies in a row on the red checked picnic rug he'd let her borrow from the boot of his car.

Unexpectedly, tears stung behind her eyelids. Hastily, she blinked them back. Family life had been wonderful for her then, but tragedy had struck: her dad had died in a car accident. She was thirteen years old when her world had come crashing down.

Her mother did her best for her, but the light had gone from her mum's eyes. Then, just over twelve months later, her mother met Bill Parsons, a local butcher, and they'd started dating.

Jackie knew she'd been, well, difficult to say the

least. She wasn't, for one moment, going to let them think anyone could ever take her dad's place. She resented Bill and gave both him and her mum a hard time, being disobedient, ungrateful and basically quite a brat. When Bill had brought home joints of beef and pork, she'd declared she was a vegetarian and sat with her arms folded, resolutely refusing to eat a thing.

Gradually, though, Bill had wormed his way into her affections. He'd bought her a rabbit (a live one), for starters. It was fluffy, white and lop-eared. Jackie called him Ringo, after Ringo Starr, the drummer with The Beatles. They'd been her dad's favourite group. Ringo would scratch behind his ear with his hind foot which thudded up and down, making him sound like he was playing the drums. Slowly, bit by bit, Bill Parsons was drip-fed into her life.

When things went so unbelievably wrong, her mum had refused to listen. She thought that Jackie had turned against Bill and was trying to cause trouble between them. Even when her mother was on her deathbed, Jackie could never forgive her.

*

She'd been in love herself once. In fact, she'd been engaged. Bret, her fiancé, had seemed so patient and caring when she couldn't face making love to him. She'd finally plucked up the courage to tell him everything, but he said that, although he loved her, he couldn't deal with hearing about what had happened. She'd felt totally bereft, but clung to him as she believed she couldn't cope without him.

One day she'd arrived back at the house they shared early. She'd opened the bedroom door to find Bret lying on top of their bed, a naked woman pinned beneath him. His pale, skinny backside was pumping up and down for all he was worth. Their faces, when they realised she was standing there, had been priceless.

'I can explain –' Bret began feebly, his willy shrivelling to the size of a walnut. The woman clambered off the bed and hoisted up her panties and mini skirt before running out of the front door in her bare feet, clutching her red patent stilettos.

While Jackie gathered up all Bret's clothes and belongings, he'd pleaded: 'I didn't want to keep pestering you for sex after what you've been through.'

She'd felt sick to the pit of her stomach, and that had convinced her she was better off without a man in her life. She'd invested so much trust, love and energy into her relationship, and for what? Men took the love-them-and-leave-them attitude with nothing to complicate things. It struck her that why shouldn't she do the same? It was easier for her to lie with a stranger to whom she felt no emotional attachment whatsoever. The only downside was the emptiness she felt afterwards.

Jackie always thought of Beth as her adopted sister, yet the closer she felt to someone, the more she kept things to herself. The last thing she wanted or needed was to see pity in anyone's eyes. She couldn't cope with that.

Beth's mum had confided in her about how much she hated the way Beth's opinions were dismissed by Paul, saying that she felt like her vibrant daughter was somehow fading.

Jackie knew Beth was good at hiding her feelings with her sense of humour, but she realised it was a mask to cover her low self-esteem. Ironic, really, that she too had huge self-esteem issues. Forever the carer, she wanted to help her friend gain a sense of self-worth – and she'd had an idea how.

Chapter Thirteen
Brussels Sprouts and Shabby Chic

Beth felt much calmer following Jackie's visit. Her friend's patience was infinite, and she admired how Jackie was a "glass half full" person. Jackie had confided in her about how Bret had cheated on her, saying that she believed that it had happened for a reason and she was better off without him. In fact, Jackie always maintained she was better off without any man in her life.

Following their chat, she felt a fresh surge of determination to better herself and gain some much needed qualifications.

Tash advised her that the first step on the long road of self-improvement was to invest in a laptop. Together they trawled around PC World, where Tash helped her to choose one from the vast array of technical confusion. Thank God Tash had set it up, she thought – or it would still be in the box! Beth was relieved she'd bitten the bullet and learned how to get by, though, with more than a little help from her daughter, who was extremely patient. That was definitely a good thing if she was going to be using ink on various parts of people's anatomies. At nineteen years old, Tash was studying for her degree in fine art. 'I want to run my own tattoo parlour eventually,' she'd announced casually over the breakfast table one day.

Paul wasn't exactly thrilled at the idea of their daughter becoming a tattoo artist. Gradually, though, and with a lot of placating from Beth, he'd come to accept it.

Tash had spent painstaking hours showing Beth how to use Google search, send an e-mail, and buy on eBay. She'd even set up a Facebook page for her, which, Beth acknowledged, was probably a mistake. There was nothing like whiling away a few hours looking at what everyone else was up to rather than tackling her own issues. Still, she reasoned, sometimes a little procrastination was a good way to unwind.

Feeling bold, Beth decided to go on an internet job hunting mission. She opened up her laptop and typed "Jobs – Worcestershire area" into the Google search engine. It wasn't a good start. The search brought up stuff like:

'Groceries online shopper. The successful applicant will have the responsibility of packing customers' orders ready to be loaded onto the delivery vehicle ....'

Ohh errr – having heard Penelope rant on about receiving two sprouts in a plastic bag from the supermarket when she'd ordered two kilos online, Beth didn't fancy that much – she knew the poor delivery guy had copped a right earful.

She read about several equally unsuitable vacancies where every employer seemed to want to recruit people with PhDs, or, at the very least, tons of experience. Beth could imagine herself in a queue of PhD educated youngsters full of confidence and fresh ideas, while she might as well sit there with a big "D" tattooed on her forehead.

Why weren't there any suitable vacancies for her, she wondered - such as: *'Fed up thirty-nine year old deserted wife and mother who can use Google search engine, buy on eBay and (on a good day), send an e-mail?'*

She made herself another coffee (her fifth, and it was only eleven o'clock), and had just taken her first sip when the door opened and Jackie breezed in. Beth looked at her friend admiringly. She looked great in denim jeans in a petite size ten. Her blue cotton top brought out her blue eyes and her honey blonde hair was piled high into a messy bun. She always achieved the look Beth would love – casual chic, whereas, Beth thought cynically, she was more shabby-chic.

Jackie's grin was as wide as a Cheshire cat's, (although Beth had never actually seen a Cheshire cat). 'Blimey, you look pleased with yourself!' She grabbed the bottle of wine her friend was swinging around precariously. 'It's a bit early for this, though, isn't it?'

Ignoring her, Jackie foraged around in Beth's muddle of a kitchen drawer for a corkscrew. After pulling out a selection of plasters and a few empty paracetamol packets with said plasters stuck to them, she finally plucked out a corkscrew and plunged it forcefully into the bottle. 'It's a celebration!' she said, untwisting the cork.

'Come on ... stop being so mysterious! What are we celebrating?'

Jackie poured two large glasses of Shiraz and handed one to Beth. 'Well, hopefully, your new job!'

'You *what?*' Beth spluttered, choking on her wine. 'What new job?'

Chapter Fourteen
CV and a Spare Tyre

'I've put in a good word with Sandra, my manager, and she wants you to come for an interview at Holly Mount tomorrow!'

Beth looked at her, aghast. 'Is this some kind of wind-up?'

Jackie shook her head vehemently. 'It's a bona fide job,' she insisted. 'You'd be a carer like me.'

'But I've never even considered looking after old people! I don't know the first thing about it!'

'It's mainly using your common sense,' Jackie said, matter-of-factly, as she topped up her glass. 'Anyway, you won't know what you can do unless you try – and beggars can't be choosers.'

'Charming! But true. Thank you, Jacks, I really appreciate it – honest.'

Jackie had worked at Holly Mount Care Home for the past twelve years. She thought the world of the residents, (or "ressies", as she fondly referred to them), always going the extra mile to make them happy.

Beth knew that caring for people was a really worthwhile job; it gave her friend a great deal of personal satisfaction. However, as much as she wished she could be like Jackie, she simply was not. She was a worrier; prone to getting in a flap, so why on earth her friend thought that she could be a carer was totally beyond her.

However, there were no two ways about it, Beth decided. She needed to earn money and, at thirty-nine, with no qualifications or work experience, people would hardly be queuing up to offer her work.

*

The next day, as she prepared for her interview, her mouth felt like the bottom of a parrot's cage. How on earth, she wondered, was she going to be able to speak to Jackie's manager? She was worried sick that she wouldn't be able to utter a word, let alone construct a sentence.

She ensured she arrived at Holly Mount early so she'd have time to park up her red Ka, calm herself down, and, most importantly, nip to the loo.

The black imposing entrance door stood between two large stone pillars. Her legs trembled as she walked into the reception area of the rambling Victorian building. She pressed the buzzer on the sturdy oak reception desk.

A couple of strained minutes ticked by and no one came to greet her. She took a deep breath and plucked up the courage to press it again, springing back in alarm as it sounded louder than she'd anticipated.

A lady, who looked to be in her thirties, came crashing through a side door. She wore a lilac tunic and black trousers; her cheeks were flushed and her fine mousey hair was scraped away from her face and tied back in a thin pony tail. She wore a name badge on her lapel: "Jodie".

She threw Beth an apologetic smile. 'Sorry about that,' her words tumbled out in a rush. 'I'm only covering reception as our receptionist's off sick, but I'm a Jack of all trades at the mo! Are you here for an interview?'

Beth returned her smile. 'Yes. I'm Bethany Bishop, here to see Sandra Sergeant.'

'No problem,' Jodie said, noting something down in a register lying open on the desk. 'If I can get you to sign in.' Handing Beth a pen, she pointed to the relevant space. 'Just write down your name, the date, and your car registration.'

As she began to enter her details, her face grew hot. She hovered with the pen poised over the space to enter her car registration. *What the devil was it?* 'Sorry,' she mumbled, hoping she didn't look as red as she felt. 'I've gone totally blank – I can't remember my car reg!'

Jodie cast her a sympathetic look. 'I can never remember mine, either. I've put it in contacts in my mobile, but sometimes I forget what I've listed it under so I have to scroll through all my contacts to find it! Just nip to your car and I'll wait for you.'

Beth felt relieved Jodie was friendly and that she didn't appear to think she was a total numpty.

'Take a seat,' Jodie said, when she'd returned. 'Mrs. Sergeant shouldn't keep you long.'

Thanking her again, Beth sat down on a grey plastic seat, yanking at the hem of her skirt as she did so. What on earth had possessed her to wear a skirt that seemed determined to part company with her knees and wriggle up to her rib cage?

Cher's '*If I Could Turn Back Time*' erupted from her bag. Oh, no, she'd forgotten Jackie's warning to turn off her mobile! She rummaged around and fished out her phone. 'I'm so sorry,' she mouthed at Jodie. As she was about to press "call reject", Paul's name flashed up on her screen. Instinctively she pressed the "answer" button. 'Hi,' she whispered urgently. 'It's difficult for me to talk right now but –'

'Look, this is important!'

She clutched the phone tightly to her ear, her curiosity piqued.

'The thing is,' he continued, 'Ben's been so awkward and uncommunicative lately and it's creating a bad atmosphere in the office. I need you to speak to him –'

'You *what?*'

She heard him give an exaggerated sigh. 'I said, Ben's being awkward –'

'I heard what you said! What did you expect?'

'Well, a bit more professionalism from him wouldn't go amiss for starters.'

'You selfish pig! No, you're not a pig - a pig's an

intelligent animal. You're – a completely selfish prick!'

'Ms Bishop?'

Blood rushed from her face down to the tips of her toes. She forced herself to turn around. A tall woman with a glossy chestnut bob stood glaring at her. Beth eyed the name tag on the lapel of her black jacket: "Sandra Sergeant – Manager".

'I'm sooo s-o-r-r-y. I didn't mean *you* were a selfish prick – or a pig – or –'

Mrs. Sergeant raised a perfectly groomed eyebrow. 'Would you come through to my office, please?'

Swallowing hard, Beth dropped her mobile back into her bag and trailed after her down the long corridor.

Once seated in a high backed chair and facing Sandra Sergeant, she understood the description her mum often used when she described someone as "a handsome looking woman". An odd description, Beth had thought, until now, but Sandra definitely fitted the bill. She looked to be in her forties, slender yet muscular. Her face conveyed authority before she opened her mouth. She wore little make-up and didn't need much, as she had flawless skin, full red lips and perfect eyebrows.

Her desk, although smaller than the one in reception, looked efficient and orderly: pens, diary and a laptop all neatly arranged. A bookshelf hugged the corner of the room, housing a host of impressive-looking leather-bound books; the book titles displayed on the spines were printed in gold script. Oak framed certificates of competence were displayed on the magnolia walls. It was all a bit dated, Beth thought, though obviously well organised.

Sandra flicked through Beth's attempt at a CV, which covered one side of A4, with her name, address and contact information, plus a few embellished details about when she helped to care for her late grandpa, Ted senior.

Looking up, she fixed Beth with an intense green-eyed stare, making her feel like a rabbit caught in headlights.

Clearing her throat, Beth tugged self-consciously at the hem of her grey skirt which had now ridden up to settle uncomfortably on top of her spare tyre. Prickly heat rash spread rapidly upwards to her chest and neck.

'So, Ms Bishop, I'd like to start by saying that it is policy to turn off your mobile when you're in the building.'

Beth hadn't thought it could be possible to feel any hotter, but now she felt as though she was about to self-combust. 'I really am sorry; I didn't realise I'd left it on, you see –'

Sandra's face broke into a smile that changed her whole demeanour. She lifted a chunky glass water jug from the desk. 'Perhaps you'd like some water.' It was a statement, Beth noted, not a question. She nodded politely. What she desperately needed more than anything at that precise moment was a wee, but she decided it might not be the best idea for her to say so. If only she'd remembered her car reg and hadn't taken that rotten call from Paul, she'd have had time to prepare herself as she'd planned.

Sandra poured the water. Beth crossed her legs as it trickled into the glass.

'So, Ms Bishop,' she continued, as Beth politely sipped her drink. 'Jacqueline speaks very highly of you, but I'd like you to tell me a little more about your experience in caring for the elderly.'

Despite her zillion rehearsals with Jackie as the interviewer, her mind went blank. All her fears came to fruition; she was unable to think of anything to say at all, let alone anything dynamic.

Shuffling around in her seat, she put a hand over her mouth and coughed to buy some time. 'I used to take my grandpa shopping,' she offered lamely.

Sandra Sergeant's eyebrows disappeared under her thick fringe. 'Have you any other experience?'

Beth held her breath. Had she totally blown it? 'Not really,' she admitted. 'But I'm good with people, and I'm very keen and willing to learn.'

Flicking through some papers, Sandra sucked in her bottom lip thoughtfully. 'You must appreciate the role of carer is a very important one, Bethany. Our residents here at Holly Mount need empathy as well as practical care. Do you think you're the person to give them that?'

Come on, Beth admonished herself, *think – think...* 'I respect everyone as an individual,' she said finally. *Phew.*

Time seemed to stand still. Beth made a conscious effort to stop her feet swinging around in mid-air on the high seat. Her heart pounded as she focused her gaze on the uninspiring mustard and brown swirly carpet.

'Would you be prepared to attend all the necessary training courses?' Sandra asked, breaking the awkward silence.

Beth nodded enthusiastically, feeling sure that, with her burning face, she'd be a good contender for the Ready Brek advert. 'Yes, I would, and I'd certainly put everything into my work,' she added truthfully. The realisation hit her that she both wanted and needed this job; *s*he longed to be successful at something other than motherhood. As important a job as that was, she knew it was time she took the bull by the horns. This was a new chapter in her life, and she wanted to fill it with things that were interesting and challenging, while hopefully earning some money at the same time.

'That's what I like to hear.' Sandra beamed. 'We want someone who's enthusiastic, willing to learn – someone who will give one hundred percent. The thing is, we can teach you everything you'll need to know about the practical care of residents, but no one can teach you compassion and empathy. That has to come naturally, from within, and, from what Jackie's told me about you, I understand you have a caring and compassionate nature?'

Beth nodded. 'Yes, I do consider myself to be a caring person.' She hated blowing her own trumpet, but Jackie had emphasised it was the only way if she really wanted to get a job.

Sandra tapped her pen thoughtfully against her lips. 'Right,' she said at last, 'I'm going to take you on for a probationary period of three months.'

Beth's face broke into a wide grin. 'Oh – thank you so much!'

'Please don't forget to turn your phone off when you're at work.'

'I won't,' she promised. 'Thank you again; that's fab!' Shut the front door, did she just say "fab"? She'd be saying things were "groovy" next if she wasn't careful.

Rising from her chair, Sandra walked around the desk and opened the door for Beth to leave. 'I'll get the wheels in motion. When your Disclosure and Barring check's come through, I'll put you on night-shift with Jackie. She'll be shadowing you for a few shifts to make sure you learn the ropes.'

Feeling giddy with a mixture of excitement, relief and nerves, Beth shook her hand firmly before dashing off to find the ladies'.

*

As soon as she got into her car, Beth called Jackie to break the news. Her friend was thrilled for her, and, following their "quick" chat, lasting half an hour, Beth phoned Paul.

'I can't see how you don't understand why Ben's not jumping for joy! After everything that's happened, how do you expect him to react?'

'I expect him to act like a professional. It's about time he grew up!'

'And it's about time you grew a pair –'

The line went dead.

Chapter Fifteen
Cocoons and Cat's Pee

Beth recalled the time Penelope had asked her what Jackie did for a living. When she'd said that she worked in a care home, Penelope's nose had crinkled in distaste. 'Why on earth would anyone want to empty commodes for geriatrics?'

'The job doesn't just involve emptying commodes,' Beth had told her crossly. 'Jackie has to do all sorts of stuff. She cares for the residents as if they were her own family.'

Penelope sniffed. 'Well, rather her than me, dear.'

Beth felt certain the residents of Holly Mount would have thought the same thing.

*

When she'd broken the news about her job to Tash and Ben, they'd both been really pleased for her. Tash had told her it was "well sick" she'd got the job and would be working alongside Jackie.

'I'm proud of you, Mum,' she'd said. Beth had to admit that, although she'd had more than a little help from Jackie, she did feel a bit proud of herself too.

*

It was a couple of weeks before Beth's DBS check came through, during which time she'd lived inside a little cocoon, thinking: 'its ages before I have to worry about this.'

She was grateful to Jackie and pleased to have actually got a job, but, at the same time, she couldn't help feeling terrified. Apart from a bit of waitressing she'd done to earn pocket money when she was at college, she'd never been out to work. She'd been a stay-at-home mum, and, she realised now, she'd become totally stuck in a rut.

*

During the build-up to starting her job, she'd had several terse conversations with Paul, including one the evening before her first shift at Holly Mount:

'If you broadened your horizons, you'd have far better choices,' he told her superiorly. 'You could've got a job as a school secretary, or something. You do know Mother's on the board of Governors at the Grammar? She could've put in a good word for you.'

Having lost track of the number of times Penelope had slipped her "status" into their conversations, Beth groaned inwardly. 'I studied complementary therapies. I've only just learned to use a laptop, and I'm certainly not trained as a secretary –'

'Anyway,' Paul interrupted. 'Who's going to walk the dog when you're not around?'

'I'll mainly be working on night-shift, so I can do it. He can use the cat-flap to get in and out of the garden and I've arranged for Dad to call round to make sure he's OK.'

Paul was silent for a few moments. 'I've never seen the point of all this holistic nonsense anyway,' he said. 'I certainly can't imagine you'd earn any sort of living from it.'

She gritted her teeth. Paul was a well-educated man, yet it never ceased to amaze her how ignorant he could be.

Chapter Sixteen
Paul

Paul swilled back his third glass of fine malt, leaned back in his chair and heaved a sigh. What the hell had he done to deserve this? All he'd ever wanted (apart from a luxury lifestyle and that went with the territory), was for Ben to be successful. He'd had success handed to him on a plate. Why the hell was his son being so bloody ungrateful and awkward?

It was as Paul had told Emily: Ben followed Bethany. Thinking of his wife, he offered up a silent prayer of thanks that at least she hadn't taken on that God damn awful job when they were living together.

Naturally, it would've been a different matter if she'd been a professional; a doctor or a teacher would have been a perfectly acceptable career. God forbid, if she'd started work at the care home before he'd left her, how the hell would he have explained to his buddies at the golf club and his colleagues at work that his wife wiped old people's arses for a living?

It was strange, though, and Paul hated to admit it, but he still felt a little protective towards his wife. He shook himself mentally. This work situation was entirely of her making; she should've held out for something better. He pulled a wry face. She was certainly getting stubborn and starting to become quite a mouthy piece too.

Paul observed Emily, who was sitting opposite, taking in her tailored suit and perfectly applied make-up. Her feet were elevated as she thumbed through the latest copy of Vogue. She glanced up, aware that he was watching her. 'Are you alright, dahling? You're going a bit heavy on the scotch this evening.'

'Yes, I'm fine.' He willed her not to start a conversation involving the Russell-Smythes. He really couldn't be doing with it this evening, and he'd noticed lately that Emily's life seemed to revolve around Jules Russell-Smythe. He wished he had Rodney to take for a walk so he'd have a good means of escape.

She gave him a seductive smile. 'Do you want one of my special back rubs?'

Paul shook his head. 'Thanks, but I'm not really in the mood.'

Blowing out an exasperated breath, she flicked over to the next page.

Chapter Seventeen
Flat Shoes and Cheap Umbrellas

As Beth prepared for her first night-shift, Rodney skulked around her legs. She popped a new squeaky teddy into his basket. 'I won't be long, boy,' she told him guiltily. She'd taken him out for a long walk and arranged for Dad to call in later, but the look her dog gave her tugged at her heartstrings.

In a desperate bid to keep him happy and tone down her guilt, she turned on the radio to keep him company before letting herself out of the house.

The sky was inky black: no stars or moon visible, and there was only the dim glow of the light from the porch to guide her. She picked her way down the long drive. Darts of rain, carried on a chill wind, whipped at her face and clothing. 'Damn!' she muttered, as she fought to put up her umbrella. She gasped as her right foot plunged into a swollen puddle, splashing muddy water up the leg of her trousers.

Thank goodness Jackie lived opposite. Beth knew she was early; it was a ten minute drive to Holly Mount and their shift didn't start until eight, but she felt sick with nerves and was anxious to give herself a chance to settle in beforehand.

Half way across the road her wretched umbrella blew inside out, propelling her along like a drunken Mary Poppins. By the time she'd reached the Old Mill and buzzed Jackie's intercom, her hair hung in rat's tails and water dripped from the end of her nose.

Jackie gasped when she opened the door. 'Blimey! You look like you've been for a dip in the River Severn!'

'Bloody cheap umbrellas,' Beth groaned, as she managed to close the offending item and shake off rivulets of water.

Her friend ushered her inside. 'I'd have picked you up if you'd hung on.'

'I know, but I didn't want Rodney to get wind that you were there. He'd have thought he was really missing out on something. Plus, I'm so nervous – I want to get there in good time.'

'We've got loads of time, so don't worry. Come on in before you catch your death. You can get dried off before we leave.'

Beth followed her along the narrow hallway, carefully negotiating her way around an assortment of china vases, jardinières and various pile of old books and bric-a-brac. Jackie loved nothing more than hunting out "antiques" from car boot sales; she hoped to uncover a hidden treasure one day and make a fortune on the Antiques Road Show.

A Grandmother clock dominated the cosy sitting room, which housed an eclectic array of Jackie's collectables.

Peering into the oval gilt-edged mirror which took pride of place above the marble mantelpiece, Beth frowned at her reflection. She rubbed her hair with a towel, and then wiped the so-called waterproof mascara from under her eyes with a tissue. 'Honestly, Jacks, I feel sick! I don't think I can do it.'

'Of course you can!' Jackie told her firmly. 'You're going to be absolutely fine. We're doing a shift-change, so most of the ressies will be in bed anyway, or they'll want to get ready for bed. I'll be there with you, so there's no need for you to look so worried.'

Beth dried herself off as best she could and visited the loo for the umpteenth time before they braved the rain and climbed into Jackie's grey Vauxhall Astra.

'What exactly will we have to do when we get there?' Beth asked, wondering why she hadn't bothered to ask this before. Honestly, she could be a real ostrich at times. Is that what had happened in her marriage? Maybe she'd buried her head in the sand, limping along because it was the easiest option.

Unaware of the turmoil in her friend's mind, Jackie checked both ways before turning the car smoothly onto the main road. 'Our first job is to check the records made by the day carers so we know what's happened during their shift,' she explained, in a professional sounding tone. 'Then we help anyone who wants to go to bed get washed and into their night clothes, get them into bed and make sure they're comfortable. We make hot drinks for ressies who want to stay up.' She paused, her brow furrowing. 'Fanny Clapp's a bit of a nightmare at bedtime, but as long as I'm not too busy, I'll sort her out. I won't throw you into the lion's den too soon.'

Beth let out a snort. *'Fanny Clapp? You're having me on!'*

'No, unfortunately, it's true.'

'Why haven't you mentioned her before?'

'It's confidential,' Jackie explained. 'Plus, when I leave work, I don't want to think about her.'

'Why on earth would anyone call their child Fanny Clapp?'

'Well, she is in her nineties – perhaps it was popular back in the day.'

'Poor sod!'

They burst into a fit of giggles.

Jackie was first to calm down. 'Try not to think about it when we have to deal with her, or you'll end up laughing again.'

Beth drew a deep breath. 'I'll have to try and think of something horrible to take my mind off it.'

'Just think about Paul, that should do the trick.' Jackie grinned. 'After that, we have a general tidy up and lay out the breakfast tables for morning. We also clean the loos, hoover the residents' lounge, and hopefully tackle the pile of ironing.'

Beth's humour subsided abruptly. There was far more to this carer stuff than she'd thought, and ironing was one of her pet hates.

'We have to do ironing?'

Jackie confirmed with a nod. 'We iron all the ressies' clothing and check their name labels before hanging the clothes or folding them, so their stuff doesn't get mixed up. Most importantly, we answer buzzers and do an hourly check on everyone to make sure everything's OK.'

Beth fell silent. This wasn't exactly what she'd had in mind for her debut career, but she reminded herself that was lucky to have a job at all.

Since living alone, she'd found herself glued to the TV most nights, the programmes acting like a kind of comfort blanket – a buffer from the real world. It was so easy to observe other people's lives, albeit on the TV, Beth thought, and think: *if I was her, I wouldn't stand for that.* But she was all too aware how real life had a habit of biting you on the backside.

After ten minutes, Jackie indicated right and they drove along the winding driveway leading to Holly Mount.

The rambling Victorian building loomed up in the night sky and Beth gulped back a lump of anxiety. It looked so different to when she'd seen it before; like the house in the Addams Family. She imagined Uncle Fester creaking open the door to a hall laced with cobwebs, and powder-fine dust frosting the furniture.

Beth glanced upwards as she climbed out of the car, a chill creeping down the rungs of her spine as she spotted the stone gargoyles peering menacingly down from the eaves, their gnarled faces seeming to mock her. At least, she hoped they were gargoyles and not the residents.

Strange, she thought now, that she hadn't noticed their presence in daylight. She realised she'd been too preoccupied with her impending interview.

Sharing Jackie's umbrella, which was a tad difficult as she was a good few inches shorter than her friend, they made a lopsided sprint towards the entrance.

Jackie pressed a code number into a panel set into the stone pillar to the right hand side of the door. There was an electronic *thunk* as it opened seamlessly.

A pungent smell, reminding Beth of a mixture of pine disinfectant and Werther's Originals, greeted them as they entered the spacious entrance hall.

Beth's heels were rubbing in the flat black shoes that she hated with a passion. She'd always adored pretty shoes; even her mules had a wedge heel.

They walked along the long black and white linoleum corridor towards the staffroom. Jackie'd advised her to purchase a pair of functional shoes, as they'd spend a lot of time on their feet. This was ironic, Beth thought, given the amount of discomfort her shoes were now causing.

As Jackie pushed open the door to the staffroom,

a plump woman charged out, almost colliding with them. She looked to be in her early forties. Her full cheeks were flushed and her blue eyes bright.

'Hi!' she greeted them pleasantly, pulling an elastic band from her hair and releasing a mass of dark curls.

Jackie grinned. 'Hi, Liz. Meet Beth, our new care assistant.'

Beth held out her hand. 'Hi!'

Liz shook it with gusto. 'Welcome to organized chaos!'

'Thanks, I think...'

Jackie went to the store cupboard and got Beth a lilac tunic. She returned with a size ten, the only spare one she could find. It strained across Beth's boobs, leaving an ugly gap displaying the front edges of her prehistoric bra which was now visible in all its grey, faded glory.

Checking her appearance in the mirror in the staff loos, Beth realised how ghastly she looked. She stuck her head under the hand-dryer to dry her damp locks, but the machine sucked up her hair like a vacuum.

She hastily jabbed the "off" button and gingerly untangled her curls, forcing them into a ponytail.

When she returned to the staffroom, Jackie was reading from a blue ledger, so Beth took the opportunity to have a look at her new surroundings. Two fluorescent strip lights lit the room, the artificial light harsh and draining. The dated carpet, which was threadbare in places, sported the same mustard and brown colour and swirly pattern as the one she'd seen in Sandra's office. However, the room did have its good points. There was a sink, a fridge in one corner, a kettle, toaster, and a hefty microwave which squatted on top of a grey Formica worktop. A red squishy sofa sat flush against one wall, and an old T.V. set on a stand was positioned in the opposite corner. Beth thought it looked like a throw-back from the nineteen eighties, or possibly seventies.

Jackie shoved the ledger under her nose. 'This is the book we use to record everything that's happened during our shift, ready for doing change-over,' she said, dragging her back to the matter in hand. She flicked open the book and pointed out the relevant page with her pen. 'Anything significant that's happened during the day is written up by the day staff. We must also record details of any medication changes. It's important to remember to check these at the start of our shift and update the records before we leave, as it's vital they're accurate and up-to-date.'

Beth nodded enthusiastically, trying her best to look all professional. Yet, despite the fact she was teamed up with her best friend, her tummy flipped with nerves. She felt as though the lives of the vulnerable and elderly residents of Holly Mount were in her hands. This may seem rather dramatic, she reasoned, but she couldn't help feeling overwhelmed before she'd even started.

Jackie smiled reassuringly. 'Don't worry. You won't be expected to remember everything right away and you'll soon get used to it.'

She took Beth on a tour of the building, pointing out, it seemed, the zillion things she needed to know. Beth had had the foresight to take a notepad and pen along and hurriedly scribbled down as much information as she could, including a brief description of each resident, a few of whom had the onset of dementia.

Jackie explained that, while some residents preferred to keep to themselves, there were others who enjoyed a natter. Beth was to be guided by them, within reason. There was Maud, who always asked for at least two cups of tea and a plate of biscuits in the middle of the night. Maud was deaf, so carers had to shout for her to hear them, and she'd keep Beth there talking all night if she'd let her.

Beth's mind swam with facts, and whether she'd be able to decipher her "shorthand" later was another matter.

Thankfully, the first part of the evening was quiet.

Jackie loaded a trolley up with a thermos jug of hot water, a plastic container of milk, a sugar bowl, tea bags, hot chocolate, Ovaltine and assorted mugs. She and Beth wheeled it into the residents' lounge.

Beth looked around the large, square room.

Mismatched, high-backed armchairs were lined up uniformly against faded green walls. Busy floral print curtains hung at the huge bay window. A couple of tatty looking floral prints hung on the far wall, and a T.V. (which she thought seemed far too small for the residents to actually watch), was suspended on brackets in the far left hand corner. A pack of cards, a battered game of Monopoly, dominos and a few more dog-eared boxed games and assorted jigsaw puzzles were stacked on a wooden table in the middle, together with a jumble of old books and magazines. Beth noticed most of the jigsaws were made up of large pieces, suitable for a child.

Everything was spotlessly clean and functional, she thought, yet, at the same time, it seemed so dismal and dated.

There were only two residents sitting in the lounge. Jackie suggested Beth should introduce herself and offer them a hot drink.

Beth walked up to the first resident, whose name was Bert. He was a rotund man with a wrinkled, lived-in face. His bald head was bordered by a halo of iron grey curls, reminding her of Sid James from the old Carry On films. Her mum always said Sid was "nice-ugly", and Bert was definitely nice-ugly. Despite being well into his eighties, he still had a twinkle in his brown eyes. Jackie told her that he'd been at the home for the past decade.

'Hi, I'm Beth,' she said, feeling as if she was

about to confess to being an alcoholic. 'Would you like a hot drink?'

Bert looked up and gave her a toothless grin. 'I'd rather have a drop of brandy, ducks!'

She smiled. 'Me too - but hot chocolate, Ovaltine or a cup of tea is all I have on offer, I'm afraid.'

He chuckled. 'Oh, ducks – I'm sure a pretty little thing like you must have plenty to offer!'

Beth smiled, but felt her cheeks flush.

Jackie shook her head good naturedly as she sat beside the old man. 'Behave yourself, Bert, or you won't get your cup of Ovaltine,' she teased.

'Is it half measures today, then?' Bert quipped, when Beth gave him his drink.

Jackie sighed. 'Take no notice of him. You're a right old troublemaker, aren't you, Bert?'

'Of course I am, ducks. And you know you wouldn't have me any other way!'

They left him to enjoy his Ovaltine and wheeled the trolley across to an elegant looking woman. Her silver hair fastened into a neat chignon. 'Hello, Evelyn,' Jackie propelled Beth forward. 'This is Beth. She's our new care assistant.'

Looking up, Evelyn gave them a paper-thin smile

'Would you like a hot drink?' Beth offered. She declined with a shake of her head. 'No thank you, dear. I think I'll go up to my room in a little while.'

As they wheeled the trolley away, Beth glanced back at Evelyn. Evelyn sat with her shoulders slumped, and she looked so lonely and dejected that it tugged at her heartstrings.

'It's so sad,' Jackie said when they were out of earshot. 'Evelyn's sister, Mae, lived here too. They shared a room and were always together, but Mae passed away a couple of months back, and now Evelyn spends most of her time in her own little world, reminiscing about the past.'

Beth shook her head sadly.

'There are a lot of ressies like that,' Jackie added. 'Some of them don't get any visitors from one week until the next. It makes my blood boil; the old dears are always on about how wonderful their sons and daughters are, yet, in a lot of cases, their wonderful offspring can't even be bothered to visit.'

'That's so rotten.'

Jackie sighed. 'The best thing we can do for them, besides giving them the care they need, is to give them a little of our time. Just a quick natter can brighten up someone's day.'

The impact of growing old swelled inside Beth's mind. She couldn't get her head around how people could treat those who'd cared for them and loved them as though they were now non-existent.

She felt guilty for her bouts of self-indulgent pity. I'm only thirty-nine, for heaven's sake, she chastised herself. I have two healthy, well-adjusted kids. It's about time I got to grips with what Tash and Ben call "getting a life".

Chapter Eighteen
Sat Navs and Cellulite

As she stacked crockery in the kitchen cupboard, Jackie checked her watch. 'Come on. I think we've earned ourselves a brew.'

Thank God for that, thought Beth. It felt like she'd been on her feet for ages, although, in reality, they'd only been working for a couple of hours.

As they headed back towards the staffroom, Jackie pointed to a mountain of ironing stacked up in the laundry. 'We should get chance to do that around midnight.'

And I want to work because...? Beth wondered. *Come on, Bethany Bishop, you know the answer to that.*

Jackie made tea for them both and lifted a pink flowery tin from the shelf. She prised open the lid, offering the tin to Beth. 'Grab yourself a few biccies. You'll need a sugar fix to make it through your first night.'

Spotting her favourite chocolate Hobnobs, Beth's mouth watered. She'd been far too nervous to eat anything beforehand and her tummy was growling. Plunging her hand in the tin, she grabbed a couple and looked at Jackie. 'Aren't you having one?'

'Not yet. I'll do a room check first.' Jackie took a couple of gulps of tea and covered over her mug with a saucer.

'Do you need any help?'

Jackie pointed to a large wall-mounted speaker. 'No, ta. You have your cuppa and, if I need you, I'll call you.'

Beth eyed the speaker suspiciously, wondering if it would echo like the supermarket speakers: *'Call please to customer checkout. Bethany Bishop to customer checkout.'*

She kicked off her shoes and sank down onto the sofa, her body sinking into the squashy material. *Ah, that was better.* Perhaps things weren't going to be too difficult after all. She took a sip of hot, sweet tea and sunk her teeth into the milk chocolate coating of the biscuit. She ate it slowly, relishing the crunch of the biscuit mingling with the sweetness of the chocolate. She was munching on her second bite when the overhead speaker crackled into life. Beth struggled to heave herself up from the sofa, hastily brushing biscuit crumbs off her tunic.

The sound of Jackie's disjointed voice filled the room. 'Beth – can you come to room thirteen – quickly?'

As she stared at the display panel lit beneath the room number. Her heart started to race. She pulled on her shoes and scanned through her notes. Harold, a quiet gentleman in his late eighties, occupied room thirteen.

A maze of corridors snaked off in every direction and room thirteen was on the second floor. Beth decided it would be quicker to use the lift. She pressed the "lift call" button, waiting anxiously for the doors to open. They remained stubbornly closed. She jabbed it more frantically this time, yet still the doors refused to budge and there was an absence of any mechanical noise.

Having been on a guided tour of Holly Mount only once, she'd need a sat nav to find her way to room thirteen. Mind you, according to Paul, she needed a sat nav to find her way around the local supermarket.

She ran around the building like a demented hamster before finally finding the right room.

Seeing her friend, she stopped in her tracks. Jackie was knelt by a motionless male figure, performing CPR. The poor old man was totally starker's.

Jackie looked up, anxiously.

Instinctively, Beth knelt down beside her. 'Page Sandra,' she said calmly. 'I'll take over.'

Jackie pressed her pager, watching wide-eyed as Beth placed the heel of her right hand on the centre point of Harold's chest and located the point approximately six centimetres down. Placing her left hand over her right hand, she pressed down briskly to the count of thirty, then pinched his nose with one hand to seal off the airway and blew steadily into his mouth.

She continued to push down on his chest.

At four a.m. a buzzer sounded. It was Maud wanting her cup of tea.

*

At the end of their shift, Jackie made coffee for them both, loading their drinks with sugar for shock.

She stopped stirring the drink and looked at Beth thoughtfully. 'Why don't men have cellulite?'

Beth blinked. 'You *what?*'

Jackie sucked in her bottom lip. 'Well, I was thinking about Harold's thighs. His skin was baby smooth – no lumps and bumps.'

At a loss as to what to say; Beth took a sip of her sweet coffee, deciding that her friend must still be in a deep state of shock.

*

As they trudged back to Jackie's car, Beth thought about a photo she'd seen on Harold's bedside table of a smiling young man who wore a cap and gown. It was a photo of his great-grandson Mark, who'd just gained his first class honours degree in sports science.

'You were great.' Jackie said, startling Beth out of her reverie. 'How on earth did you know what to do? I didn't know you'd had any training!'

'I don't feel very great,' she replied dolefully. 'I've seen them doing CPR on *Casualty*, so I just copied it. It didn't help poor Harold, though, did it?'

Chapter Nineteen
Eastern Europeans and a Splash of Cold Water

Rodney stood on his hind legs, performing his little welcome dance as Beth walked in. It was only seven thirty a.m., and she decided to take him out before collapsing into bed. She felt drained both emotionally and physically, and she was worried that, once she'd climbed under her covers, she wouldn't want to get up again.

They strolled along together; the cool morning air smelt fresh and clean following the previous night's rainfall. She was glad to rid herself of the stuffy detergent infused atmosphere of Holly Mount. Her mind raked over the night's events. Could she have done more to save Harold, she wondered, unable to shake off the image of him lying there.

They walked on further than she'd intended, and, before she'd realised it, they'd reached the bronze statue of Sir Edward Elgar which stood opposite Worcester Cathedral. There was a bench close by, and she sat down to rest. Rodney lay at her feet. It was strange to see the town so quiet, she thought. No shops were open yet. Except for a couple of strutting pigeons and a café owner unlocking his door in readiness for the day ahead, the normally bustling street was deserted.

Rodney stood up and pulled on his lead. Beth rose from the bench, and they made their way home.

*

When they got back, her limbs were heavy with tiredness, but even after her walk, her brain stubbornly refused to switch off. What an awful first night.

She made her way wearily upstairs with Rodney trotting behind, seemingly unfazed by this new routine. This was OK in the interim, she realised, but she was worried about what she'd do when they had to move house and there would be no one to check on him.

The outside world was gradually coming to life. Car doors slammed and engines fired up as people headed out to work or took their children to school. Things Beth had never been aware of before were now sharp in her mind. It was a strange thought that as her day was ending; most people would be starting theirs

She cleaned her teeth and pulled on her PJs before climbing into bed and snuggling under her duvet.

Rodney didn't seem too keen on the idea of going to bed anymore. After all, he'd slept during the night, and, although he'd been for a walk, he was still full of energy. Deciding it was time to play; he leapt off the bed and raced downstairs to fetch his favourite purple squeaky ball from his basket. Scrambling back up onto the bed, he nuzzled the ball towards an exhausted Beth.

Feeling the persistent nudge of the ball in her side, she sighed with frustration. The squeaking sound went straight through her. She tried in vain to persuade Rodney to lie down, but finally gave up.

After consuming two more cups of coffee and playing with Rodney for almost an hour, her eyes were sore and dry, and a dull ache throbbed at the back of her skull. She simply must get some shut-eye before her next shift started, or she'd be good for nothing.

Finally climbing back into bed, she pulled her duvet up over her head. Rodney, now content, settled down, too. Beth laid her head on the soft feather pillows and let her eyelids close.

Seconds later, she sprung bolt upright. Clasping her hand over her mouth. She made a dash for the bathroom. Bile rose from the pit of her stomach and up into her throat, the acidic burn making her eyes water.

Shivering uncontrollably, she knelt down next to the loo, retching and vomiting.

Beth felt so dreadful that she spent the remainder of the day lying on the sofa.

Later that afternoon, Paul phoned to check how Rodney was.

'Rodney's fine,' she croaked.

'God, you sound awful.'

'I haven't slept – I'm not feeling too good.'

'What did I tell you?' he said accusingly. 'You'll have picked up something nasty from the wrinklies.'

*

At seven thirty p.m., Beth pulled on her tunic. It felt like twelve minutes rather than twelve hours since she'd worked her last shift. She really wasn't feeling up to it tonight, but Jackie had gone out on a limb to recommend her to Sandra. No matter how rubbish she felt, she had no intention of letting her friend or herself down.

She called for Jackie at seven forty-five p.m. as arranged, and they headed to Holly Mount.

Taking in Beth's ghostly pallor, Jackie's face was etched with concern. 'Are you sure you're alright?'

Giving her a watery smile, Beth nodded. As well as feeling like death warmed up, she was still shaken up after what had happened to Harold.

*

The lift repair guy, Tom, waved to them as they walked into the building.

Beth looked at him in approval. Tom had sleek, dark hair, a cheeky smile and the red tee-shirt he wore showed off his muscular physique and the half sleeve tattoo on his arm.

He grinned as he began packing his tools away into his large metal workbox. 'Good evening, ladies.'

'Evening,' they replied in unison.

Closing the lid of the box, he stood up, giving Jackie a wink. 'I hope to see you again very soon.' He whistled as he picked up the heavy looking box with ease and strode off down the corridor. Beth grinned as she nudged Jackie. 'He looks like he should be on the advert for Diet Coke, and it's obvious he fancies you.'

Jackie shrugged. 'I've known him for ages. He's friendly to everyone.'

'Whatever,' Beth replied, her grin widening.

It was Beth's turn to check on the residents whose rooms were upstairs. She pressed the lift button, waiting nervously until she heard a reassuring noise as it glided down to the ground floor. The door slid open. She walked inside and pressed the button to take her up to the second floor.

Making her way along the corridor, she checked each room in turn to ensure the residents were OK. When she came to room thirteen, she peeked around the door. All Harold's personal possessions had already been removed, leaving a single bed, a walnut wardrobe with matching chest of drawers and a bare bedside table. It was if all traces of him had been erased, as if he'd never been there.

A lump of emotion lodged in her throat. She knew from what Jackie'd said that this room had been Harold's sanctuary. Now, she thought sadly, it would soon belong to someone else. She realised it was probably something she'd have to get used to, but that didn't lessen the impact.

With the exception of some fairly unpleasant commode emptying, to her relief everything went well.

Reaching room twenty-two, Beth took her

customary peek round the door.

'Ssshhh!'

Beth started as Violet, the room's occupant, shot upright in bed. The old lady's face was grey in the pale glow of the nightlight. Her pink scalp was just visible through her fine, white frothy-cloud hair that framed her tiny, bird-like features. She put a knotted finger to puckered lips, her forehead creasing into a frown. 'Stop making such a din, you silly girl. You'll wake them up!'

Beth tiptoed to her bedside. *'Who will I wake up, Violet?'*

'The Eastern Europeans!' she said, as though Beth was totally clueless, which, of course, she was.

Beth stared at the assortment of blankets strewn across the floor. 'What are these for?'

The old lady looked at them blankly for a long moment, before her top lip began to tremble. 'Oh, dear, oh, dear. They've gone. They've all gone away.'

Feeling totally out of her depth, Beth pressed the buzzer to summon help. She put a comforting arm round Vi's shoulders while they waited.

Jackie walked into the room and quickly assessed the situation. 'Your friends will come back, Vi,' she soothed.

'They've gone – they've all gone,' Violet repeated dolefully.

'Don't you worry about it,' she said reassuringly. 'Why don't you lie down and we'll get you a hot drink and make you all warm and cosy.' She looked over at Beth. 'Will you collect the up the blankets, please?'

Glad of something useful to do, Beth knelt down and began gathering them up and folding them neatly.

Violet's eyes were glazed with sadness. 'They will come back, won't they? It's cold outside and Mother hasn't given them any breakfast.'

Beth swallowed as she busied herself stacking the folded linen. Jackie caught her eye, and gave a nod of understanding as she straightened the old lady's bed covers. 'I'm sure they're all going to be OK, Vi, you'll see.'

Vi's face brightened. 'Yes, dear – they will, won't they?'

She turned to look at Beth. . 'What are you doing in my room?'

Beth gave a reassuring smile. 'I'm Beth, Violet.

I work here. I'll go and make you a nice, hot drink.' Violet seemed placated.

'Can you empty Vi's commode before you make that drink? I'll finish getting her sorted,' Jackie asked.

Beth covered the top of the commode with a plastic lid, and held it a foot away from her body as she headed off to the loo.

Finally, after what seemed like another never-ending shift, Beth dropped Jackie home and turned her car into her own driveway. She'd only worked a couple of nights, yet she felt drunk with tiredness. The fact that she'd had no sleep, due to her weird working hours, was already playing havoc with her body clock. She wondered for the millionth time how her friend had done it for so long. Still, she thought, at least she didn't have to go in tonight, so she'd be able to catch up on some much needed shut-eye.

As she pulled up in her driveway, Penelope appeared in the doorway. What on earth was her mother-in-law doing, letting herself into the house without asking?

Penelope walked outside and stood on the top step, her back ramrod straight, her hands placed on her slender hips, as though she was mistress of all she surveyed. Her face could curdle milk from behind a closed door, thought Beth.

With a weary sigh, she pressed the automatic key fob to lock her car. 'So you're back, then,' Penelope remarked tartly.

Well done, Miss Marple. Beth turned to face her mother-in-law. 'Why have you let yourself into my house?'

'There's no need to take that tone with me. Your father rang Paul. Apparently, his car wouldn't start and he was worried about the dog. Paul was busy, so he asked me to call round to make sure Rodney was alright. I came as soon as I'd seen his message this morning.'

Feeling guilty that she'd seemingly misjudged her, Beth mellowed. 'Thank you. That was good of you.'

Penelope followed her as she headed into the house. Beth hoped fervently that she wouldn't want to hang around, but she decided it would be rude not to offer her a drink after she'd come to do her a favour.

After making a fuss of Rodney, Beth went into the kitchen, Penelope at her heels. She did a double-take; it looked like something out of House & Home magazine! Not one piece of clutter blemished the gleaming granite work surfaces, and even the floor tiles sparkled with a new lease of life.

Her mother-in-law watched her. 'I've cleaned up. It looked as though you could do with the help,' she said airily.

Taking a deep, calming breath, Beth decided it would be easier to say nothing. She was far too worn out to argue. She reached into the cupboard for a cup and saucer. Naturally, Penelope would never use a mug: "They're crude – for workmen, dear".

As Beth wasn't quite tall enough to reach the top shelf, she groped around for the china that she kept for best, while Penelope sashayed through to the sitting room, clutching a copy of the Financial Times.

Muttering a few expletives under her breath, Beth threw a herbal teabag into a cup and poured on boiling water. She let it steep for a couple of minutes before carrying it through.

Penelope took a tentative sip and frowned, her cup clattered as she banged it down on the saucer. 'You've forgotten to add a dash of cold water – you know I can't drink it without –'

With an exasperated sigh, Beth snatched the cup out of her hand. The tea splashed over the rim. 'Oww!' Beth yelped, the hot liquid scalding her fingers. The cup fell to the floor where it rolled around, splattering steaming yellow liquid everywhere.

Penelope's hand darted to her mouth. 'Now look what you've done –'

The door to the sitting room swung open, and Tash breezed in, her smile changing to a puzzled frown when she saw the mess on the carpet. 'What's going on?'

Penelope conjured up a smile which didn't reach her eyes. 'It's nothing for you to worry about, Natasha, dear. It was just a silly little accident, that's all.' Tash threw Beth a *what the hell?* look, but, before Beth could say anything, Penelope leapt up and hugged her granddaughter. 'Never mind about that, dear.' She indicated the spilt tea. 'Your mother will soon clear it up.'

Tash glanced at Beth. Beth rolled her eyes. 'It's so lovely to see you, Natasha,'

Penelope continued, 'but what on earth have you done to your beautiful hair?'

'It's only temporary, Gran,' Tash replied nonchalantly. 'I fancied a change.'

Tash's normally gold-blonde hair was streaked with vibrant pink hues. She was wearing her favourite black skinny jeans and a plain white tee-shirt, showing off a tattoo that depicted a dove, below which the word "Peace" was inked on her right upper arm. Her tawny, almond shaped eyes were heavily lined with black kohl and bright scarlet lipstick emphasised her perfect Cupid's bow lips.

Penelope pursed her lips. 'A change is buying a new dress or trying a different perfume, dear. Not ruining your crowning glory.'

'It does wash out, Gran,' Tash explained with more patience than she felt.

Beth gave her daughter an apologetic smile. 'I'd have picked you up from Foregate Street Station if I'd known you were coming home, love.'

'It's half-term, Mum – I always come home for the holidays!'

'Oh, no! How could I have forgotten?'

'No worries. I got a taxi. You've had enough on your plate.'

'You should've called your father, Natasha.' said Penelope. 'He never forgets important things.'

The look Tash gave Beth spoke louder than words ever could.

Chapter Twenty
Aztec Patterns and Three Witches

Bright sunshine seeped in through Beth's bedroom blind and she heaved a contented sigh. She didn't have to work tonight, and having her daughter home made her feel more positive than she had in a long time. She showered and dressed before heading downstairs with Rodney following. Paul would never have allowed the dog on the bed, but she felt comforted having him beside her.

As she walked through to the kitchen, Penelope was perched on a stool at the breakfast bar. Beth's face dropped.

'Natasha let me in,' her mother-in-law informed her curtly, before she'd had chance to speak.

She bit her lip. She could hardly send her packing when her daughter had invited her in.

Penelope looked as elegant as ever in a smart Stella McCartney black tailored skirt teamed with a cream cotton blouse.

'Anyway,' Penelope said, breaking the tense silence, 'I trust you're feeling better this morning?'

Beth frowned. 'Yes, I'm fine, thank you. Why d'you ask?'

Penelope sucked in her bottom lip and then blew out a long breath. 'I'm quite concerned about you, dear. You really should go and see your GP. I think you're going through the change – your head's been all over the place and you've been so snappy and forgetful of late –'

Beth felt a hot flush coming on and it had nothing to do with the menopause.

'The reason I forgot that it's half-term is *nothing* to do with being on the change! I'm tired out and I've got a lot on my mind, that's all.'

Penelope tapped the side of her nose knowingly. 'There's really nothing to be ashamed of, dear,' she said, as though she was an expert on all things menopausal. 'The change affects women in many different ways.'

Before Beth could protest, Tash sauntered in dressed in yesterday's tee-shirt teamed with a pair of skimpy tartan shorts. She raked a hand through her tousled hair. 'Morning, Mum! Gran's called to see me.'

'So I see,' Beth replied quietly.

Tash sniffed the air. 'Mmmm – something smells nice.'

Penelope inflated with pride. 'It's my new Versace, dear. I'll treat you to some if you'd like?'

'Cheers, Gran!' Tash lifted a mug from the mug tree and scooped in a teaspoon of coffee granules.

'In fact,' Penelope added, her face brightening, 'why don't we all go into town? We could have a girlie day out!'

Beth's eyes widened in horror; she'd rather walk barefoot over hot coals. Tash, too, looked stricken at the thought of a girlie day out with her Gran, but felt too awkward to refuse. She gave Beth a sideways glance, as if silently pleading not to have to do it alone. Reluctantly, Beth relented.

*

Beth and Tash felt like a couple of minions as they followed Penelope along Worcester's busy High Street. They'd already ventured into several "posh" shops, and Penelope had made numerous purchases which they'd somehow been left to carry. Beth thought affectionately of her own mum who always took a House of Fraser carrier bag with her when she visited the local charity shops. Mum would have a fit if she'd seen how much money Penelope spent on clothes and cosmetics. How Beth wished they were out shopping with her mum instead.

'We'll have lunch at the Ginger Pig in Copenhagen Street,' Penelope instructed.

Beth made wide-eyes at Tash, silently transmitting that it wasn't worth the hassle of suggesting anywhere else. Plus, she was starving and in no mood for an argument.

As they strode purposefully past McDonald's, Tash glanced longingly through the window. Beth looked at her and shook her head; Ronald McDonald's would be a definite no-no for her mother-in-law.

Despite Tash's misgivings, the Ginger Pig had a fresh and contemporary feel, the walls were painted in a muted shade of green and the staff were friendly and welcoming. Best of all, there were triple cooked chips on the menu, which more than made up for missing out on McDonald's.

Beth opted for soup of the day – cream of tomato, piping hot, served with hunks of crusty bread. Penelope ordered a salad with a light dressing and a cup of green tea (which Tash referred to as "cat's piss").

Tash laced her chips liberally with salt and vinegar and Beth slathered her soft, crusty bread with best golden butter, looking enviously at her daughter's trim figure as she did so. Tash didn't have to worry about putting on weight, whereas Beth thought she'd probably put on at least a couple of pounds by just looking at the chips.

They all thoroughly enjoyed their meals, and, feeling comfortably full, Beth felt her spirits lift. With Penelope in a good mood, perhaps it wasn't going to be such a bad day after all. In fact, she wondered if her mother-in-law had undergone some sort of personality transplant. As well as buying Tash her perfume, she'd even offered to treat Beth to some new clothes.

'Say "yes", Mum,' Tash whispered.

Beth really wasn't keen on the idea, but, as Penelope was making such an effort, she decided to accept her offer gracefully, so as not to upset the apple cart.

The women left the Ginger Pig and headed for the House of Fraser.

Inside the spacious, well organised store, Beth flicked idly through rails of colourful spring wear dresses. Her eyes lit up as she picked out a slinky ankle length number printed with Aztec patterns in bold reds, blues and gold. She smoothed her fingers over the silky material. 'This one's gorgeous!'

Penelope took one look and shook her head. 'That would suit someone tall and slim, dear.' She placed an OPI pink painted fingernail on her bottom lip and flicked through the rack of clothing before finally plucking out an uninspiring navy blue cotton pinafore dress. She held it up against Beth's body and stood back, looking at her admiringly. 'Now, *this* is definitely more you.'

Beth swallowed, unable to find words to express just how ghastly she thought the dress was. Tash dug an elbow into Beth's ribs, inclining her head towards two rapidly approaching figures. Beth looked up to see Emily and Miss Pink Lycra Pants heading towards them. Emily was wearing a figure-hugging deep purple dress teamed with chunky, silver jewellery, and a black tailored jacket. She hated to admit it - but she looked great.

Miss Pink Lycra Pants wore shocking-pink cling-on shorts with black opaque tights, long black leather boots, a white crop top exposing her trim, fake bronzed waist, complete with a pink jewelled piercing in her navel. A shaggy brown fur gilet completed her mix and match look.

Beth's heart plummeted at the exact moment Penelope's eyes lit up. Penelope bundled the pinafore dress into Beth's arms and glided over to greet them, air-kissing Emily. 'How lovely to see you, dear. I do so love your dress; it really suits you. Karen Millen, is it?'

Emily's expression was that of the cat who got the cream. 'Yes, it is!' she cooed. 'I just adore her designs.'

Penelope looked Miss Pink Lycra Pants up and down, her brows rising as she observed the cling-on shorts.

'This is Julie Russell-Smythe; she's married to Giles,' Emily informed her. 'Julie's recently joined our accounts department.'

Beth's eyes widened. So Miss Pink Lycra Pants was none other than Jules Russell-Smythe, married to the boring and pompous Giles! She thought it strange to think of her as a Julie; she'd always imagined her more as a Portia or Hermione or something equally pretentious.

Emily's lips twitched as she spotted the dress Beth was now desperately struggling to hide behind her back. 'Is *that* for you?'

Beth's face burned. *Witch*.

'I've picked it out for Bethany,' Penelope said proudly. 'Don't you think it's simply made for her?'

'Without a doubt,' Emily agreed, looking Beth up

and down. 'It's definitely you, Bethany. It must be *so* difficult to find nice things, with you being so short.' Before Beth could form a response, Tash snatched the dress out of her hands. 'It's not my Mum at all!' She shoved the monstrosity back onto the rail and picked out the Aztec print dress, sliding it off its hanger. 'This would look sick with heels, Mum.'

Penelope's brow puckered. 'Must you use that awful turn of phrase, Natasha?'

Beth gave her daughter a grateful smile. 'I'll go and try it on,' she said, pure relief washing over her that her humiliation was over. She headed off to the changing rooms with Tash, leaving the three witches of Eastwick stirring their cauldron.

Chapter Twenty-One
Quality Time and a Mystery

Ben and Sam had called in to see Tash before she returned to uni, but they were on their way to a party, so hadn't stayed long.

Beth noticed that her son seemed preoccupied, and worried he was letting his dad's relationship with Emily affect his work. She decided to have a word with him as soon as she had a chance.

It would be great for her to be able to spend some quality time with her son and daughter, she thought, but, throughout the half-term, Penelope had arrived unannounced on several occasions, sometimes alone and sometimes with Clive in tow. What with that and her working nights, then having to catch up on sleep during the day, it had been difficult for them to get any private time together.

The day after Tash returned to uni, Jackie and Beth had to stay after their shift for a staff meeting. Sandra announced that they were short staffed during the day, asking if anyone would be prepared to change shift to cover the hours.

With a knot of uncertainty in her stomach, Beth decided to volunteer. She'd really miss working alongside Jackie, but she was fed up with feeling exhausted. Jackie was used to working nights, they no longer affected her body-clock, but said that she wouldn't mind filling in for the odd day shift.

Due to a lot of chattering and coffee drinking following the meeting, it was after ten a.m. when Beth dropped Jackie off at the Old Mill and turned into her own drive. She yawned as she climbed out of the car, thinking longingly of her bed. That was when she saw it, in all its dominating, formal glory: a white board headed with bold red lettering, *Harrison Estate Agents - For Sale – View by Appointment Only.*

All traces of tiredness disappeared in an instant. She'd known this was coming, yet it felt like she'd been hit. It was really happening; her old life would be gone. It was now up to her to make a new one.

The house seemed eerily quiet when she opened the front door; not even her usual enthusiastic greeting from Rodney. She guessed he must be out in the garden answering the call of nature and went through the kitchen to open the back door. 'Rodney!' she called.

For a nanosecond, she wondered if Penelope had driven over and taken him out, but she knew her mother-in-law wouldn't allow him in her BMW, and she certainly wouldn't bother taking him out for a walk: "I don't 'do' dogs, dear".

The heaviness of unease settled in the pit of her stomach. Something was very wrong.

*

'Sorry, love,' Mum said worriedly, when she answered Beth's call. 'Your dad hasn't brought Rodney here.'

Beth clutched the phone tightly. 'Was Rodney OK when Dad came round?'

'Yes, he was fine. Hang on, love. Dad's right here – She heard her mum giving her dad a quick explanation about Rodney's disappearance before handing over the phone.

'Hi, love,' Dad said anxiously. 'Rodney went outside and did a wee but he was back in his basket and snoring when I left. D'you want me to come and help you look for him?'

'No, thanks. I think I might have a very good idea where he is. I'll keep you posted.'

'OK, but I'm only a phone call away if you need me.'

Beth hung up the phone. Her heart hammered as she scrolled down to Paul's number on her mobile, but, when she rang it, it went straight to voicemail. She left him a garbled message, and then rang off to dial his office number.

'I'm sorry, Mrs. Bishop,' Claire, the receptionist, said, in her annoying sing-song voice. 'I'm afraid Mr. Bishop's out of the office today.'

'Do you know when he's likely to be back?'

'No, sorry,' Claire trilled. 'Can I take a message?'

'Can you put me through to his PA?'

'I'm sorry,' Claire repeated. 'I'm afraid she's not available. Can I take a message?'

'Just ask one of them to ring me as soon as possible, please. Tell them it's urgent.'

She rang off and scrolled through her contacts once more, finding home and mobile numbers for Penelope. She called her home number and, when there was no reply, she tried her mobile.

'This is Penelope Bishop's telephone. I'm afraid I'm busy right now. Please leave a message after the tone and I will get back to you.'

'Do you know where Rodney is?' Beth gabbled. 'Please ring me as soon as you get this message.' She pressed the "end call" button and raced over the road to Jackie's, holding her finger on the buzzer until her friend's sleep-fogged voice sounded through the intercom. *'Keep your bloody hair on! Is there a fire?'*

Chapter Twenty-Two
Fifty Shades of Grey and a Luminous Green Cat

Knowing only too well that her friend would be shattered, Beth felt guilty, but she just had to talk to her. 'Jacks – they've taken Rodney!'

Jackie was wide awake in an instant. 'Come on up!'

Beth stood in Jackie's kitchen, nursing a mug of coffee. 'How *dare* they take him? Paul's had everything else; he's not taking my dog!'

Jackie, who was clad in a rumpled pink tee-shirt and lacy black knickers, put a comforting arm around her shoulders. 'Don't worry, we won't let him. Drink your coffee while I get dressed. We'll drive round to Emily's – Penelope might've taken him there.'

It only took them a few minutes to drive to the sprawling modern building at Diglis. The apartments were very distinct, many sporting Juliet balconies. Beth knew that Emily's apartment, number ten, faced the river.

Jackie parked up in a place reserved for visitors and they headed towards the entrance, before taking the lift up to the second floor. Once there, they crossed the hallway, soon finding number ten. With a heavy heart, Beth pressed the buzzer. No barking meant no Rodney.

The elderly lady from apartment twelve shuffled out onto the landing, an acre of wrinkled cleavage spilling over her silk nightie. She wore a garish orangey lipstick that had bled at the corners of her mouth, the residue of white cream lingered on her skin. Beth noticed that, even though she was in her nightwear, a heavy gold charm bracelet dangled from her wrist. She wore a pink hairnet, stretched taut over six neat rows of yellow sponge rollers. Bizarrely, they reminded Beth of mini Swiss rolls.

'Is everything alright, girls?' she enquired, in a plum-in-the-mouth tone.

Beth smiled politely; worried she might think they were casing the joint. 'Sorry if we've disturbed you. We're looking after Munter – sorry, Emily's cat, you see, and I've done something silly and left the key at home.' She heaved an exasperated sigh for good measure before turning to Jackie. 'We'll just have to go back for it.'

Hairnet Lady smiled, her garish mouth and white face, together with the sponge rollers, making her a dead ringer for Ronald McDonald. 'Don't you worry about that, dear. Emily told me someone was coming to feed Celine. I always keep their spare key in case of emergencies; they're such busy folk, bless them.'

Jackie's eyes widened, but Beth jumped in

quickly. 'Oh, yes, they are – always busy,' she agreed. 'Thank you so much – that will save us a journey.'

'How did you know Emily has a cat?' Jackie whispered, as Hairnet Lady disappeared inside to get the key.

Beth blew out a relieved breath. 'Paul mentioned it, thank goodness.'

A few moments later, Hairnet Lady returned with the key. 'I would have fed Celine for them; they're such a nice couple, but I'm allergic to cats, you see, dear.'

Beth felt a surge of annoyance that Paul and Emily were perceived to be "such a nice couple".

'Well, you're a lifesaver, thank you so much.' 'It's no problem at all,' Hairnet Lady said kindly. 'Just pop it back through my letterbox when you've finished. I'm going back to bed for a while with my book,' she added, patting her rollers. 'I'm reading that Fifty Shades of Grey, you know.'

Beth's eyes widened. She risked a sideways glance at Jackie, who had changed a few shades of red herself. 'Oh, err, that's nice...'

Jackie stifled a giggle.

Back across the landing, Beth unlocked Emily's door, trying hard to shake off the disturbing image of Hairnet Lady and bondage.

They exchanged 'OMG' looks as an ocean of snow-white carpet greeted them. Jackie voiced exactly what Beth was thinking. 'If the lady at number twelve thinks we're here to feed the cat, someone else must be coming to do it, so we'd better be quick.'

Beth frowned. 'I don't understand why anyone would have to. Surely he's fed before they go to work and again when they're back in the evening?'

'It is very odd,' Jackie agreed. 'But we might uncover a clue as to Rodney's whereabouts, so let's get a shifty on with our investigation.'

Beth thought that maybe her friend was starting to take this detective thing a bit too seriously.

Jackie picked up a hand-written note propped up by the telephone on the hall table. *'Please remove shoes before entering,'* she read aloud.

They looked at each other before removing their shoes and padding along the hallway, their feet leaving imprints in the carpet's plush pile.

'I feel like a secret detective,' Jackie whispered conspiratorially.

They walked a few steps and froze. Holding their breath, they stared at one another in horror. A strange whooshing sound met their ears, followed by the sweet, heady smell of vanilla drifting along the hallway. Beth released her breath when she spotted an Ambi Pur air freshener, the fragrance blasting intermittently in short bursts.

The first door they opened led to the kitchen. It was pristine and clinical, like a dentist's surgery (and rather like Emily herself, Beth thought), all white tiles, high-gloss units and black marble worktops. She picked up a colour coded list of instructions. Various coloured marker pens had been used to detail Celine's daily dietary requirements. There was a selection of cat biscuits also coded accordingly. Scanning through the note (which had been written by Emily), she read that Celine was to have her special milk (right hand side, third shelf down in their huge American fridge freezer). *This must be warmed slightly in a saucepan. DO NOT use the microwave to heat up the milk. Celine must not be subjected to radiation.*

Beth shook her head, imagining a luminous green cat emitting radioactive rays. Judging by the stainless steel monster of a cooker, that gleamed as if it had never been used, Emily didn't apply the same rules to herself and Paul.

Further instructions regarding Celine's welfare were attached onto weighing scales. They stated the precise quantities of nutritionally low carb biscuits (made for cats with a delicate digestive system), which MUST be weighed out at all times.

Beth rolled her eyes. 'Blimey! It's a cat – not Posh Spice!'

They explored the other rooms of the immaculate apartment.

As they ventured into a palatial bedroom, Beth spotted a pair of Paul's slippers next to the king-size bed. A black framed photo of Paul and Emily gazing into each other's eyes was strategically placed on the bedside table, along with the gold cufflinks Beth had given to him for their twentieth wedding anniversary.

It felt as though her husband had traded their years together for a different, more pristine life, a life he now shared with, as Penelope had so delicately put it, "his intellectual equal".

She waited to feel something stomach-clenching; some kind of hurt to cut beyond the quick. What she felt instead was a steely determination; it was a liberating feeling. Paul had his new life. She was now more determined than ever to have hers.

Unable to find anything relating to Rodney's whereabouts, they decided to call it a day. Beth was about to drop the key back through Hairnet Lady's letterbox when Jackie grabbed her by the arm.

'What's wrong?'

'I think I must've dropped my phone in Emily's apartment!'

They doubled back and let themselves in. Sure enough, the phone was lying on the floor next to the breakfast bar. As Jackie bent down to retrieve it, they heard a strange kind of strangulated cry behind them. They turned around slowly and saw the biggest bruiser of a cat either of them had ever laid eyes on. Celine's solid body seemed to fill the narrow doorway. His black, bushy fur stood to attention as he fixed them with a steady green-eyed gaze.

'M I A O WWWW!!!!'

Cautiously, Jackie crept towards the cat, rubbing a forefinger and thumb together. 'Here, kitty, kitty!' she soothed.

The cat continued to stare, his tail swishing angrily, but he made no move.

Throwing caution to the wind, Jackie made a grab at him and bundled the ball of shrieking black fluff into her arms. 'You're a softy really, aren't you, kitty?'

Celine, who was singularly unimpressed with being manhandled, latched his claws into her sweatshirt, making contact with her skin. 'Oww!' she yelled, struggling to unhook the cling-on cat.

After a great deal of manoeuvering they finally managed to detach Celine. His tail swished from side to side as he leapt away and disappeared through the doorway.

'I've had enough of this malarkey,' Jackie said. 'Let's get out of here.'

Beth nodded in agreement. As they went to walk out of the kitchen, a key turned in the lock.

'Quick - hide!' Beth mouthed, diving behind the kitchen island. Jackie quickly followed suit.

Their hearts pumped in sync as someone walked in.

Jackie gripped Beth's arm so tightly, she had to bite her bottom lip to stop herself crying out.

'Hello, puss. What have you been up to then, eh?' said a male voice.

Blowing out a rush of air, Beth shrugged Jackie off and they scrambled to their feet.

'HOLY SHIT!' Ben cried. 'What the hell are you two doing?'

'I'm really sorry we scared you, love,' Beth said, her heart rate slowly returning to normal. 'We're looking for Rodney – it's a long story.'

Emitting a long breath, Ben dropped onto a stool. 'God, Mum, you nearly gave me a heart attack –'

'We're ever so sorry,' Jackie cut in. 'But Rodney's been taken and your mum's worried sick. Anyway – what are you doing here?'

'Dad and Emily are away on urgent business,' he explained, almost apologetically, and Beth guessed he might somehow feel disloyal to her by being in Emily's apartment. 'I'm meant to be feeding Celine for them. Dad said Mrs. Pearce at number twelve had a key, but when I called there she said someone was already here.' He paused, frowning. 'But why would you be looking for Rodney here?'

'When I got home he'd gone,' Beth explained. 'Your granddad hadn't taken him and your receptionist said neither your dad nor Emily was available. We put two and two together and thought your dad or gran might have brought him here.'

'Dad didn't mention anything about Gran or Rodney. Are you absolutely certain he hasn't gone through the cat flap and got out of the back garden?'

Jackie shook her head doubtfully. 'He wouldn't go anywhere without your mum.'

Ben knew she was right. 'I don't understand it. Have you called to ask Gran if she knows what's going on?'

'I've left her a couple of messages, but I haven't heard from her yet –'

'Why's a male cat called Celine?' Jackie asked. Beth shook her head. *She had great timing, did Jackie.*

'It's because Emily loves Celine Dion,' Ben explained. 'And when she first got him, she thought he was a she.'

That, Beth thought, was arguably the only good taste the woman had. 'Well, we're not getting anywhere here. Let's go and pay Penelope a visit and try to find out what the devil's going on.'

Leaving Ben to feed Celine, the women headed off. Neither of them had slept for eighteen hours, but both were still spiked with adrenalin.

*

Penelope stepped graciously out of her grand entrance door, her eyes narrowing as she spotted the approaching car. Jackie pulled up and they clambered out into the fresh air. Beth walked up to face her mother-in-law. 'Do you know where Rodney is?' she demanded.

'Paul collected him last night, just as you'd arranged.'

'I arranged no such thing!'

Jackie stepped forward. 'Paul and Emily have gone away on business –' she chipped in.

Penelope frowned. 'They can't have – he would have told me.'

'So where is he, then?' Beth challenged.

'If my son's gone away at short notice, it's through no fault of his, of that I'm certain. He will have made adequate provision for his dog, so there's no need for all the dramatics.'

'Rodney's *my* dog. How dare he take him?'

Penelope sighed. 'Paul loves that animal and he'll make sure he's fed and watered.'

Beth clenched her fists. 'For the sake of peace I've put up with so much crap from both of you – but I won't put up with this, do you hear me? I want my dog back now!'

Her mother-in-law fingered the hem of her green Yves St Lauren jacket. 'I know you're upset, Bethany,' she said, '…and you may or may not believe me, but I really don't know where Rodney is.'

Beth was shocked at her hurt tone.

'But you know as well as I do,' Penelope continued, 'that Paul wouldn't do anything detrimental to the dog. Someone must be caring for him in his absence.'

Beth couldn't, for the life of her, understand what Paul was playing at, but she had to admit her mother-in-law was right. He would never harm Rodney.

Both despondent, they got into the car and drove back to Emily's apartment. Together with Ben, they searched the place high and low in case they'd missed any clue as to where Rodney might be.

'There's nothing here – not even a hint as to where he's gone,' Beth said dolefully.

Ben put his arm around her shoulders. 'Try not to worry too much. I'm sure you'll hear from Dad soon.'

Chapter Twenty-Three
Unexpected Visitors and a Chippy Pong

Unable to settle, Beth wandered from room to room. The house felt so desolate without her dog and she was glad to be working days. The change of duties would help to keep her busy and help to take her mind off things. Her vivid imagination had already run riot. She had to keep reminding herself that, for all his faults, her husband wouldn't let anything bad happen to Rodney. But what if he'd re-homed him just to spite her? What if Emily had egged him on? It certainly wouldn't be out of the question, she thought worriedly.

*

As Beth drove home from work late on Friday afternoon, she decided to stop off at the chip shop. She hadn't eaten properly since Rodney went missing and she was living on a diet consisting mainly of toast, porridge and tea.

When she got in, she settled down with a large glass of wine and her fish and chips, still in their paper wrapper, sprinkled with lashings of salt and vinegar. She sniffed the parcel appreciatively. She wouldn't have been able to indulge in this simple pleasure if Paul had been there. Since he'd turned into such a snob, it was unheard of not to use a plate when eating. Recently, she'd derived a secret pleasure from all the things that would totally piss him off.

Her mouth watered as she bit into a chip buttie; the fresh, crusty bread with hot chips melting into the creamy butter, tasted delicious.

The doorbell chimed, interrupting her feast. She plonked her supper tray down on the sofa, with an irritated sigh, and heaved herself up to answer it.

Locking eyes with a tall, dark stranger, Beth blushed. His black hair bore hints of steel grey, which she thought made him look distinguished, and he was dressed formally in a grey suit, white shirt and navy silk tie. It took her a few moments to register that he was not alone; a young couple had climbed out of an estate car and were now heading towards her front door. 'Mrs. Bishop?' the handsome guy asked pleasantly.

Beth nodded.

He gave her a wide smile, displaying an impressive set of overly white Simon Cowell teeth. 'I'm Greg Harrison from Harrison's Estate Agents. I'm here to accompany Mr. and Mrs. Edwards on their viewing.'

She frowned, puzzled. *'Viewing?'*

'I left you an answer phone message yesterday asking you to let me know if the time wasn't convenient for you.' Greg's tone made him sound as though he was talking to an imbecile. Beth felt a prickle of annoyance. 'I didn't get any message,' she told him firmly.

He pulled a leather-bound notebook from his briefcase and flicked through the pages before reading out a mobile number. 'That is your number, isn't it?'

'It's one digit out.'

'Oh – I'm so sorry. My assistant must've keyed it in incorrectly.'

Greg smiled again, and Beth felt her annoyance ebbing away. He sounded apologetic, and he was certainly handsome.

'Please, call me Beth.'

'OK, Beth – would it be at all convenient for Mr. and Mrs. Edwards to look around now?' Greg asked hopefully. 'They both work, you see, so it has to be an evening appointment, and I promise we wouldn't keep you long.'

'Well –'

'We can rearrange, if it's not convenient,' he cut in amiably.

'No, no – its fine, but you'll have to excuse the mess,' she said, swallowing down her panic. 'I was just about to have dinner.'

'Of course – I'm sorry we've interrupted you. Thank you, Beth.'

Despite the fact that she'd been dreading people viewing her home and invading her personal space, Beth warmed to the young Mr. (and heavily pregnant) Mrs. Edwards.

She asked Greg to show them upstairs first, and as they all trooped up, she hurried back into the living room and grabbed her tray; whizzed through to the kitchen and dumped her bag of fish and chips unceremoniously into the cold oven, and then stuffed anything else on show into the cupboard under the sink.

She blasted enough floral air freshener to singularly destroy the ozone layer. At least, she thought, it masked the chippy pong.

When they came to view downstairs, things looked quite presentable. Beth crossed her fingers behind her back that no one would open a cupboard.

'You have a lovely home,' Mrs. Edwards told her, as she showed them out.

Beth smiled and thanked her. It was difficult, knowing that soon she'd have nowhere to call home. She noticed the loving way in which the young man looked at his wife and the small gestures he made, like holding her arm to steady her as she climbed down the steps, and knew that it was something she'd never had. She could picture them living here, a happy couple and their new baby, and swallowed a lump of emotion as she wished them all the luck in the world.

Chapter Twenty-Four
A Polo and a Manky Mint Imperial

'Why didn't you tell that smarmy estate agent where to get off? You don't *really* want to leave, do you, Mum?' Tash asked Beth during their weekly phone catch-up.

'He's not smarmy, love. In fact, he seems quite nice. Anyway, I've made my decision. The house doesn't feel like my home anymore. I think it's time to make a fresh start.'

Tash paused for a long moment, taking this in. 'Well, I guess so,' she admitted reluctantly.

Beth understood why her daughter didn't want to sever ties with the house. It had been home to her and Ben since they were born.

Mum and Dad had suggested Beth move back home, but, although she loved them dearly, she felt that, at this stage in her life, it would be a backwards step. She was really grateful to Jackie for offering her and Rodney a place to stay in the interim, at least until she could afford to rent somewhere.

At the sound of her mobile, Beth shot upright in bed, and glanced at her clock. Panic rose in her throat – it was only four thirty a.m.

'*Beth.*' Mum's voice croaked down the line.

'Whatever's the matter?'

'It's Aunt Lena – she's been rushed into hospital.' Beth's hand was clammy as her grip on the receiver tightened.

'She's had a heart attack.' Mum sniffed. 'She's all wired up and looks so frail, bless her.'

Holding the phone crooked against her shoulder, Beth pulled on yesterday's leggings. 'I'll be there as soon as I can.'

Grabbing her bag and car keys, she hurried out into the cool night air.

It was only a fifteen minute drive to Worcester Acute Hospital, yet every minute seemed like an hour before she finally turned into the car park. She sighed with frustration when she saw that there were no available parking spaces; she'd never guessed it would be so busy this early in the morning. She drove around and around, mentally willing someone to pull out and leave her a space.

A car horn blared, making her jump.

'Look where you're going, woman!' an irate guy mouthed at her through his windscreen. In her panic, she'd driven straight in front of his green V.W. Polo.

'*Sorry,*' she mouthed back, crunching the gear stick into reverse.

V.W. Man shook his head crossly and made a right palaver of revving up his engine before screeching off.

What a knob, Beth thought crossly.

*

Eventually she found a space. It was a large area for a little car, yet her nerves were in tatters and it felt like she was handling a double-decker bus.

Heat rose from the soles of her feet and rushed through her body when she realised she'd forgotten to pick up some coins to feed the greedy parking meter.

She pulled her purse from her bag and opened it. It held her debit card and a few coins, mainly copper. *Why didn't she keep some emergency change like her mum had always advised?* If she'd had time, she'd cry.

Tipping the bag upside down, she emptied the contents onto the passenger seat. *There must be some money in here somewhere.* She rooted through her stuff: a mushed up lipstick; a few old till receipts; a key (for God knows what); a twenty pence piece; a comb and a manky mint imperial.

Deciding she had no choice other than to leave the car ticketless and face the consequences, she clambered out, locked the door and began sprinting towards the hospital entrance.

V.W. Man hung out of the window of his car, waving a parking ticket at her. 'It looks like you're in a hurry. D'you need this? It has another couple of hours on it.'

Beth's stomach contracted as she walked over to his car

'I didn't realise it was you, at first,' Greg

Harrison said.

'I'm sorry – I don't normally drive around like a maniac, but, you see, my aunt's had a heart attack and been rushed in and –'

He raised his hand and flashed his Simon Cowell smile. 'No need to explain.' He handed over the parking ticket, his hand accidentally brushing against hers. A tingle coursed through her body at his touch. Although she knew it was the most inappropriate thought in the whole world right now, she wondered what it would be like to feel his strong arms around her. She also wondered if other people had inappropriate thoughts if they were scared or nervous. 'Thank you,' she said weakly.

Greg smiled. 'Anytime.'

As she hurried into the reception area, she wondered what Greg was doing visiting the hospital at this hour.

The steel doors of the ICCU unit (Intensive Critical Care Unit) opened, and the strong antiseptic, clinical smell invaded her nostrils, making her feel slightly nauseous. She joined her anxious parents at her aunt's bedside and sat down next to Mum, threading her fingers through hers. Dad, seemingly grateful for something to do, wandered off down the corridor to get them all a coffee.

A monster of a machine squatted next to Aunt Lena's bed, bleeping rhythmically. Beth swallowed.

Her aunt looked so vulnerable. Her pallor was grey, her face sunken and hollow. The lady lying there was so far removed from her robust, capable aunt, that it hit her again how fragile people are and how lives can change in an instant.

Chapter Twenty-Five
Ideas and Old Tat

Following a long wait, the consultant said that Aunt Lena's condition was stable.

Beth wanted to be around in case her parents needed her. She phoned Sandra to explain. Holly Mount was still short-staffed due to holidays and illness, but Sandra told her she'd work the rota so she could take the day off.

It was eight-forty five a.m. when she finally arrived home. The first thing she did was to make herself a strong coffee. Mum and Dad had gone home for some rest, although she didn't imagine, for a moment, that they would sleep either. Knowing her mum, she was probably cleaning everything in sight and Dad would be pottering around in the garden or working in his shed.

Beth wandered around aimlessly. She missed her dog so much. Normally, she'd have been able to take him out for a walk and clear her head after the antiseptic stuffiness of the hospital.

Desperately in need of something to keep herself busy, an idea formed in her mind. She raced upstairs and pulled down the loft ladder. She climbed through the hatch and clicked on the light switch, soon finding the cardboard boxes she was seeking. After gathering them up, she threw them down onto the landing.

She wasn't going to wait until things happened to her, she thought determinedly. She'd be proactive and start her packing in readiness for her move.

She started work on the kitchen, pulling everything out of the pantry, and only keeping enough stuff back to enable her to cook simple meals. She'd just emptied the third of the drawers and sorted out some old utensils when Jackie walked in.

She looked up at her friend in surprise. 'Hi! – I thought you'd be at work –'

Jackie shook her head. 'No – I was called in last night. Kate didn't turn up again. She'd told Sandra she'd come down with a virus or something, but knowing her, she'd probably fallen out with her fella.'

A worried expression clouded Jackie's blue eyes as she regarded her friend. 'Sandra's told me about Aunt Lena. I can't believe it; she always seems so fit and well. How's she doing – and how are you coping?'

Beth sighed. 'Well, she's stable, thank goodness, and I'm OK, but it was awful to see her like that. She looked so old and vulnerable.'

'You must've been really shocked to get the call. I take it you haven't had much sleep?'

Beth shook her head. 'I can't settle, so I thought I'd get some of my stuff sorted out. Anyway – what about you? You must be knackered if you worked last night.'

'I can't sleep either,' Jackie told her. 'I was worried about you and your parents, and, judging by those dark circles under your eyes, I'd say I was right to be worried. Let me give you a hand – it looks like you've got a lot of stuff to sort out.'

Beth blew out a long breath. 'You could say that. Honestly, I can't believe how much I've packed up from just one room!' She pointed to a box full of old china and pots and pans, jelly moulds, and an assortment of wicker baskets. 'These look like they've come from out of the ark!'

Jackie's eyes widened as she examined the goods. 'No way!' Some of this stuff's really collectable.'

'*What* – this old tat?'

'They're vintage,' Jackie said knowledgably. 'People go mad for this sort of stuff. It's called "kitchenalia". You've got some money's worth here.'

Beth was surprised at her friend's awareness of the subject. An idea rushed into her mind. 'If Aunt Lena's doing OK by the weekend, how d'you fancy doing a car boot sale with me before hospital visiting hours this Sunday? We can split the profits.'

Jackie nodded eagerly. 'Definitely, but baggsie first dibs of some of this stuff!'

Chapter Twenty-Six
Only Fools and Rodney

'How are you?' Beth asked Aunt Lena, when she visited later that evening.

'Don't you get worrying about me, love.' Lena gave her a weak smile. 'I'm doing OK.'

'I'm glad to hear it – you gave us all a fright.'

Mum fluffed up her pillows. 'She's coming to stay with us to recuperate once she's discharged.'

'I don't want to be any trouble,' Lena protested.

Dad shook his head. 'Then don't argue. You know your sister won't take "no" for an answer.'

*

Beth got home and threw off her coat. She looked with satisfaction at the boxes stacked up in the dining area. At least they were all contained in one room. She could go in the sitting room to watch a bit of mindless T.V. She flopped down onto the sofa and picked up the remote, idly scrolling through the programmes and settling on something light-hearted: a repeat of Only Fools and Horses, her all-time favourite show. She'd met the cast when they were in Margate in 1989, filming for the Christmas special, "The Jolly Boys' Outing".

It had always been tradition for Beth and her parents to visit Margate at the same time each year.

Beth was twelve years old and she'd been super excited to see David Jason (aka Del Boy), and the gang.

The cast was brilliant: really approachable and friendly. Beth shook her head as she remembered making a total numpty of herself. Nicholas Lyndhurst (aka Rodney – she'd named her dog in his honour) had asked her which episode she'd most enjoyed. She'd told him with the honesty of a young girl, 'I loved the one with the blow up dolls!' She couldn't understand why Mum's face had turned crimson and why everyone erupted into loud guffaws.

She hadn't realised the impact that hearing the name "Rodney" every few minutes would have, and found herself blubbing for England. Turning off the T.V., she headed upstairs to seek solace in the office, the only room that had yet to be blitzed. She sat down and gazed out of the window onto the back garden. It was a bright, sunny day, not a cloud in the sky, yet nothing could lift her mood.

The sound of her mobile startled her, and, worrying that her aunt might have taken a turn for the worse, she dived to answer it.

'Hi, Beth – it's Greg Harrison.' She let out a relieved breath.

'Are you still there?'

'Yes – sorry, I thought it might be news about my

aunt.'

'Oh, I see. How's she doing?'

'She's doing OK, thanks, though it's still early days

'I hope all goes well for her.'

'Thank you.'

'Anyway,' Greg continued. 'I wanted to let you know that Mr. and Mrs. Edwards have put in an offer on the house, which your husband's accepted.'

Beth stiffened. 'You've spoken to my husband – *today*?'

'Yes,' Greg confirmed. 'He's back from his holiday.'

'Holiday?'

'Yes – he's back,' he repeated carefully, as if wondering whether he'd somehow put his foot in it.

Thanking him for letting her know, she hurriedly hung up the phone.

She was busy hatching plans for Paul's slow and painful demise when she heard the distinct sound of a dog barking. Like a mother can tell when her own baby cries, she could recognise her dog's unique bark.

The barking became more insistent as she hurried along the hallway. She yanked the door open, and, as she knelt down to scoop him into her arms, a bundle of tan and white fur leapt at her, smothering her face with affectionate licks. 'Oh, Rodney - I've missed you so much, boy!'

Paul clicked the key fob to lock his car and headed towards the door. If Beth had been a cartoon character, she'd have steam pouring out of her ears.

Hitching a writhing, excited Rodney onto her hip, she glared at him. 'What the hell do you think you're playing at?'

Paul spread out his hands in a pleading gesture. 'Look, I'm sorry. But you know I wanted custody of the dog, yet you refused!'

Her mouth fell open as he continued to dig himself into a deeper hole.

'I... *we* thought Rodney would be better off living with us. I'd planned on taking him into the office during the day, then back to the apartment in the evening, but, as soon as I got him home, he and Celine fought, like – well, like cat and dog, I suppose.'

'What did you think they'd do?' Beth raged. 'You had no right to take him in the first place – how *could* you? Common sense should've told you what would happen!'

'It was done with the best of intentions. We thought -'

She bristled at the second mention of "we".
Did he have a death wish?

'Oh, *we* thought, did *we*? That's just it – neither of you thought at all; you never do. All you and Emily ever think about is yourselves and it's to hell with everyone else! You even told Ben you were away on business! Are you so used to lying that it's become second nature?'

'Never mind what I was doing,' Paul replied, scuffing his foot against the door jamb. 'The simple fact is that you can't look after Rodney if you're out at work.'

'You know damn well he'd be fine on his own for a few hours! Dad calls in, so he's never alone for long. Anyway, just tell me this,' she ploughed on, 'how do you think the poor dog felt, being taken away from me and everything he's familiar with? I can't understand why on earth you'd take him when you were going away on holiday! It just doesn't make any sense.'

'I didn't know we were going away,' Paul protested. 'Emily arranged for us to visit the Niagara Falls as a surprise for our anniversary. I knew nothing of it until I'd taken him back to the apartment.'

Beth's eyes widened. 'The Niagara falls - *in Canada?*'

'Well – the Falls are in Canada,' he said, in a condescending tone. 'To be more precise, Niagara is a collective name for the three waterfalls straddling the international border between Canada and the United States. Specifically, they lie between the province of Ontario and the state of New York.'

Jeez. Beth shook her head crossly. She hadn't asked for a geography lesson.

Paul took her stunned silence as his cue to continue.

'Look, taking Rodney wasn't my idea –'

'So why didn't you bring him back as soon as you realised? Where did you take him?' 'Surely you didn't pack him off to kennels?'

'It was more like a five star canine hotel,' Paul said indignantly. 'The dog whisperer was going to sort out Rodney's behaviour towards Celine.' He raked his fingers through his hair, which somehow infuriated Beth even more.

'And did he?'

He shrugged. 'Nothing's changed,' he replied flatly. 'As soon as Rodney set eyes on the cat, he tore after him. Celine climbed up onto the roof and refused to come down. Emily's going frantic.'

'You've done many hurtful things, but, believe you me; I won't forgive you for this.'

He opened his mouth to speak, but Beth put up her hand in a "stop" gesture. 'I don't want to hear any more of your excuses –you're pathetic!'

With Rodney in her arms, she turned on her heel and slammed the door shut.

Chapter Twenty-Seven
Offers and Bargains

A fat woman dressed in a stained grey bomber jacket thrust three jelly moulds at Beth.

''Ow much, luv?'

'They're four pounds for the lot.'

'I'll give yer three pounds-fifty for 'em,' the woman persisted, dangling them in front of Beth's face.

'I'll do them for three seventy-five,' Beth told her firmly. 'They're vintage and very collectable.'

'Oh, go on then,' she agreed reluctantly, rummaging in her purse and handing Beth a couple of two pound coins. Beth sorted her change from the cash box.

Jackie laughed as the woman waddled off with her purchase.

'Look at you – wheeling and dealing!'

'I'm really enjoying myself! The only thing bothering me, apart from Aunt Lena, of course, is how we're going to get all your stuff back home.'

Looking at her own purchases stashed next to the car, Jackie nodded in agreement. They included a huge Oriental jardinière, which someone had already tried to purchase from her, and a large stuffed bear. 'I know.'

She sighed. 'I'm taking more home than we brought, but I just couldn't resist.'

Beth grinned. 'You never can!'

At the end of the day, Beth did a quick tally-up of their takings before they packed away. They'd already decided to drop off what little was left to a charity shop on their way home.

'We've made one hundred and ten pounds and forty four pence! If we take out the money for our float; that leaves us fifty-one pounds each!'

Jackie started reloading the boot. 'When I take out what I've spent I'll be left with about a fiver! It's been great fun, though.'

'It certainly has.' Beth agreed. 'I'm going to save mine to buy stuff when I can get a place of my own.'

*

They drove to the charity shop to drop off the remaining goods before heading to Jackie's. Beth helped her to carry her stuff in before collecting Rodney from her parents.

After recent events, she hadn't wanted to risk leaving her dog on his own – not even for a few hours. She'd arranged for Jackie to look after him the following day while she was at work, too.

*

Beth's day at Holly Mount had gone smoothly. As she drove to Jackie's to collect Rodney, she felt a weight had been lifted off her shoulders. She had her dog back and her mum had left her a message to say

Aunt Lena had been discharged from hospital.

When she got to The Old Mill, her friend opened the door and Rodney launched himself at her.

'He's missed you loads,' Jackie said. 'I think it's going to take him a while to get over his Pampered Pooch experience.'

'Yes, I think it is. Poor Rodney. Thanks so much for having him.'

'No problem –' Jackie hesitated.

'Was he naughty?' Beth asked anxiously.

'I don't know how to tell you this –'

'Tell me what?'

Jackie heaved a sigh. 'Someone's complained about a dog being here. The landlord called round to see me and pointed out the tenancy agreement states there are strictly no pets allowed, except for a budgerigar or a caged bird,' she explained. 'I hate seeing birds in cages.'

Beth swallowed a rising bubble of panic.

'I'll put the kettle on,' Jackie said. 'Perhaps we can think of Plan B.'

They wound their way down the hall past her "antiques" and into her small kitchenette. She took two heart-embellished mugs from a mug tree and popped a teabag in each. 'I can't believe someone's dobbed him in –'

'Look, Jacks, it's not your fault.' Beth's upbeat tone belied how she felt. 'Please don't worry. I'll sort something out.' What the heck she was going to do now, she wondered. It felt like she'd taken two steps forward and three back.

'You could stay with me if your mum and dad could have Rodney for a while.' Jackie offered.

Beth was grateful for the offer, but being parted from Rodney again would definitely be a last resort.

Despondently, she made her way home and phoned her mum to check on Aunt Lena. Mum invited her to dinner the following evening, suggesting she brought Rodney to cheer her aunt up; Lena had always loved him. Beth decided not to mention her living arrangements, or lack thereof, for the time being. Her parents had had quite enough to cope with lately.

*

Holly Mount

When Beth walked into the staffroom, Liz was scrutinising her face in her compact mirror. 'God, it's been an awful night,' she groaned. 'My eyes look like piss-holes in the snow!'

Beth smiled as she poured herself a coffee. 'D'you fancy a cup?'

Freeing her hair from the confines of an elastic band, Liz shook her head, her mass of curls bouncing freely. 'No, thanks. My neck and shoulders are killing me! I just want to get home and lie down in a darkened room.'

Beth thought for a moment. 'Would you like a neck and shoulder massage before you go? It'll help to ease the pain.'

Liz raised an eyebrow. 'Really? Are you trained?'

'I studied at college for a year, though I didn't get to sit my exam.'

'Well, I have every faith in your abilities, and that offer sounds too good to refuse, if you're sure you don't mind?

Beth smiled. 'Not at all. I love giving the treatment; it calms me down too.'

Liz sat down while Beth washed her hands before beginning the massage.

She used sweeping movements to perform a series of gentle strokes called effleurage to warm up Liz's muscles.

'How does that feel?'

'Ohhhhh – that's lovely,' Liz replied dreamily. 'I could fall asleep. Last night was bedlam.'

'Why? What happened?'

'It was Fred Thompson, the newbie in room thirteen. He's made it obvious he fancies our Vi and poor Bert's fuming. He's been holding a torch for her for months!'

'Oh, dear,' Beth sympathised.

'Bert's been in and out of his room all night to make sure Fred didn't sneak in to see her,' Liz continued. 'I've been up and down like a bloody yo-yo – I've not had a minute's peace. You'd think these men were teenagers, not pensioners, the way they carry on.'

Beth began to knead the knots out of Liz's

shoulders. 'And what does Vi think of all this male attention?'

'Secretly I think she's lapping it up,' Liz said, relaxing at Beth's touch. 'She said she's told her Eastern European friends and apparently Mr. Dervischi's going to punch Fred if he goes anywhere near her!'

'What's Fred like?'

'Well, apart from being a bloody pain in the proverbial, I suppose you could say he's what's known as very dapper. You'll see what I mean when you meet him later.'

By now Beth was dearly wishing her shift was ending instead of beginning.

Sandra appeared in the doorway. 'That looks good,' she commented, watching as Beth used the heel of her hand to create small friction movements on each side of Liz's upper back and across her shoulders.

'It's absolute heaven,' Liz said.

Heidi and Claire, a couple of day carers, arrived and watched as Beth finished off the massage with smooth strokes over Liz's back.

'I'd forgotten you'd trained in massage,' Sandra said, as a fully relaxed Liz reluctantly rose from her chair and pulled on a cardigan over her tunic.

Beth smiled. 'My aunt's the expert, but I've always enjoyed doing it.'

'You can put me down for some of that! My shoulders are as hard as iron!' Claire said.

'I'll give you a massage sometime, no problem,' Beth told her, before turning to Liz. 'Would you like a drink before you go?'

'I'm OK, thanks. That was just what I needed after a long and difficult night.'

'Well, make sure you drink plenty of water,' Beth advised, 'and try and take things easy.'

'Are you sure you don't feel refreshed enough to stay on longer?' Sandra teased.

Liz grinned at her boss. 'As much as I love my job, I'm looking forward to a good kip and then watching a recording of *I'm a Celebrity*. I reckon eating kangaroo balls and drinking crocodile pee would be easier than working nights sometimes!'

Liz set off and Claire and Heidi went to start their shift.

As Sandra went to sit down with a cup of coffee, her mobile bleeped with a text message. She read it and looked at Beth. 'I'm sorry to ask you at short notice, but I wonder if you can cover reception today? Jodie's daughter's been taken ill and she needs to go home.'

Beth nodded her agreement, although she knew working on reception was a huge responsibility: important calls came through regularly from G.P.s and pharmacists regarding medication, as well as more general calls from residents' families. There was also the worry that a resident suffering with dementia may try to leave the building.

Sandra smiled. 'Thanks, Beth. Jodie will show

you the ropes before she leaves, and you can ring through to my office if there are any problems.'

Beth's stomach twisted with nerves, yet her nervousness was mingled with excited anticipation. *She could do this!*

Chapter Twenty-Eight
Rolling Days and Bright Ideas

Jodie showed Beth how to operate the switchboard and enter calls manually into the register. She also gave her a typed-out list clarifying what she had to do.

Beth's stint on reception went by surprisingly quickly; fortunately, without a hiccup. She was knelt down, filing away the last of the paperwork, when the bell rang. She scrambled to her feet to see Evelyn. The old lady's face was pale and drawn, her normally immaculate chignon tumbling loose around her shoulders.

'Are you alright?' Beth asked her gently.

The old lady's chin wobbled, her eyes were bright with tears.

Shoving the bundle of files she was holding onto the filing cabinet, Beth caught hold of her hand. 'It's nearly the end of my shift. Why don't I finish off and we can have a cup of tea together in the lounge?'

'I don't want to keep you from getting home.'

'I was going to make myself a cuppa before heading off, anyway – I haven't had time for one this afternoon. I'll come and find you when I've finished up here.'

*

There were a few of the residents seated in the lounge, and Beth's heart dipped, as it always did, when she saw that some of them just sat there all day, not exchanging a word with one another, just waiting for one day to roll on into the next.

Evelyn sipped her drink in contemplative silence whilst Beth sat beside her. After a couple of minutes, as the old lady placed her cup on the table, a single tear slid down her pale cheek. Beth put a comforting arm around her shoulders.

'I miss her so much,' Evelyn murmured.

'Mae?' Beth clarified, remembering what Jackie had told her about Evelyn's sister.

She nodded. 'Today's her birthday. She'd have been eighty-three. Sometimes I wonder why I bother getting up in the mornings, now she's gone.'

'To lose someone you love is hard enough, but it must be even more poignant on special days, like birthdays and Christmas. I can only imagine how you must miss her.'

'I miss Mae all the time, my dear, all the time.' Beth gave Evelyn's hand a gentle squeeze.

'How did you and Mae celebrate?'

'We'd always go to see a show.' Evelyn, told her, her face brightening. 'We both loved our pop music, you know: Elvis Presley, Roy Orbison and Gene Pitney. We'd find a tribute act in town, but Elvis was our favourite. We'd get all dolled up to go and see him.' This revelation surprised Beth. She'd have imagined Evelyn enjoying classical singers, maybe the Three Tenors or something. She realised how wrong she was to have made such a sweeping judgment.

'I'd always buy Mae a bunch of yellow roses and a nice box of Belgian chocolates, they were her favourites, you see.'

'That sounds lovely. They must've been special times.'

A smile hovered on the old lady's lips at the memory. 'Oh, yes, they were, dear. They were truly wonderful.'

Beth spent a while with Evelyn, who told her more about herself and Mae, how they'd grown up on their parents' farm and how they'd always done everything together.

'We were sisters, but we were more like twins. We even had a double wedding, you know, marrying two brothers.'

'Wow, that's amazing!'

Through their conversation, Beth realised, more than ever, what a gaping hole the loss of her sister had made in the old lady's life. A nugget of an idea formed in her mind.

Before she left for the evening, she sought out Sandra and put it to her.

She also had a chat with some of the other residents, and finally met the notorious Fred Thompson.

Fred was exactly as she'd imagined through Liz's description: tall and ruddy-cheeked, his thick steel-grey hair in a side parting. He wore a tweed waistcoat with brass buttons fastened down the front, his top pocket sporting a silk handkerchief (navy with white dots). His shirt was brilliant white; the collar starched to attention and finished off with a navy cravat, his brown leather brogues polished to a high gloss shine.

Poor Bert, thought Beth. What with the debonair Fred and the imaginary Mr. Dervischi to contend with, he had his work cut out if he wanted to gain Vi's affections.

Chapter Twenty-Nine
Oil over Troubled Waters

Beth smiled as she walked into her parents' sitting room. Aunt Lena was relaxing on their well-worn tapestry sofa, and it was good to see her aunt's cheeks had regained their rosy glow. Rodney strained on his lead to reach Lena's side.

'Your mum's feeding me up, love,' Lena said, with a wink. 'Now, let me give that lovely boy of yours some fuss.'

She let Rodney get close enough to sniff her outstretched hand. The dog seemed to sense Lena wasn't herself and made no attempt to jump up, simply resting his head in her lap.

Lena smiled. 'Ah, he knows I've been poorly, don't you, sweetie? But Auntie's much better now, and I'll be able to come for walkies with you soon.'

Antimacassars covered the faded arms of the chair on which Dad sat. He glanced up from his newspaper and rolled his eyes. 'You're all too daft with that dog. It'll make him a right softie.'

Ignoring him, Lena pointed to a wooden box sitting on the glass topped coffee table. Beth's eyes lit up as she recognised it.

'That's for you,' Lena told her.

'You can't part with that!'

'Yes, I can – now open it up!'

Beth unlatched the clasp and carefully lifted the wooden lid. The concertinaed drawers spread open to display amber glass bottles containing pure essential oils which were labelled and colour coded according to their notes: top, middle and base. She recalled the top notes were the lighter oils such as bergamot and neroli; the middle were more complex and comprised the focal point of the blend, such as clary sage and chamomile; the bottom or base notes were the ones upon which the foundation of each perfume was built, such as patchouli and sandalwood.

'I want you to have it.' Lena pointed to a large hessian bag. 'There are a bundle of books here, too, and I want you to have them all.'

'I don't know what to say –'

'You don't need to say anything, love. But you can *do* something.'

Beth raised her eyebrows. 'What's that?'

'I want you to do something for yourself for once,' her aunt replied, her voice serious. 'I'd be so happy if you would go back to your studies and put all that talent to good use. It's like I've always said since you were a little girl - you should never give up on your dreams.'

Mum walked into the sitting room, wiping her

hands on a tea towel. 'What's going on?'

'I've just given my aromatherapy stuff to my favourite niece.'

Beth laughed. 'I'm your only niece!'

Mum simply nodded, not in the least bit surprised, and Beth guessed she'd already known what Lena had planned to do. 'Listen to your aunt and make good use of it.'

'I will,' she promised.

'Anyway,' Mum continued, 'Ben rang earlier to check on your aunt. He's suggested that, if she feels up to it, perhaps we could all meet up for a carvery at The Ketch on Sunday? He's already called Tash and she says she can make it.'

Still feeling emotional at her aunt's generosity, Beth gave her a wobbly smile. 'That would be lovely.'

Lena nodded in agreement. 'I'd really enjoy that.'

Mum tucked in the ends of the crocheted shawl lying on Lena's lap. 'We'll make sure you're feeling well enough first. You don't want to run before you can walk.'

*

As soon as Beth got home, she placed the treasure box on the kitchen worktop, caressing the smooth mahogany surface with her fingertips. She'd always loved the box. As a young girl, she'd believed it was magic. With the healing properties of the oils, she supposed, in a way, that it was.

As she lifted the lid, she inhaled the scent of

lavender, bergamot and neroli, stirring memories of her childish eagerness to mix the "magic" potions. She pulled one of the aromatherapy books from the bag and began to read. A couple of hours ticked by before Beth closed the book and put it back into the bag for safekeeping. The amount of things she could remember from her college days surprised her. She could've kicked herself for dropping out; she'd enjoyed her course and was doing so well, but with Paul and the children to look after, it had seemed like it wasn't meant to be.

She felt a flutter of excitement – perhaps her aunt was right, maybe she could return to college and follow her dream! The only problem was that she needed to earn cold, hard cash to make a living.

The sound of Cher from her mobile dragged her from her daydream.

'Hi, Beth,' said a male voice. 'It's Greg.'

'Oh – hi...' It was late for a call from the estate agent.

'I know it's rather late,' he continued. 'I've tried to call you to let you know contracts have been exchanged.'

She fell silent as panic swelled inside her.

Where on earth were they were going to live?

'I know I could've phoned you in the morning,' Greg continued,'... but I do have an ulterior motive.'

'Oh,' Beth replied distractedly. 'What's that?'

'I wondered if you'd fancy meeting up with me

for a drink – un-work related?'

There was an awkward pause as she mulled this over. 'Err – OK – that'd be nice,' she managed finally.

They made arrangements before she hung up the phone.

Why on earth had she said "yes"? She couldn't imagine going on a date! It had been, well – years. And she had nothing to wear for starters, let alone having to make a full blown conversation with Greg. Apart from the house sale, would they have anything in common to talk about?

She flopped down onto the sofa and Rodney jumped up, snuggling into her side. 'God, Rodney – what have I just agreed to? As if I haven't got enough to worry about already.'

He let out a gentle snore. *Oh, to be a dog,* thought Beth.

Chapter Thirty
Roast Beef and Revelations

The enticing smell of roast beef and Yorkshire pudding wafted through the restaurant.

Beth smiled across the long table at her son. 'It was a lovely suggestion for us all to get together for lunch.'

Ben returned her smile, causing her to momentarily catch her breath – sometimes his likeness to Paul was uncanny, but she acknowledged that this was only in the looks department, and not in personality.

'It certainly was thoughtful,' Lena agreed. 'You're a very thoughtful young man.'

Ben blushed, and Tash, who was sitting opposite her brother, rolled her eyes good-humouredly.

Dad raised his pint glass of real ale into the air. 'Here's to good health!'

Everyone else followed suit. 'To good health,' they chorused.

The dinner tasted as good as it looked: golden roast potatoes crisp on the outside and fluffy in the middle, tender slices of beef, succulent roast parsnips, cauliflower cheese, carrots and broccoli with lashings of rich, steaming gravy.

Amid all the chatter and laughter, Beth observed her son. He was making an effort to laugh in the right places, yet, knowing him so well, she could see he had something on his mind.

Once they'd eaten and enjoyed their meal, the family wandered into the bar area and Beth took the opportunity to pull him to one side. 'Is everything OK?'

Ben shook his head. 'No, Mum – not really. I've left my job.'

Beth blinked, struggling to take this in. 'I hope this isn't because of your dad and Emily?'

'It's not just that – it's complicated. I don't really know where to start.'

Having overheard them talking, Sam walked over to join them. 'Ben's been unhappy at work for ages,' he explained. 'In a strange way, the situation with his dad and Emily's helped him make up his mind.'

Beth looked from one to the other anxiously. 'Make up his mind about what?'

'You know how I hate what Dad's done to you, to us, by going off with Emily. I won't lie; I hate seeing them together and having my nose rubbed in it every day, but take all of that out of the equation and I'd still be unhappy working there.'

'I'm so sorry, love. I had no idea you felt like this,' Beth said, reaching out to touch his arm.

Ben heaved a sigh. 'I never wanted to train in law

in the first place. It's been what Dad always wanted for me – what he expected of me.'

'But you've worked so hard! I can't believe you've been so unhappy – why didn't you say anything?'

He dropped his gaze. 'I didn't want to disappoint anyone. I feel such a bloody failure.'

'Oh, love, you know I'd never be disappointed in you! You could do whatever you want as long as it makes you happy – that's all I've ever wanted for you and your sister.' Beth gave him a hug. 'And you'll never be a failure. *Do you hear me?*'

Everyone was now looking over at them curiously. Ben cleared his throat. 'You may as well all know,' he said. 'I'm going to train as a nurse.'

There was a collective sharp intake of breath before Tash spoke. 'Good on you, bro,' she told him. 'What does Dad have to say about it?'

'He wasn't best pleased, as you can imagine. He told me to collect my stuff and clear off if I was going – he called me a few choice names too. I feel crap for letting him down, but nursing's what I want to do. I know in my heart it's the right thing.'

Dad clapped him on the back. 'Well done, son. That took guts to face up to your father.' He lifted his glass once more. 'Let's drink a toast to your future.'

Seeing the look of relief wash over her son's face, her eyes filled with tears.

Chapter Thirty-One
Wise Words and Deaf Ears

Holly Mount

Opening a filing cabinet, Sandra plucked out a form which she handed to Beth. 'Ask Ben to complete this and get it back to me as soon as possible so we can get his DBS check sorted.'

'Thank you,' Beth said. He can fill it in tonight and I'll bring it back tomorrow.'

At their family lunch, Ben had gone on to tell everyone how it was becoming more and more difficult to cope with doing something his heart simply wasn't in. He'd managed to line up a nursing course starting in September, and it was a requirement of this that he gain experience in the caring profession. Beth had mentioned it to Sandra. It was a stroke of luck that, due to staff shortages, there were temporary vacancies at Holly Mount.

*

Beth drove home pleased for her son and looking forward to a quiet evening. Turning on her mobile, she saw she had a missed call from Paul. She sighed, hoping that he wasn't going to rant on about Ben's decision, although she knew that he would. Reluctantly, she returned the call and he answered after the third ring. Beth heard Emily's voice in the background, *'Do hurry up, dahling – we're going to be late!'*

'I missed a call from you,' Beth said without preamble.

'Look, I don't know what the stupid lad thinks he's doing, but I don't have time to discuss it right now. Can't it wait?'

'No! You're the one who phoned me, remember, so I want to hear what you have to say.'

There was a pause before he spoke again. 'I want you to try and talk some sense into him before he completely flushes his life down the toilet. That's the trouble with Ben – he's like you. No drive and no ambition! Doesn't he understand how privileged he is, for God's sake?'

His words struck a low blow; her heart rose up into her throat. 'Ben's an adult now. It's his life, *his* decision, and I'm really proud of him. I only wished I'd had the courage to do the same years ago. And I'll tell you something else: He's kind, caring and loyal; twice the man you'll ever be.'

Shaking with anger and in desperate need to off-load, she went to see Jackie. Her friend listened patiently, not passing comment until she'd poured everything out. 'The reason Prat face said all that stuff,' she said finally, 'is because he's a dickhead and you're better off without him!'

And Beth had thought she was going to say

something profound.

Perhaps, she decided, it was good that some things never changed.

Jackie handed her a cup of tea. Beth stirred it thoughtfully. 'With everything that's going on, I think I should cancel my date.'

Jackie shook her head determinedly. 'No way, madam!'

'I don't feel up to it, Jacks,' Beth said with a sigh.

'Oh, come on – you can't sit around and worry about Ben; he's a grown man, you've said so yourself,' Jackie reasoned. 'You've helped him to find work and you're supporting him all the way – there's nothing else you can do.'

'I guess you're right,' she conceded, 'but there's the imminent problem of where I'm going to live. I've been wondering if I could rent a place now. I'm not exactly rolling in cash, but, with the extra for covering shifts; maybe I can rent somewhere half decent – as long as Rodney's allowed to live there too.'

Jackie blew out her cheeks. 'I'm still fuming about whoever complained about him.'

Putting down her cup, Beth reached out and touched her friend's arm. 'I know, but it could've been worse. It's a good job we hadn't moved in with you lock, stock and barrel. Imagine having to shift all my stuff out again – what a nightmare!'

Jackie sat deep in thought for a few moments, and her face brightened. 'Why don't you ask Greg about properties to rent? His company deals with letting as well as sales, doesn't it?'

'I hadn't really thought about it,' Beth said pensively. 'But at least it'll give us something to talk about.'

Jackie grinned. 'Now you can sort out your glad-rags and look forward to a night out.'

'Oh, don't – I'm still dreading it!' Beth laughed nervously. 'God knows why I agreed to go in the first place. What if he turns out to be an oddball?'

'OMG, you're right – he could be a serial killer!'

She gave her friend's arm a friendly slap. 'Pack it in or I won't go at all!'

'Don't worry. I'm sure he's perfectly fine. I know where he works and I know where you're meeting him.' She looked at Beth's anxious face. 'And remember, you haven't agreed to marriage – it's just an informal drink and a chat.'

'I guess so,' Beth said resignedly. 'Will you pop round to help me get ready?'

'Yes, of course I will.'

'Come early so we can have a drink. I think I'm going to need one – or two!'

Chapter Thirty-Two
Paul

Paul reversed his car into the second allocated space outside Emily's apartment. It was safe in the covered and gated area, but he missed the wealth of space his own driveway had provided. He missed the double garage too. It had been his "man cave". Although he didn't like doing anything too technical with the car, it was nice to go in and have a tinker around sometimes. It certainly made a change from dealing with some of the weeping women and broken men who formed a large proportion of his client base. The other good thing about the garage was that Beth had respected it as his domain and never entered unless it was to bring him a cup of coffee.

As he walked towards the main entrance, he noticed a familiar blue escort parked in one of the spaces reserved for visitors. A tight ball of anger welled up inside him – *the Russell-Smythes!* Hadn't he seen enough of that pillock last night at dinner as well as being with him in the office all day? He'd never been so bored at a so-called dinner party in all of his life. Giles had droned on all evening about holiday destinations he'd visited during the last decade, which had been followed by Paul having to sit and look at endless photographs and oohing and ah-ing in all the right places. He really couldn't have given a damn whether the Russell-Smythes holidayed in Miami or bloody Skegness.

It was all very well for Emily – she and Jules seemed to be joined at the hip these days. The photograph viewing had been punctuated at regular intervals by their irritating and constant chatter and laughter.

He hesitated for a moment, tempted to jump back into his car and drive away. If he was lucky he might not be spotted. His shoulders slumped as he decided he'd have to go in, or Emily would be on his case for the next month.

When he walked in, Emily was seated next to Jules, whilst Giles looked thoroughly at home in *his* chair. A fresh burst of irritation flooded through him. He raked his fingers through his hair. All he'd wanted after a busy day was to enjoy a nice relaxed meal and a few drinks. The fact that his son had walked out on a brilliant career kept clawing at his mind and the last thing he needed was meaningless chit-chat with people who, ironically, he considered to be as shallow as a puddle.

All eyes turned to look at him.

Emily shook her head in mock-stern fashion, letting out a tinkling laugh. 'You're rather late, dahling. I thought you'd be home early, knowing I'd had the afternoon off.'

He refused to join in her laughter. He also refused to meet her gaze. Emily's face grew hot with embarrassment. How dare he show her up in front of her friends?

At the same time, Paul wondered how she dare humiliate him in front of his staff.

Flicking her silky blonde hair over her shoulder, Jules flashed an embarrassed smile. 'I'm sorry if we've come at a bad time,' she purred. 'But we have some exciting news! I only found out this afternoon and I was simply dying to share it with Emily.'

Paul frowned. 'What news?'

Giles stood up, grasping his hand in a vice-like grip, pumping it up and down vigorously. 'It's really good news, old boy.' Paul observed beads of perspiration glistening on Giles's forehead and blanched as his halitosis breath reached his nostrils. God, he thought, the man is revolting. Paul was at least a decade younger than Giles too, and took exception to being referred to as "old boy".

'My wife's a clever girl,' Giles continued jovially, oblivious to Paul's disgust. 'She surprised me when I got home. Of course, I was as pleased as Punch! I wanted to come over and view it straight away; we've always fancied living in one of these apartments.'

Paul stood speechless. It felt as though he was being subjected to some sort of Chinese torture.

'Oh, dahling, it really is the best news ever,'

Emily added. He assumed that she thought he was just being a misery guts because he was tired.

'It certainly is,' Giles agreed. 'We're going to be neighbours, buddy! Perhaps we could car share when we're working the same hours?'

Over my dead body, he thought, gritting his teeth, and why is the idiot calling me his buddy?

Loosening his tie, he walked over to the dresser to pour a double whisky – heaven knows he needed it. He took a long glug before glancing over at Emily. 'I didn't know there was an apartment for sale.'

Emily rolled her eyes. 'I *did* tell you, dahling. You know I never forget things like that.' She turned to face Jules. 'I've got a photographic memory, you know.'

Paul shook his head in annoyance but, unperturbed, Emily looked at him as she continued. 'It's Mrs. Pearce from apartment twelve. She had a fall last week and she's decided to move in with her daughter.' She gave another tinkling laugh. 'I have to admit I'm glad; she was rather common and did lower the tone.'

Paul bit back his annoyance. The old lady was certainly a colourful character; there was no doubt about that. She reminded him of a pantomime dame, but she had a heart of gold, always offering to help others. There was no need for his girlfriend to be quite so mean-spirited.

Emily smiled indulgently at her guests.

'Honestly, men!' she exclaimed. 'Fancy him forgetting that – now, let me pop into the kitchen and get you that brochure. She rose from her seat and Paul followed her. 'What the hell's going on?'

Emily sighed. 'I do so wish you wouldn't get all worked up over nothing. Mrs. Pearce told me of her plan to move a few days ago. She wanted a private sale. I mentioned it to Jules. I did tell you, Paul. I know I did.'

'I have no recollection of you telling me whatsoever,' Paul hissed. 'And I'll tell you this for nothing: I'm not spending one more minute with that prick than I have to!'

Emily shook her head in annoyance, her elfin crop remaining immaculately in place. It always made her look so young and vulnerable, but he realised she was a wolf in sheep's clothing.

She heaved a sigh at his negativity. 'Look, I've also already told you that Daddy's treating us to a long weekend away of our choice, which is jolly decent of him. I really think you should show him some gratitude if you want to be senior partner. It'll be good to spend time in New York with Jules and Giles. You can get to know him properly and do man stuff while Jules and I go shopping. It'll be a hoot.'

Paul clenched his fists. 'I think you mean it'll be a scream,' he said sarcastically, 'and I'm the one who'll be bloody well screaming! How could you do all this behind my back for God's sake, Em?' He fought the desperate urge to go back into the sitting room and demand that the Russell-Smythes leave there and then, but he realised that he would be in big trouble if he did. On top of his longed-for promotion, there was also the tiny matter that the apartment where he now lived belonged solely to Emily.

'It is good of your father,' he agreed tersely. 'But the key part of what you've just said is that it is "our choice" where we should go, and you chose to make that decision behind my back. What I'd like to know is: when has my opinion ever come into it?'

'Ssshhh!' Emily inclined her head towards the door. 'They'll hear you.'

Paul shrugged. 'So what if they do? I'm getting heartily sick of being told what to do.'

Emily gave him a hard stare as she snatched the brochure for bespoke kitchens from the drawer and wandered back through to the sitting room.

Paul remained in the relative quiet of the kitchen for a few minutes, waiting for his anger to subside. If it wasn't for Emily's daddy dearest and the promotion that must surely come, he'd be out of that front door faster than a greyhound out of a trap.

Chapter Thirty-Three
Piccadilly Circus and Verbal Diarrhoea

Jackie gave a low whistle. 'Wow! Give us a whirl'

Beth felt a bit silly, but she swivelled round on her heel as her friend looked at her admiringly.

'You've lost so much weight,' Jackie said. 'That dress looks gorgeous on you.'

Flushing slightly, Beth smoothed down the soft fabric of the Aztec patterned dress with her fingers, scrutinising her tummy and hips in her wardrobe mirror. 'God knows how I've done it – I struggled to fasten the zip when I tried it on in the House of Fraser, but I was determined to get into it. There was no way I was going to put it back on the rail and give Penelope and Emily the satisfaction!'

Jackie smiled. 'You certainly don't need to wear your super compresso underneath that!' (Mum's super compresso was Tash's nickname for Beth's Spanx). 'You've been so busy with your job and everything that you haven't been scoffing chocolate and junk food.'

'That's true – I haven't thought about a bag of

peanut M & Ms for weeks!'

'And how are you feeling about tonight, now you're looking all glam?'

'To be honest, I'm still scared stiff,' Beth admitted.

After being with one person for over half of a lifetime, it was a mammoth task to imagine being with anyone else. The mere thought of anything approaching intimacy felt terrifying to her.

'You'll be fine when you get there,' Jackie placated. 'You know it's often the thought of doing something, rather than actually doing it, that's the scarier prospect.'

The sound of the doorbell startled them. Rodney let out a bark and ran downstairs.

'Carry on beautifying yourself,' Jackie said as she took in Beth's stricken face. 'I'll get it.'

Left alone to reflect, Beth was glad she'd given herself the luxury of a couple of hours to get ready. If she had to go through this rigmarole before she went on a date, her nerves wouldn't take it. But, she berated herself, maybe that was wishful thinking – this might be the only time she'd have to worry about it.

Rodney trotted back into the bedroom, his tail wagging. Assuming Jackie had got rid of the caller; Beth twirled around in front of him. 'Well, what do you think, Rodders?'

Her dog looked up at her quizzically, his gaze

dropping down to her feet. He knew if she was wearing boots or wellies it was time for walkies or if she was in her flatties it meant she was going to work, but he looked totally puzzled by her new black heels.

Holding a long string of black beads to her neck, Beth swivelled round on her stool and looked at her reflection in mirror. Her eyes widened as reflections of Tash and Penelope appeared behind her. She swivelled round, looking anxiously at her daughter. 'Please don't tell me I've got your term time muddled up –'

Tash shook her head. 'No, don't worry – it's nothing like that. I had some free time, so I've come to see Gran.'

Beth looked from one to the other suspiciously, thinking how strange this was. Tash never called in on her Gran voluntarily.

Penelope, who had been unusually quiet, looked Beth up and down. 'Your dress looks ... very nice, dear.'

'Thank you,' she replied, swallowing her surprise.

Her mother-in-law gave her a tight-lipped smile. 'Natasha wanted to see you, so I thought I'd come along, too, to check how you are now the sale's gone through. I've been very concerned about you.'

Beth held her gaze. 'Everything's fine, thank you.'

'I'm glad to hear it,' Penelope replied stiffly.

'Are you off somewhere nice this evening?'

'I'm meeting a man for dinner,' Beth replied boldly.

Penelope pursed her lips and, out of the corner of her eye, Beth saw Jackie's pained expression. She could guess what she must be thinking: Why hasn't she told the old trout to mind her own blooming business?

The doorbell rang for a second time. Rodney raced off downstairs once more, his paws skittering across the wooden floor as he reached the hall.

Jackie rolled her eyes. 'Flipping heck – it's like Piccadilly Circus tonight!'

This time Beth left them to it and went downstairs. *Why on earth had her mother-in-law turned up tonight of all nights? As if she wasn't stressed enough already.*

A thought dawned on her: had she got her wires crossed? Maybe Greg had said he'd pick her up, yet it was far too early for it to be him, and she was quite certain they'd arranged to meet outside The Fox at Branford, a few miles outside Worcester. She painted on a smile just in case, before opening the door.

Beth did a double take. Ben and Sam, together with Paul and Emily were standing on her doorstep. Quickly gathering herself together, she ushered them inside. 'Whatever's wrong?'

Ben bundled an excited Rodney into his arms. No one spoke as they followed her through to the sitting room.

The others came downstairs to join them, Tash

glowering at Emily, although her expression softened when she looked at her brother. 'Are you OK, Ben?'

He nodded. 'I'm not too bad, shrimp. I'm going to be working with Mum soon.'

'Mum's told me. Sick.'

Penelope rolled her eyes. 'Do you really have to use that vulgar expression, Natasha, dear?'

Tash ignored her. Penelope turned to face her grandson. When she spoke again, her tone was ominously quiet. 'I asked your father to bring you here tonight, Benjamin, so we could all talk. I must say I'm very concerned and disappointed to hear you're throwing away your future.'

Heat seemed to rise from the soles of Beth's feet through her solar plexus and radiated into her cheeks. Her eyes bored into her mother-in-law. *So this was the reason for the unexpected visit.*

'How dare you speak to him like that?' she demanded. 'Ben's future's in nursing; it's what he's always wanted to do. And if it wasn't for your control freak of a son, he'd have pursued it a long time ago.'

Seven pairs of eyes were now fixed on her, soundless mouths gaping open and shut.

The tick of the clock seemed amplified a hundred times and her heart beat in sync with it.

'That's both unfair and untrue!' Paul's voice shattered the silence. 'All I've ever done is put this family first.'

His words were like a red rag to a bull.

'You're as deluded as your mother!' Beth cried, unable to stop herself now. 'Oh, yes, you've always put your family first – that's why you went off with that … that stuck up cow! Of course your mother's going to side with you, just like she always does –'

Jackie grabbed her hand. 'Calm down, Beth,' she whispered.

'No!' Paul snapped. 'Let her finish! Is there anything else you want to add?'

There was a lot that she could add, Beth thought to herself, but she fell silent.

'Well, Bethany, if that's how you feel, perhaps I'd better go,' Penelope said.

Beth nodded. 'That sounds like a good idea.' A sob caught in Penelope's throat as she rose from her seat and hurried from the room.

Paul drew a long breath. 'Well, thanks very much for that performance. It's just what Mother needed right now.'

Beth swallowed. She knew she'd gone a bit too far, but how had he expected her to react when his mother was verbally attacking Ben?

'I'll go and check if Gran's OK,' Tash offered, shooting her mum a sympathetic look before dashing off.

Beth felt as if she was standing outside the headmaster's office waiting to hear her punishment for talking in class.

'Are you OK, Mum?' Ben asked.

Beth managed a thin smile and nodded.

Paul headed towards the kitchen. 'We need to talk – in private.'

'Do you need me to stay?' Jackie offered her face anxious.

Beth shook her head. 'I'll be alright, thanks – I'll call you later.'

The front door clicked shut as her friend left, and suddenly Beth felt very alone.

Paul loosened his tie as he stood in the door aperture. 'Well, this was going to be difficult anyway, but –'

Emily rose from the sofa and pointed a red-tipped finger at her Rolex. 'Dahling, do you really have to do this *now*? We're going to be frightfully late –'

Paul's eyebrows beetled together. 'Give it a bloody rest for once, can't you?'

Emily shrank back in her seat, her face reddening.

'Me and Sam will take Rodney out while you and Dad talk,' Ben told Beth.

She nodded her agreement and they headed off. She took a brief glance at Emily, who wouldn't look her in the eye, before following Paul through to the kitchen. She had no idea where this was going, but she knew that, whatever it was, it certainly wasn't good. She also knew she didn't want to end up in a full scale row; there had been quite enough drama for one day.

Beth watched as Paul leant his back against the granite worktop, realising, for the first time since he'd arrived, how drained he looked. 'What's wrong?'

He took a long, deep breath, breathing out slowly before speaking. 'Father's left Mother.'

She took a step back, unsure if she'd heard him correctly. 'What do you mean – he's left her?'

'He's not coming back from Antalya.'

'Why not?'

He sighed wearily. 'Apparently he's met someone else and he says he has no intention of returning. He said his life's been miserable for years and he's had enough.'

They stood in silence, each absorbed in their own thoughts.

'Mother was heartbroken when I told her,' Paul continued eventually. 'She was so distraught I had to call Tash to stay with her while I went to a meeting.'

That explained why Tash had gone straight round to her gran's.

'I'm sorry,' Beth told him truthfully. Although she could understand Clive's feelings, she didn't like the way he'd gone about it and realised what an awful shock it must've been to her mother-in-law.

She looked up at Paul and they locked gazes for a moment. Before she realised what was happening, Paul was standing before her and reaching out his hands, trying to pull her towards him.

Chapter Thirty-Four
Red Bull and Prickly Heat

Once the house had emptied, Beth poured herself a large glass of red wine. *What a day.* She'd assumed everyone was there to have a go at Ben. Never in a million years would she have believed that her mild mannered father-in-law would have cleared off for good.

The very last thing she felt like doing was going on a date, but it was now seven thirty p.m. and she was meeting Greg at eight; it would be unfair of her not to turn up. She dialled the taxi firm's number before she had time to change her mind, then dashed upstairs to do a quick make-up repair job.

As her taxi pulled up outside The Fox, she saw that Greg was already waiting. He was dressed casually in stone coloured chinos and a black cotton shirt, and grinned at her as she walked over to him.

'Hi,' Beth said, feeling the attractive glow of prickly heat rise up into her throat.

'You look stunning,' Greg replied smoothly. Beth swallowed; he looked more handsome than she remembered.

They headed into the pub, which was busy, yet not overcrowded, the hum of conversation comforting rather than intrusive. Although her insides were jelly, she decided maybe the evening would be alright after all – at least it was a distraction after the afternoon from hell.

Greg pointed out a candlelit table in a secluded corner, and Beth took a seat and waited while he went up to the bar to order drinks: a glass of house red for her and a Red Bull for him. *Unusual choice, she thought.*

He joined her, placing their drinks on the table, and pulled out a chair. 'How's your aunt doing?'

She absently swirled the stem of her glass between her fingers. 'She's doing well, thanks for asking. I meant to ask you before; I wondered why you were at the hospital that night?'

Greg blew out a rush of air. 'I had to do a mercy dash – '

Beth raised her eyebrows. 'Oh, dear –'

'You see, my sister's waters broke. It's her first baby and it was panic stations.'

'Goodness – I bet that was a shock! Isn't the baby's father around?'

He shook his head before taking a long swig of his drink. 'Marie's a lone parent.'

'Was everything OK – I mean, with your sister and the baby?'

'Yes – it was all good. She had a boy – Marcus.

They're both doing well.'

'I'm glad to hear that.'

Greg raised his glass. 'Cheers!' He leaned over and whispered in her ear, 'It gives you wind.'

What the hell?

Beth took a large gulp of wine before answering. 'Oh, never mind,' she said, trying to sound matter-of-fact. 'It *is* very gassy –'

His eyebrows furrowed. *'Pardon?'*

'Well – that must be the reason it gives you wind.'

Greg's eyes widened. He swallowed as he put his glass down on the table. 'That would have to go down as the most unromantic thing I've ever said! What I actually said was, "It gives you *wings*".'

Oh God!

'I'm so sorry,' Beth stammered, her face burning.

His smile was half-hearted. 'I can assure you it doesn't give me wind!'

Beth considered making a dive for the door, but she knew that wasn't really an option.

Their conversation from then on was awkward and stilted.

Greg asked if she'd eaten. Although she hadn't had anything since breakfast, she couldn't face eating anything now.

How the heck could this day have gone from bad to worse? Mentally, she willed time to go by quickly, but every minute felt like an hour.

They did touch on the subject of property rental, though, and Greg said he'd check if there was anything suitable for her plus one dog on his books.

After a second drink and a bit more forced polite chit-chat, he seemed as anxious as she was to call it a night.

Having said their goodbyes, Beth breathed a sigh of relief as she climbed into her taxi. As soon as she got home, she called Jackie, pouring out the whole sorry saga, firstly about Penelope and Clive, and, then, "date-night".

'The guy's obviously got no sense of humour,' Jackie said, when she'd managed to calm down from a fit of the giggles.

Beth blew out a long breath. 'You can say that again.'

'I can't believe it about Penelope, though,' Jackie added.

'As much as I dislike the woman, I can't quite believe it myself – they've been together for all these years.'

'Perhaps it's karma for all the hassle she's given you.'

Being superstitious, a part of Beth wondered if maybe she was right. Clive had put up with so much from his wife, as her unwavering devotion to her son meant he'd always come a shoddy second place in her affections.

'Is she staying on at Downton?' Jackie asked.

'No. Paul said it has to be sold. Apparently she'll be moving in with him and Emily.'

'Blimey – that's a turn-up for the book! I wouldn't have thought Emily would want another woman in her kitchen, especially one like Penelope. But, as far as I'm concerned, they all deserve one another. As long as that woman's not your problem, you should thank your lucky stars.'

Chapter Thirty-Five
Paul

Paul raked his fingers through his hair. *What the hell had just happened?* He'd made a lunge at his ex, that's what.

He poured himself another glass of Johnnie Walker's and strolled out onto the balcony, rubbing his throbbing temples and letting the gentle lap of the waters of the River Severn soothe his frazzled brain. He threw back his head and downed his scotch in one, enjoying the sensation as the warm liquid hit the back of his throat.

And what on earth was his son thinking? Jesus Christ! The stupid boy had had it all on a plate. Why the hell would he want to wipe old folk's arses and be a general dog's body?

Natasha hadn't studied law as Paul had hoped she would, but at least she'd dug her heels in at the time and he knew she'd be successful in life. What a great pity she hadn't been the male. Ben just didn't have that same drive, determination and ambition. He simply pottered on in his day-to-day life and, thought Paul, just like Beth, Ben was a dreamer, not a doer.

He rested his glass on the steel rail of the balcony,

his fingers gripping the base to steady it, and let out a resigned sigh. He could finally see with clarity that the reason his marriage had lasted for twenty-three years was because he and Beth were so different. He hated to admit it, even to himself, but he missed her.

On top of all this, Emily was proving a challenge.

If she wasn't so demanding, perhaps things wouldn't be so dire. But her expensive tastes were certainly taking their toll.

His mind turned to Christmas once more, and how Emily had insisted on a Michelin starred restaurant for Christmas lunch. Truth be told, Paul would have preferred a few drinks with his golf buddies at the club, followed by a home cooked Christmas lunch with all the trimmings. Beth had never been Nigella, but he had to admit she could always rustle up a decent roast.

He knew he'd offended his parents by not inviting them to have Christmas lunch with them, too. He just couldn't have stumped up the extra cash. If Emily kept spending at this rate of knots, he'd be bankrupt within a year. Now, to add insult to injury, his father had buggered off with some floozy in Antalya, leaving him to shoulder the burden of his mother, who had turned from a stoical, forthright woman into a total wreck, seemingly overnight. He'd been shocked when Emily'd suggested his mother come to live with them – very shocked indeed. Although, when he'd really thought things through, he'd decided it could be a plus. She could look after the apartment and the moggie, allowing him and Emily the freedom of impromptu breaks, as long as they didn't involve the Russell-Smythes. Oh boy, did he fancy feeling the sun on his back right now.

Ah, well, he speculated, at least things couldn't get any worse. The company would eventually be his, even if his dream of "Bishop & Bishop" adorning the brass wall plaque would never be realised.

Chapter Thirty-Six
Friendship and Sleeping Dogs

What an absolute disaster today had been, Beth thought, from Penelope undermining Ben to hearing the news that Clive had left. Then last, but of course by no means least, her dreadful date!

She climbed into bed and sat nursing a cup of Ovaltine with Rodney curled up alongside her, but even with her comforting milky drink and the lavender oil under her pillow, her brain simply refused to switch off. She lay staring into black nothingness, soothed somewhat by the rhythm of Rodney's gentle snoring. She wondered what he could be dreaming about – perhaps he was chasing a cat up a tree or digging up a bone. She envied the seemingly simple life of a dog – well, her dog, anyway.

Finally giving up sleep, she rolled over and clicked on her lamp. Opening the drawer of her bedside table, she picked up a detective novel and began to read, but, having read the same paragraph twice and not being able to take a word in, she shoved the book back and shut the drawer with a sigh.

Her whirring mind flicked to her relationship with Paul. She remembered how some of her friends were envious when she and Paul became an item. Even from that young age, she guessed, they realised he was destined to make something of himself.

Many lads the same age as Beth would hang around nightclubs with their fake I.D.s and their swagger, hoping to score with the girls. She'd known instinctively Paul was different. He'd been popular with both his peers and his teachers – he was a grafter, committed to studying for his future, but, as he didn't find the work too arduous, it meant he could spend time with her too. She'd really admired his grit and determination.

In complete contrast, she'd never been particularly academic, and she wasn't very popular with her teachers, although, with her kind and helpful nature, she, too, had been popular with her peers. Her end of term reports usually read along the lines of, *"Bethany can work well, but is easily distracted"*.

'That's the trouble with you, Beth,' Paul had said many times. 'You have a butterfly mind. You're always flitting from one thing to another. That's why you never finish a job properly.'

Although she'd been annoyed at the time, she grudgingly knew he was right. Yet she believed that, if she'd been able to continue at college and had pursued her passion, she'd have done well. Her tutor, Mrs. Drew, had praised her, saying she had an aura of calm about her, an empathetic nature and an instinct for nurturing people.

She pounded her pillow and then laid her head on it, trying to find a cool spot. It was going to be one of those nights that went on forever. She closed her eyes, willing herself to sleep, but it was about as effective as it had been when she was eight years old, anxiously waiting for Santa to come. Mum always told her to close her eyes and think nice thoughts and she'd soon fall asleep. But the lavender oil had failed to work on that particular Christmas Eve, too. Beth smiled to herself as she remembered it was almost six o'clock on Christmas morning before her Dad was able to tiptoe into her bedroom to leave her stocking at the foot of her bed. She'd peeped over the top of the quilt and watched him. When he'd looked in her direction, she'd snapped her eyes shut. She knew there wasn't really a Santa Claus, but hadn't wanted her parents to realise; it was more fun that way. Besides, there was always an extra gift from Santa in her stocking on Christmas morning.

She realised that, in normal circumstances, most people reach a stage when the "honeymoon" phase of their relationship comes to an end and real life kicks in. Sometimes the things about your partner that used to make you smile can, after a while, make you want to scream. She'd almost forgotten how Paul would ask her to take a shower before they made love. He'd made it sound like some sort of foreplay. Beth cringed inwardly at her naivety.

She also realised that, in most relationships, with understanding, compromise and a bit of give and take, you can strike the status quo. It hadn't been like that between her and Paul, especially since he'd joined Charles Mortimer's company. He'd become every inch the alpha male and hated it if she voiced an opinion which differed from his own. She knew he'd found many of her quirky ways irritating. He'd roll his eyes whenever she painted each of her fingernails in a different colour and he'd moan about the funky clothes she bought from charity shops. Her favourite purchase had been a pink woollen jacket, which he'd grumbled made her look like a teddy bear.

For the past year, Beth had felt as if she'd been house sharing with a virtual stranger, yet she acknowledged that, when the kids were young, their marriage had worked; she'd been the butterfly whilst Paul was the worker bee, buzzing with ideas, clever, astute, sensible.

When Ben and Tash were small, she'd done all the mumsy stuff: taken them to playgroups, run around with them in parks and mixed with other mums. Beth remembered with fondness the "school gate mums" – Celia Bateman, who'd been a dab hand with a sewing machine and would run up costumes for the school plays; Annie Harris, whose son, Simon, shared his birthday with Ben. Beth and Annie would host joint birthday parties. One year, Beth forgot to buy candles for the birthday cake. Annie had the brainwave of sticking matches straight into the icing, but it looked more like a blow torch than a cake once they were lit.

She heaved an indulgent sigh. It was things like that that made good memories.

Eventually, Tash and Ben went to Worcester Grammar and Celia's daughter, Helen, to Cheltenham Ladies' College, whilst Annie and her family moved to Devon. They'd all kept in touch at first, but now it was scribbled notes added hastily to the bottom of Christmas cards (the internet was even more of an alien concept to Beth then). Now she was more computer savvy, she'd managed to find Annie on Facebook.

Simon was in the Police force, something he'd always dreamed of as a child. It had brought a lump to Beth's throat when she'd seen his photo on Annie's home page. He'd looked so proud and smart in his uniform.

Paul hadn't been interested in Beth's friends.

Secretly, she'd harbored the thought that she embarrassed him. After all, she'd never been "dynamic" enough or a "go-getter" like Emily. In fact, you could write what she knew about divorce law on the back of a postage stamp and still have room for the address. It wasn't because she hadn't been interested in Paul's work, quite the opposite – but Paul was a true professional, networking in influential circles; handling confidential client cases. With the exception of the odd comment here and there, he'd never discussed his work.

Now she came to think of it, she didn't really know anything about Paul's friends – well, nothing of significance, anyway. He played golf at weekends and had sometimes mentioned a few of his golfing buddies. Occasionally, they dined at the homes of his work colleagues. She'd always dreaded these dinner parties which were stuffy and formal affairs. The wives would gather into a little clique, comparing their latest Jimmy Choos and designer handbags, but what annoyed her most was their competitiveness. She'd overheard Grace, the wife of one of his colleagues, discussing her daughter. "Tamara's already booked into that wonderful pre-school in Hagley", she'd said, in her plummy voice. "It's got an "outstanding" from Ofsted. I simply wouldn't entertain sending her anywhere else ". Tamara was six months old.

The men communicated with one another using the latest law "buzzwords". As far as Beth was concerned, they may as well have been speaking Japanese.

Although she often felt out of place, she'd always made an effort to mix for Paul's sake. He hankered for her to magically become Nigella Lawson overnight, but the thought of not only having to put up a front for these people but to actually have to cook for those with "acquired tastes" made her want to run to the hills.

On one occasion Audrey Russell-Smythe served up fois gras. Beth had to grit her teeth, the thought of the cruelty involved made her want to vomit, and she'd pushed her plate away untouched, whilst Paul had glared at her across the table.

The Russell-Smythes were now divorced. Giles,

who worked in accounts at Mortimer's, had re-married. She'd hoped that his new wife would be an improvement, but she'd been gob smacked when the new Mrs. Russell-Smythe turned out to be Miss Pink Lycra Pants!

The worst guests ever seen on *Come Dine with Me* would've had nothing on that lot, Beth decided.

She had had one ally, though, a legal executive named Ruth.

'I have a confession to make,' Ruth had confided tipsily, when they'd enjoyed a sumptuous Italian themed meal. 'I'm hopeless at cooking – I even burn toast!'

'But the food was delicious!'

Ruth put a finger to her lips. 'I had it delivered from the finest restaurant in town. I'll give you the number, if you promise to keep it to yourself.'

Ruth's confession had made her feel so much better and they'd become friends, exchanging the odd phone call and sticking together at the tedious dinner parties. She guessed that working for both Paul and Emily, Ruth now felt too awkward to continue their friendship.

She'd thought about giving her a call, but she didn't want to make things awkward for her, so, in the end, she'd decided to let sleeping dogs lie.

Rodney shifted to a more comfortable position, giving little yelps as he slept. Beth stroked his head gently, soothing him until he was quiet, then lay back against her pillow, her thoughts turning to Jackie. It was like a breath of fresh air when they'd met.

The day after Jackie'd moved into an apartment in the former Georgian merchant house now known as The Old Mill, she'd locked herself out. Beth had arrived home from a rain soaked walk with Rodney as she'd come scurrying down their garden path, her hair and clothing dripping wet. Even then she'd looked so pretty with her big blue eyes and her warm, friendly smile, Beth remembered.

Beth had struggled in vain to stop an excited Rodney jumping up. Jackie'd laughed and patted his soggy head. 'Do you live here?' she'd asked, pulling a wet tendril of hair away from her damp cheek.

Beth nodded. 'I'm sorry about my dog – are you OK?'

'I'm fine – although I must look a right state.

I've moved into one of the apartments –' She'd waved her hand in the direction of The Old Mill, '…and I've managed to lock myself out. My mobile's inside too – only I'd be stupid enough to do that.'

'No, you wouldn't,' Beth told her. 'Believe me – it's something I've done too!'

Jackie sighed. 'It wouldn't be so bad, as the landlord has a key. But its sod's law he's away for a few days. I wondered if I could use your phone to call a locksmith.'

They'd gone into the house and Beth had handed her a towel. While Jackie called the locksmith, she'd put the kettle on to boil. Soon, they were drinking steaming mugs of hot chocolate and chatting away as if they'd known each other for years. They'd discovered they shared the same sense of humour and love of animals. That was the start of their friendship.

Jackie had told her that her mother had died of a heart attack and her natural father had been killed in a car accident. Although her mum remarried, she hadn't got on with her stepfather. She'd never gone into detail, and Beth didn't like to press her for more.

As soon as Jackie met Beth's parents, it was as though Brenda and Ted were her surrogate mum and dad. Beth thought of her as a surrogate sister too; she'd always wanted a sister, someone to talk to and share things. Mum was unable to conceive after having Beth and now Beth considered herself lucky to have been able to choose her own "sister". There could be no better sister, and they supported one another through thick and thin. Although, Beth thought solemnly, Jackie seemed to be doing all the supporting of late.

Chapter Thirty-Seven
Beggars can't be Choosers

Greg unlocked the door to Flat One, Slade Terrace. Biting her lip, Beth did her best to quell her embarrassment over their date night.

The large, box-like nineteen sixties' house had been split to make two flats. It stood uniformly next to a row of houses that all looked similar in design and build and all had well-tended gardens.

A curtain twitched and she spotted a bald headed guy peeping out from behind it. She thought about giving him a wave, but realising she'd seen him, he disappeared.

'I'm surprised to find a nineteen sixties' house in the depths of the country,' she said, taking in the large green field opposite.

'It was built by a housing association to provide affordable housing,' Greg explained. 'Then it was sold on privately.'

He unlocked the door and stepped aside for her to enter. 'It's basic,' he said matter-of-factly, and she knew that, if an estate agent played the house down, she should be worried. If it was the size of a postage stamp, they'd say something like: *'This bijou apartment boasting a cosy interior...'*

She followed him through the flaky green painted front door and into the narrow hallway, stepping over a pile of junk mail and leaflets. He flicked a switch and a single opaque bulb suspended from white flex emitted dim sodium light. The sitting room was small and square, with tatty blue marbled linoleum which was plainly visible where the stained beige carpet didn't quite reach the corners.

Greg registered the look of distaste on Beth's face. 'Nothing a lick of paint won't fix,' he said over-cheerily.

She swallowed down her disappointment and tagged along behind him into the kitchen. To describe it as cramped was putting it mildly – Greg had to edge out before Beth was able to walk in. A fluorescent light flickered overhead, sending a cloud of dust motes into the air. The gaudy blue painted units with cracked white plastic handles looked like they were a throwback from the nineteen sixties.

There were two bedrooms, both of them square boxes, lacking in either charm or character. Greg gestured to the magnolia walls in the main bedroom, which was roughly a foot wider than the other bedroom. 'This room's been given a fresh lick of paint.'

She sucked in her lip and nodded, trying to look more enthusiastic than she felt.

They left the bedroom and Greg opened the door to what appeared to be a cupboard. He flicked on the light switch. 'The loo,' he announced.

Beth cringed when she saw the grubby orange toilet cover perched on top of an avocado loo.

'Don't worry,' Greg added quickly. 'There's a separate shower.'

When they walked into the shower room, her eyes widened. It was surprisingly large. Although it would definitely need a pair of Marigolds and the use of some industrial strength detergent, it was painted a muted shade of green except for the tiles, which were plain white.

'Can I see the garden?' she asked, a spark of hope rising that perhaps this could be the piece de resistance.

They headed over to the back door and Greg put the key in the lock. He fumbled around with it for a few moments and frowned. 'Damn! Sadie must've given me the wrong key. I'm afraid you'll have to see the garden through the window.'

Brilliant, she thought. With the amount of grease and grime on the glass she'd be lucky to see her own reflection.

Despite her best efforts to keep a stiff upper lip, to her horror tears pricked at the backs of her eyes. Greg placed a reassuring hand on her shoulder. Although she felt acutely embarrassed, Beth was grateful for the gesture. 'Remember, there are plus points to this flat,' he pointed out firmly. 'It's within your budget, it has a rear garden area, there's only one neighbour, and, most importantly as far as you're concerned, your dog would be allowed to live here.'

She sighed resignedly. 'I'll take it.'

He raised a quizzical brow. 'Don't you want a little time to think it over?'

She shook her head, remembering the phrase Jackie'd used when she'd gone for her interview at Holly Mount: "*Beggars can't be choosers*".

On her way home, she made a detour, calling round to tell her parents the news.

'You know you could stay with us,' Mum told her worriedly. 'Me and your Dad would love to have you here, and your Aunt Lena would be over the moon!'

Beth nodded. 'I know, and I appreciate it – I really do. But you've got enough on your plate as it is. You've no idea how long Aunt Lena will be staying, and I've made up my mind. Anyway,' she added, 'it'll look better after some elbow grease and a few homely touches.'

'If you say so, love.' Mum sounded unconvinced. 'If you have second thoughts, just let us know.'

She wrapped her arms around her and gave her a hug. 'Thanks Mum. Is it alright if Rodney stays here, though? It would only be for a night or two while I get things sorted.'

'You know it is, love.'

*

The phone rang as soon as she walked in through the front door.

'Hello. It's me –' Paul said, using the monotone flatness to which she'd grown accustomed over the years.

'Hi –' she replied hesitantly, knowing he wouldn't have called for a natter.

'Look, I'll come straight to the point – I'm filing for a divorce.'

She bristled; he'd made a grab for her and now he was saying he wanted a divorce. 'That's fine!'

'You knew it was on the cards –'

'Look, *whatever* – I'm too busy to discuss this right now. I'll try and call you tomorrow.' She hoped this made her sound vaguely interesting and worldly. Inside she felt hollow; the shift in her life was now happening at an alarming rate. Paul was a pompous idiot – and a lot more besides. Yet she'd loved him once; she'd spent twenty-three years of her life with him.

When she hung up the phone, her mind went into overdrive. What if he'd already had the best years of her life? What if they were all behind her and there was nothing but a giant black hole stretching out in front of her, or a vortex of space sucking her into a vacuum of nothingness?

Ben and Tash had their own independent lives, albeit Tash was studying and Ben was about to embark on his nursing career. Where did she fit into life's rich tapestry? What was her purpose, her function, now she was no longer a wife and no longer a mother in the sense of actually looking after someone?

Her new-found resolve was wavering big time. She pondered as to whether men had these thoughts too. They didn't have to go through having periods, giving birth or the menopause. As Jackie had pointed out, they didn't even have to worry about cellulite, so she guessed they probably didn't.

Wandering into the office, she sat and stared through the window onto the garden below. It dawned on her that she had the daunting task of unlearning the ingrained habits of almost a lifetime.

Chapter Thirty-Eight
Paul

Paul leaned back in his chair and lit a cigar. Thank God both his mother and Emily were in Birmingham on a shopping trip, no doubt parading around Selfridges. Still, he thought, it might cheer his mother up.

Why were women so bloody difficult, he wondered? Although he dealt with divorce matters on a daily basis, he'd never envisaged himself going through the same thing as his clients. How bloody humiliating, let alone downright unnecessary.

And why on earth did Emily have to keep banging on about marriage? He'd left Beth and was living with her, surely that should be enough? But obviously not: when Emily got her teeth into something, she was like a terrier with a bone.

He sighed heavily as he ground out the barely smoked cigar in an empty mug. Emily would have a fit if she knew he'd smoked indoors, but it was either that or downing a scotch. If he started on that he wouldn't be able to stop at one.

A copy of Tatler lay open on the coffee table. Paul picked it up and found the corner of a page turned over strategically. He leafed through the magazine until he came to the indicated page. A glossy advert for diamond engagement rings by Tiffany stared at him and cold panic clawed inside his chest. *How the hell was he going to pay for one of those?*

Chapter Thirty-Nine
Pastures New

It was a blustery Friday afternoon as Beth and Jackie struggled to load all Beth's worldly goods into the back of the hire van.

Following their visit to the boot fair, Paul had insisted they sold the remainder of the furniture. To Beth's astonishment, after a prick of conscience, he'd split the money between them.

All she had to take to her new home were numerous boxes of personal items she couldn't bear to part with – things Penelope had dismissed as clutter.

'Honestly, Bethany,' she'd said, 'I've never seen so much clutter! What are you going to do with it all?'

She'd gritted her teeth as Penelope prattled on. *'Honestly, Bethany. Honestly, Bethany.'* She'd sounded like a demented parrot, programmed to inflict on her some kind of brain washing technique. The cheek of her! That so called "clutter" was of great sentimental value. There was her Buddha collection for starters. Aunt Lena told her you shouldn't buy a Buddha for yourself, but if you have one given to you as a gift, it's supposed to bring good fortune. Ben and Tash always brought her one back from their travels. She was now the proud owner of fifteen in total, all different sizes and features; no two the same. She was still waiting to cash in on the good fortune, and kept rubbing their plump bellies, just in case.

Her candle collection had begun when Ben was at junior school. He'd saved up his pocket money to buy her a Yankee candle ("Fluffy Towels" fragrance). Friends and family added to it over the years. With over twenty candles, including tapers which exuded different fragrances, container candles and votives, it was pretty impressive.

The wind tore at their clothes and hair as they struggled to load the boxes. Jackie jammed her knee against the rear door of the van to keep it open and they heaved in the final box. 'That's it – all done,' she puffed. 'Are you OK?'

Beth gave her a weak smile. 'If I'm honest, I'm terrified – but not about leaving the house. It stopped being a home when the kids left.' She cast her eyes downwards as her lip started to tremble. 'It's you I don't want to leave.'

'Don't – you'll start me off.' Jackie sniffed as she hugged her. 'Anyway, you won't be very far away – it's only a twenty minute drive.'

Beth sighed. 'I know. 'I'm just being silly, but I'm so used to you being on the doorstep – literally.'

Jackie headed off in the van and Beth took a final look around the house. She realised the only thing she'd really miss about it now was the space. She'd guessed it would always be difficult to down-size, but one day she was determined to own her own home.

On the bright side, the flat did have a garden; although she'd yet to see it, and she was keeping her fingers crossed it was going to be big enough for Rodney to run around. She wondered anxiously if he'd settle down quickly in their new home, or if he'd pine for the old one.

She was also worried about living with a new neighbour on top of her, so to speak. Greg said a guy lived in the flat above. *What if he hated dogs or played loud music into the early hours, or had house parties every weekend?* Ah, well, she'd just have to cross that bridge when she came to it.

With a final glance in her car mirror, she headed down the driveway for the last time. She needed to drop off her keys and collect the ones to Slade Terrace, so she parked up on the road outside Harrison's. As she walked through the door, she caught a glimpse of her reflection in the window and self-consciously ran her fingers through her wind-blown curls.

Beth was unable to resist taking a peek at the "For Sale" brochures displayed on the walls. Her eyes feasted greedily on a "chocolate box" black and white timbered cottage complete with wood burning stove and an Aga in the spacious kitchen/diner. It also boasted undulating views towards the Malvern Hills. If only.

'Can I help you?'

A young woman dressed in a formal navy skirt and jacket teamed with a white silk blouse snapped her out of her reverie. Her auburn hair was piled high on top of her head and styled away from her face. Her plum-coloured lipstick emphasised her full lips and HD eyebrows framed attractive chestnut coloured eyes. Beth thought she looked the epitome of the brains plus beauty business woman.

'Is Greg here? – Greg Harrison,' she added needlessly.

The woman shook her head. 'I'm afraid he's busy at the moment. I'm Sadie, his PA. Can I help?'

Just then, a side door opened and Greg strolled in, his mobile jammed to his ear. He acknowledged her presence with a curt nod and continued his conversation. 'Yes, of course. That's absolutely no problem at all, Mrs. Jarvis. I'll see to it myself.'

Beth pursed her lips. It would seem that whatever Mrs. Jarvis wanted was obviously far more important than dealing with her. She smiled at an expectant Sadie. 'I'm Beth Bishop. I've come to hand in the keys to Britannia Square and collect the keys for Slade Terrace.'

Sadie scrolled through a typed list of names and addresses attached to a clipboard. 'Ah, yes. That's fine.' She indicated an entry with the end of her biro. 'If you could just sign to say you've both given and received keys, I'll write you a receipt and get your keys.'

Sadie wrote out the receipt and unlocked the

metal cabinet which sat on the wall behind her desk. The assorted keys jangled as she rummaged through them. She checked the handwritten label, ensuring they were the correct ones, before lifting them down off the hook. 'There are two front door keys and one back door key to Flat One,' she said as she handed them to Beth.

Thanking her, Beth slipped them into her pocket. 'Please thank Greg for his help, too.'

Greg glanced up from his phone conversation and gave her a warm smile. She smiled back. Maybe he wasn't so bad after all.

Sadie walked around from her desk and pulled open the office door. 'I do hope you'll be very happy in your new home.'

Beth crossed her fingers behind her back. *So do I.*

Chapter Forty
Ryan

It would be good to have a new neighbour. Well, at least, Ryan Morgan hoped it would.

Mrs. Lucas, the former tenant of the downstairs flat, was a lovely old dear. She'd baked Ryan a fruit cake when he'd first moved in. It was delicious, full of raisins and spices.

When he told her how much he'd enjoyed it, not only had she given him the recipe, she also insisted on showing him what to do!

She'd arrived at his door armed with a loaf tin, a bag of ingredients and some weighing scales (he didn't have any of this paraphernalia himself), and, under the old lady's eagle-eyed supervision, he'd set about the task in hand.

Mabel Lucas (aka Mrs. L), had gun-metal grey curls framing a fresh, full face. Her cheeks had a natural glow and she had surprisingly few wrinkles for a woman in her late seventies. Her husband, Alfred, had died a few years back, and she'd shared the flat below Ryan with Alfie, her Staffordshire bull terrier, named in honour of her late husband.

She'd tied a red flowery apron around her ample

waist before setting out the ingredients on Ryan's Formica table, and then washed her hands at the kitchen sink. 'There now, that's better,' she'd said, patting them dry with a towel. 'Now, Ryan, the first thing you do is to line your loaf tin with greaseproof paper – like this, see?'

Ryan had nodded. 'OK, Mrs. L.'

Mrs. L had brought one she'd prepared earlier, like on Blue Peter. Strange, though, he thought, that the oblong tin was called a loaf tin when he was going to be baking a cake.

She'd set the tin to one side. 'Now,' she'd said, her blue eyes shining, 'this is the fun part. First you rub the butter into the flour until it looks like fine breadcrumbs.' She'd demonstrated the rubbing action and Ryan had taken his turn. 'That's right – well done,' she'd encouraged. Ryan had felt as if he was back at school, but in a good way.

He'd followed the rest of Mrs. L's instructions. While the cake was baking in the rickety oven, they'd shared a cup of tea together.

'Wow! Would you just look at that?' Ryan had exclaimed when he'd seen the result.

Mabel smiled. 'There – I told you it wasn't difficult.'

'It was you who made it look easy, Mrs. L! Let's hope I can make one like that when you're not on hand to help.'

That had been the start of Ryan's love affair with

baking. He'd now acquired several books on the subject, including one from Mary Berry and Paul Hollywood. Before she'd moved away, Mabel had given him one by Fanny Craddock, a very odd name, he thought, certainly not one he'd heard of before.

Ryan heaved a contented sigh. It was therapeutic to get your sleeves rolled up after a hard day's digging or sometimes after a difficult stint working as a sexual abuse support volunteer. It would take his mind off everything as he carefully weighed flour, fruit, or chocolate, to create something delicious.

In a way, it was like his day job, he thought to himself. Just as he'd sift through soil and scatter seeds to grow into fragrant blooms with feather soft petals and vibrant hues, he'd sift the flour and scatter the fruit, all the while anticipating the hopefully moist and juicy mouth-watering outcome. Sometimes, when things became too harrowing, baking was his form of escapism.

Wrestling with his oven gloves, Ryan blew his sandy fringe out of his eyes and opened the oven door, licking his lips in anticipation as the tantalising smell emanated through the kitchen. He hadn't baked this cake to eat himself; it was a welcome gift for the new tenants of Flat one, whom he'd yet to meet.

He lifted out the oblong tin carefully, carrying it to the table and firmly tapping the bottom. The cake slid from the tin with well-practiced ease.

Ryan planned on waiting for it to cool, but he saw

a white van pull up outside and a red Ford Ka was parking behind it. Boxes were piled up in the back of the van. He pondered whether he should offer to help, but, not wanting to appear a nosey neighbour, he decided to leave what he felt was an acceptable amount of time before knocking the door.

Chapter Forty-One
Misgivings and Worldly Goods

As she pulled up outside Slade Terrace, to Beth's surprise, Jackie had just parked in front of her. She'd thought her friend would've arrived there a while ago.

Jackie pressed a button to open the electric window and poked her head out. 'I stopped off at my place to collect my overnight bag,' she said. 'I'm not leaving you on your own until I know you're going to be OK.'

Feeling a weight lifted from her shoulders, she gave her friend a grateful smile. 'Thanks, Jacks. You're a star.'

Jackie got out and opened the van door, throwing her overnight bag onto the pavement. 'When are your mum and dad coming over?'

'I've got to call them when we're ready – I thought it would be best if we get the place cleaned up a bit first. Mum would have a fit if she saw the state it's in!'

Beth opened the front door and flicked on the light switch. The gloomy lone bulb barely lit the hallway in the dullness of late afternoon; and her heart dipped. She'd almost forgotten how grotty it actually was. She desperately hoped she'd done the right thing. She scooped up yet another pile of junk mail before walking through to the kitchen and throwing it down on the worktop.

Jackie opened the rear doors of the van and together they heaved out the first of the sturdy brown cardboard boxes. 'What are your parents bringing?'

'You know what Mum's like.' Beth grinned. 'She's worried I'll catch my death of cold, so she's got an electric fire she's had stored in the garage and about six thick blankets. Dad's managed to pick up a washing machine he found in an ad in the local paper, and there's a brown leather sofa and an oak dining table and chairs that Aunt Lena's donating.'

'Sounds like they've got everything sorted,' Jackie said, with a knowing smile. 'But how will they get it all here? It'll never fit into your dad's car.'

'He's borrowed his friend's truck,' Beth explained. 'He used to work on the council gardens with him, apparently. There are several pairs of curtains, too, that Mum's got from the charity shop – she says they're bound to be useful, even as dust sheets.'

They stumbled up the kerb, half carrying and half dragging the box up to the front door.

'There's a gas cooker that was left here – it's been safety checked and I've brought loads of cleaning stuff and towels and bedding, but I can't believe the total sum of my worldly goods. It doesn't amount to much for twenty-three years of marriage, does it?'

Jackie sighed. 'I guess not – but you've got Tash and Ben. They count for a great deal.'

Beth nodded thoughtfully. It was sometimes too easy to lose sight of what she did have in her life.

With Beth walking slowly backwards and Jackie directing her, they carried in the box and placed it down on the living room floor. Jackie gazed around, silently taking in the dated woodchip walls and threadbare carpet. Watching her, Beth sighed. 'I bet I know what you're thinking – '

'I bet you don't! I was thinking that we'll soon have it feeling like home.'

Bless her friend's enthusiasm, she thought.

Chapter Forty-Two
Marigolds and Fruitcake

Beth was anxious to see the rear garden. Relieved she now had the correct key; she turned it in the lock and pulled open the back door. Her mouth fell open. The garden was certainly big alright, but so was the jungle of brambles and weeds.

'Jesus!' Jackie exclaimed. 'It's like The Day of the Triffids!'

Beth blanched. 'How can Rodney live here? It'll take ages to sort this lot out – and money I haven't got. It's far worse than I could've imagined.'

'Look,' Jackie said gently. 'Don't think about the thing as a whole. Let's get the flat sorted first. When your parents come over, we can see what your dad thinks. He's a good gardener, isn't he?'

'He is, but I couldn't expect him to tackle anything this big.'

'No, of course not,' Jackie agreed. 'At least, not on his own. But I'm sure we can all put our heads together and round up some help.'

A couple of hours later, Beth flung down her Marigolds and topped up the kettle; she'd ensured it was the first thing she'd unpacked.

She looked around, surprised and pleased at how much their cleaning efforts had already started to pay off. The windows were now grime free thanks to using white vinegar as Mum had advised. The cooker and work surfaces were scrubbed clean and even the dreaded loo and shower now looked respectable; the ghastly orange loo cover was bagged up ready to take to the tip. She knew she'd have to live with the avocado suite for the foreseeable, but she envisaged the sitting room painted in a warm pale gold with a ruby-red feature wall. Although she couldn't run to the cost of a wood burning stove for a while, she'd seen an electric replica in a second hand shop, and the logs and flames looked very realistic. She decided to use some of her boot fair money to buy it, along with a couple of tins of paint.

Jackie joined her in the kitchen. 'I'm covered in cobwebs,' she grumbled light-heartedly, pulling a long, silvery thread out of her hair. 'I'll just have a quick freshen up while you make the brew.'

Beth rummaged around in a box. 'I'll see if I can find any biscuits – I was sure I put a packet in here somewhere.'

Jackie disappeared into the bathroom as the doorbell rang. It was too early for Beth's parents to arrive; they weren't coming round until she phoned. She wiped her face on a square of kitchen roll and raked through her curls with her fingers before answering it.

She stared up at the young, slightly dishevelled guy who was taller than her by a good few inches. A trace of stubble outlined his chin and his sandy hair flopped over one eye. He raised a hand, subconsciously sweeping it away.

Colour rose into her cheeks as she took in his blue-grey eyes and the way they crinkled attractively at the corners when he smiled. He was wearing black jeans and a navy shirt, open at the neck. 'Hi! I'm Ryan from the upstairs flat.'

A friendly voice, too, Beth noted, with what she thought may be a slight Midlands accent.

She smiled. 'I'm Beth.'

Ryan handed Beth a foil wrapped package. 'A welcome gift.'

She let out a small gasp as she felt warmth radiating from it.

He looked familiar, but she just couldn't place him.

As she peeled away a corner of the foil, a tantalising smell of baked fruit cake permeated the air. Nostalgia gripped her and she was transported back to when she was a child. Lena always baked a fruit cake for her weekly visit, and it was something Beth had looked forward to. She sniffed the parcel appreciatively. 'Mmmm! It smells delicious. That's really kind. Thank you.'

Ryan gave a lopsided grin which made him look kind of cute, she thought, although she knew "cute" was a word men didn't appreciate.

Ryan raised an eyebrow. 'I hope you don't think it's a bit bizarre, some random guy bringing you a cake?'

'No – I think it's a lovely gesture. Did you bake it?'

He nodded. 'I find baking quite therapeutic.'

'Oh, that's – super!' She blushed, wondering what on earth the matter with her was. She always managed to sound like she was a child if she felt nervous. She looked around anxiously to see if there was any sign of Jackie, but her friend was still in the bathroom.

'My friend's helping me to clear up, and we're taking a tea break,' she told him, 'so a slice of cake would go down a treat. D'you fancy joining us?'

What was Jackie doing in there, Beth wondered. She was taking ages! She really wanted her to meet her dishy new neighbour.

Ryan held up his hand. 'That's a tempting offer, thanks. I have to go out soon, but definitely another time.'

'Yes, that would be great. And thanks again.'

He made to leave, but stopped suddenly and turned around. 'Is anyone sharing the flat with you?'

'No, it's just me and Rodney.'

Was it her imagination or did he look disappointed?

'Well, if you need anything at all, just knock. I

know Mrs. L struggled to keep on top of things before she moved in with her daughter; she was a fiercely independent lady. Not that that's a bad thing –' he tailed off awkwardly.

'I work in a care home, so I know what you mean.'

Ryan looked relieved. 'Well, I hope you'll both be very happy here. Is your husband at work?'

Beth frowned. 'My husband?'

'*Rodney?*'

'Oh – Rodney's my dog, not my husband!'

'I see!' Ryan laughed. 'Anyway, I'll let you get on. It's great to meet you.'

With a start, Beth realised where she'd seen him before – the disastrous Christmas day dog walk!

She drew in a deep breath. 'I hope you're OK with me having a dog here – the landlord said –'

'I love dogs!' Ryan assured her. 'Mrs. L had Alfie, a Staffordshire bull terrier. He was a lovely dog, but, of course, he was her companion and she took him with her. I used to enjoy taking him for walks. Anyway, like I said – just knock if you need anything.'

'Thanks – I will.'

He frowned thoughtfully. 'You know, I'm sure I recognise you from somewhere.'

'I think you may have seen me out walking my dog,' Beth replied hastily, hoping he wouldn't realise she was the idiot who'd snapped his head off for no good reason.

'Ah, yes, that's probably it – it's a small world. Anyway, I hope you'll enjoy living here, Beth.'

She flushed with pleasure, deciding she liked Ryan from upstairs.

*

Beth cut into the fruitcake and handed slices out to her parents, Jackie and Aunt Lena.

'Well, well. A dishy guy who likes dogs and bakes cakes – what more could a girl want?' her aunt said, with a wink.

Beth stirred her tea with more enthusiasm than was necessary. 'Give over! I'd only put him in his late twenties, anyway.'

'Your point being?' her aunt enquired.

'Well, he's too young for me, that's for certain.'

'Says who?' Lena chuckled. 'What do you think, Jackie?'

'I don't think age comes into it,' Jackie replied. 'If he's nice, then she should go for it. There aren't many nice guys around.'

'I wonder if he's any good at gardening,' Dad piped up.

Beth smiled ruefully. 'Well, judging by the state of the garden, I'd guess the answer to that one's a "no".'

Chapter Forty-Three
Interrogation and a Bird's Nest

Leaning on his spade, Dad mopped his brow with a hankie. 'Blimey, this root's as tough as old boots!'

Beth handed him a mug of strong tea heaped with his usual four teaspoons of sugar. He took a sip. 'Ta, love! That's just what the doctor ordered.'

Mum rolled her eyes. 'I doubt that!' She chastised him. 'Not with that many sugars in it, anyway.'

Aunt Lena sat perched on a stool at the kitchen window and Beth waved to her. Her aunt smiled and waved back. It was a fine, warm day and Lena had been out in the garden for the first half an hour, until Dad had more or less ordered her to go in and have a rest. She'd done as she was told for once. Beth was relieved; her aunt was definitely not up to standing around for hours.

Rodney pottered happily in and out, sniffing his new surroundings and also lending a paw to dig the soil. 'I suppose Rodney could stay here,' Beth said thoughtfully. 'He does seem to like it.'

'Get yourself sorted out before the boy comes back,' Dad said. 'You've got enough to do without worrying about him for now.'

Mum knelt down on the grass, absorbed in attacking a wild looking rhododendron with her secateurs. Beth took a mug of tea over to her. 'Have a break for a bit, Mum– your back must be killing you.'

Mum struggled to her feet and rubbed the small of her back. 'Gosh, it is – a bit. I must be getting old.'

'You're doing too much,' Beth berated her. 'You're not twenty-one anymore.'

Mum raised her eyebrows. 'And don't I know it!'

'Why don't you go in and keep Aunt Lena company?'

Kneeling down, Mum placed her mug on the ground, before attacking the bush once more. 'I'll just finish this first,' she said determinedly.

Beth sighed. She knew from experience there was no point arguing with her.

'Is Jackie coming over?' Mum asked, clipping away at the stray branches.

'No – she's covering for me at work, bless her. We're really short staffed, but she'll pop over when she can.'

'That's good, love. I'm so glad you've got her in your corner. When do you have to go back?'

'Not 'til next Monday. Sandra's given me time off and put it down as holiday so I can get sorted.'

Mum glanced up at her. 'You've got a very understanding boss.'

She nodded in agreement. 'She's been as good as gold about all this.'

'Well, you must be a good little worker; otherwise I don't think she'd be so obliging.'

'Oh, I don't know – she's just a kind person, and with Jackie stepping in –'

'Nonsense!' Dad said as he strolled over to join them, cradling his mug of tea. 'Your mum's right – you must work very hard. We're both proud of you, you know – the way you're coping with everything. It can't have been easy.'

A lump rose in Beth's throat. Her dad was not one to show his emotions. She knew things hadn't been easy for her parents, either.

She hugged Dad impulsively. 'Careful or I'll slop my tea!' He laughed.

They all looked up as the gate creaked open. Ryan grinned as he strolled into the garden. 'Hi everyone!'

Beth felt herself blush. Why did she have to look such a state, covered in dirt and with her hair resembling a bird's nest? 'Hi!' she called. 'Mum, Dad, this is Ryan from upstairs.'

Ryan walked over to Dad and shook him firmly by the hand. 'You've got your work cut out for you with this lot – would you like some help?'

Beth's eyes widened. 'Are you any good?'

Ryan grinned and her blush deepened.

'I think what my daughter means is: are you any good at gardening?' Dad added, with a chuckle.

'Well, I'm not bad, as it happens. I do it for a living.'

Everyone gaped at him and his grin widened. 'I bet you're wondering why this garden's in such a state?'

Beth cleared her throat. 'Well, errr –'

'I used to do all the gardening here, but I've been away for a few weeks, helping to look after my mum.'

Mum's face creased with concern. 'Oh, was she poorly, dear?'

'She passed away, I'm afraid.'

'You poor boy. I'm so sorry to hear that. Is your dad still alive? Do you have any brothers or sisters?'

Beth rolled her eyes, wishing her mum wouldn't ask so many personal questions.

Ryan shook his head. 'Dad died a few years back. I've got a sister, Meg, who's older than me by a couple of years. I've also got an older brother, Josh, but I don't see him much.'

Beth looked at Ryan, picturing him at his dying mother's bedside until the end before coming home to his empty flat. And then she pondered if she was being fanciful; for all she knew he could have a girlfriend.

Dad pointed to the weeds, some of which stood over a foot tall. 'And you think you're up to the task, eh, lad?' he asked, lightening the mood.

Ryan nodded. 'I sure am. I'm not bad in the DIY department, either, if you need any help.'

Beth's eyes lit up. 'I certainly won't say no to an

offer like that,' she told him gratefully.

At five o'clock, everyone had had enough of the great outdoors. They packed up their tools and trooped inside for something to eat.

'I haven't got much in yet, I'm afraid,' Beth apologised, foraging fruitlessly in the fridge for something edible.

'Why don't you let me get us all some fish and chips?' Ryan suggested.

'There's no chippie round here, is there?' Dad asked, in surprise.

'Not a chippie per se,' Ryan told him. 'But there's a caravan site a couple of miles on, and the restaurant does take-away as well as eat-in. Their fish and chips are delicious.'

Everyone nodded in appreciation at the suggestion; they were all hungry and really fancied the idea.

'I'll drive round and pick them up,' Ryan offered.

'Thanks, lad – as long as you don't mind. But I'm paying – a thank you for all your help today,' Dad said. 'We wouldn't have got anywhere near that amount of work done if you hadn't helped out.'

'I've enjoyed doing it – and it's been great to meet you all.'

Chapter Forty-Four
Ryan

After enjoying a relaxed and tasty fish and chip supper with Beth and her family, Ryan met up with his friend, Alex, for a drink.

He'd had a great day, he reflected. He'd been anxious about the garden in its overgrown and unkempt state, but he hadn't had time to tackle it sooner.

It'd been hard, looking after his mum. She'd had cancer, and he'd watched as the awful disease ravaged her body, which seemed to wither and shrink before his eyes until she was skin and bone.

Ryan's sister, Meg, had been her full-time carer. Ryan worried it was a cop-out, him being self-employed and needing to get his gardening business off the ground, although both Meg and his mum hadn't seen it like that at all; they'd fully understood his position. He'd been determined to be there when things had taken a turn for the worse. He couldn't and wouldn't leave it all to Meg; she'd had enough to cope with.

Meg was married to Mark, an accountant. They owned their own house and were financially stable. She'd been quick to take up the gauntlet when their mother became ill – her patience and caring nature, Ryan thought, were just two of her many virtues. It would have broken their mother's heart if she'd known what had happened.

There was something about Beth that reminded him of Meg. Perhaps it was the love in her eyes when she talked about her children and how she obviously adored her parents and her aunt.

Ryan had never married. He'd come close once, but it hadn't worked out. Sometimes he regretted not settling down and having kids, but life didn't always work out the way you hoped. He'd come to see himself as a bit of a loner, more at one with nature than anything else.

A cool breeze nipped the air. The trees' branches rustled as he sat on a wooden chair in the pub garden, waiting for his friend. It was a good thing he was used to the outdoors, as he knew Alex would be anxious for his fag fix. They'd been friends since meeting at horticultural college, but now Alex had moved in with his girlfriend, Kate. They lived in a tree- lined, salubrious area of Worcester. Ryan wondered how he was getting along with his new neighbours. Alex played on drums with a band in his spare time, practicing at every given opportunity. He hoped, for Kate's sake, that they had a soundproofed room.

Alex raised his hand in greeting as he spotted Ryan. He ambled across the grass to where he sat, his dark wiry hair sticking out at odd angles over the collar of his pink flowered shirt. He pulled out a chair and sat down, crossing his long legs, and jammed his steel framed glasses further onto his nose. Unable to get comfortable on the wooden seat, he held onto the table and leaned back so that the front legs of the chair lifted off the ground. He grinned at Ryan before sliding a cigarette out of his gold packet of Benson & Hedges. 'Been up to much lately, then, mate?' He tapped his pockets to find his lighter.

Ryan, whose mind was still focussed on the time he'd shared with Beth and her family, lifted his pint glass off the table. 'Yep, I've been quite busy. I've been helping my new neighbour sort out the garden today.'

Alex lit up his cigarette and took a long drag. He sat back thoughtfully, blowing a fat line of smoke into the air. His green eyes narrowed suspiciously. 'What's she like, then – this new neighbour of yours?'

Ryan raised his eyebrows. 'How did you know she was a she?'

'Could be the reason you look so pleased with yourself, mate.' Alex smirked. 'Is she fit?'

'She's nice,' he said, non-committally, and then took a long swig of lager.

Alex frowned. 'Nice? What sort of a word is "nice"? Has she got a good rack?'

Ryan rolled his eyes. 'She seems like a really nice person, good to talk to – '

Alex's smirk widened. He stubbed the end of his cigarette out on the wooden table, and Ryan shook his head. 'For God's sake, mate, use the ashtray.'

Alex shrugged. 'Whatever. I worry about you, mate. You haven't had a bird in – how long?'

'I've told you. I'm not interested.'

'If you say so,' Alex replied. 'Sarah was a bitch of the highest order. I'm telling you, mate, the law of averages says you won't be that unlucky again.'

Ryan swilled the amber liquid around in his glass. He'd lived with his ex, Sarah, for three years. She'd owned her own floristry business. With Ryan starting up his gardening enterprise, it had seemed like the perfect match. That was until he'd arrived home early one day to find her in bed with his brother, Josh. Sarah had begged him for forgiveness, saying it was a big mistake. It had taken a long time, but Ryan had forgiven them both. However, he'd never forget.

He sipped the froth off the top his beer, his thoughts flicking now to the way Beth's smile lit up her face, how the breeze had whipped her red curls. She'd laughed and declared she must look a right mess, but he thought she looked great.

Ryan tried to brush the thoughts away; he was off to Canada soon, working on a lucrative landscaping contract for an accountant friend of Meg and Mark's who'd recently emigrated. Yet, despite this, he still desperately wanted to get to know her better.

Knowing Alex couldn't keep anything quiet, he decided it would probably be better to keep these thoughts to himself.

They'd downed a couple of pints and caught up on their news, when Ryan's phone bleeped with a text message. He picked it up and flicked the screen, his eyes widening as he read. It was a bit late for a visitor, but he always welcomed Louise. At least this time he'd made up the spare bed. He quickly typed out a reply before saying goodbye to Alex and making his way home.

Chapter Forty-Five
Clutter and Dirty Evidence

Beth opened the back door and Rodney padded outside. She couldn't believe how much they'd all managed to achieve the previous day. Ryan had been a fount of knowledge about making the garden dog-friendly. She hoped the, now large, outdoor space would soon become a haven for herself and Rodney. She wanted him to be able to explore and romp around safely, so she'd have to take care not to plant anything poisonous. Ryan suggested using soft mulch as it was gentle on paws, bordered with ornamental grasses and a long, winding path to provide Rodney with plenty of exercise. He'd also suggested planting perennials, such as japonica, or, as he'd specifically said, anemone japonica, explaining that it was a pretty, daisy-like flower in pinks and whites.

Dad had come up with the idea of laying some smooth stone "landing pads" to denote an area for dining and entertaining. He had an old wrought iron table and chairs in his garden shed which he'd told Beth she could have and paint up.

Ryan promised to help her achieve her dog friendly haven, and also agreed to help with the painting inside the flat. With lack of money an ongoing issue, Beth was grateful. He'd told her he'd provide as much as he could for her garden "gratis".

She smiled to herself. The garden was now weed and rubbish free and Rodney seemed totally at home in his new surroundings. She'd never been remotely interested in gardening before, mainly because Paul had employed a gardener. She felt a buzz of excitement at the prospect of designing her own space. She had to admit she was also feeling rather excited at the prospect of working alongside Ryan Morgan too.

It wasn't until Beth was alone for the first time that the reality of her situation hit home. She poured herself a glass of wine and stood gazing from the window out at the field, but it was too dark to see anything. With a sigh, she closed the curtains.

It sounded wonderful, she mused, to say that you lived in the country and had a view of a lush green field, but the actual reality didn't quite match the perceived outlook. Yes, it was great to see open space, but when it went dark in the countryside, without the benefit of street lamps one couldn't actually see a thing. And the thing she missed seeing most of all was the light from Jackie's flat which had been visible from her bedroom window. When she'd been on her own, looking out and seeing Jackie's light shining made Beth feel she wasn't alone. That little glimmer of light was like a beacon to her: welcoming, encouraging, safe.

It wasn't so bad during the summer months, and

she acknowledged it was late in the evening, but if she felt like this now, how was she going to feel when the clocks went back and darkness fell early?

Annoyed with herself, she let out an exasperated sigh. She knew she was being melodramatic again; it was a great failing she'd had of late. She could be too melancholy, too set in her old ways. Only last night, during their telephone conversation, Tash had reminded her that she needed to embrace her new life, make the most of what she had. Beth knew she was right.

She walked away from the window, threw on a coat over her PJs, slipped on her boots and gathered up Rodney's lead. From her experience a good cure for a bout of the blues was a brisk walk with her dog. Rodney was only too happy to oblige. He leapt off the well-worn, yet comfy leather sofa, and Beth noticed the indent he'd left on the seat. That was the beauty of leather, she thought. Wear and tear didn't make it ugly; it lent it charm and character; that comforting lived-in look. She wondered if she had the lived-in look too. Had she worn well with a few years on the clock, or did she indeed look rather frayed around the edges?

She attached Rodney's lead to his new posh bejewelled collar (a gift from her mum), and ventured out into the warm night air.

Rodney performed a few wees and then, to her surprise, he decided he didn't want to continue this late night crusade after all. He wanted to curl up in comfort on Beth's bed, and staged a sit down protest to demonstrate the point.

Frustrated, she tugged at his lead. 'Come on, boy – *walkies!*' she cajoled. Rodney wasn't having any of it. Heaving a sigh, Beth gave in and turned around, retracing her steps. As she reached the flats, Rodney decided he needed to poo after all. He squatted down next to the main entrance door, and, to her horror, an automated light clicked on illuminating them both. She glanced up at the upstairs window. Ryan was peering out, a grin spreading across his face. Beth looked away in embarrassment. Having relieved himself, Rodney was trying to scuff imaginary dirt over the giant, steaming turd.

'Oh, Rodney,' Beth groaned. 'Why do you always have to show me up, you stupid dog?'

Rodney, obviously well put out at being called "stupid", looked at her as if to say, "It was your idea to go out in the middle of the night, you stupid human!"

She fumbled in her coat pocket for a poo bag, but, in her haste, she'd forgotten to put one in, so she let Rodney in before hurriedly rummaging through the kitchen drawers in search of a bag. She finally found one amongst the clutter and fished it out, thinking to herself how easy it was to collect clutter when you'd only been in a house for five minutes. She went back outside to scoop the poop. As she did so, she glanced up once more at Ryan's window, intent on showing him she was going to clean up after her dog, that she wasn't one of those dreadful people who left it and walked off, but his curtains were drawn. She felt embarrassed at the thought of bumping into him again.

Chapter Forty-Six
Jackie

On her way home after a long shift, Jackie heaved a sigh. *Teabags!* She'd meant to pick some up before work, but hadn't had time.

Pulling up outside the local Co-op, she fished her purse out of her bag and went in. She browsed the well-stocked shelves and selected her usual box of PG Tips, then headed to the counter.

She paused, distracted by a shelf stacked with an array of mouthwatering confectionery. Her hand hovered over a bar of mint Fry's Chocolate Cream, her taste buds tingling at the thought of the smooth dark chocolate and cool, sweet fondant filling. Oh, why not? She hadn't had one in ages! She picked up the chocolate bar and joined a queue of four people at the checkout. As she neared the front, the burly bald guy in front of her slammed his newspaper down onto the counter and pulled his wallet from the back pocket of his paint splattered jeans. He emptied out his change onto the counter and began sorting through it.

Something made Jackie glance over his shoulder. As she scanned the front page, an icy tingle crept down her spine.

Mumbling an excuse to the woman behind, Jackie broke away from the queue and grabbed a copy of the local paper from the display rack.

When she'd let herself in, she locked the door, spread the newspaper out over the kitchen counter and read:

'Seventy-one year old William Parsons (Billy) died after his Vauxhall Zafira was struck by a lorry on a dual-carriageway of the A449 near Worcester on Friday 2nd May....'

Her knuckles blanched as she gripped onto the counter to steady herself, her vision blurring as panic swelled inside her.

Come on, her mind whirred. Breathe – breathe.

She gulped in a rush of air and her breathing began to return to normal. The blurred edges of her vision gradually cleared. She dragged herself over to a stool and sat down heavily.

After sitting quietly for a few minutes, she picked up the newspaper and tore out the page, ripping it into strips and crushing them into a ball in her fist. She hurled it into the rubbish bin where he belonged.

That night, unable to sleep, Jackie got out of bed and stared out of the window at the black, starless sky. Tears pricked at the back of her eyes. Blinking them back determinedly, she knew something had to give; secrets ate you up inside. She couldn't live a lie any longer.

Chapter Forty-Seven
All Shook Up

Beth dried off after her shower and pulled on her uniform. Rodney looked up at her, his eyes beseeching and his tail down. 'I'm sorry, boy, but I have to go to work.'

The dog lay down, resting his jaw on his front paws, and looked up at her like a petulant child.

'You know I don't like going out and leaving you, don't you?' Beth said, over her shoulder. She went to his treat cupboard and took out a beef flavoured chewy bone which she placed in front of him as a treat. He ignored it. Did she really think he could be fobbed off so easily?

With a final glance backwards, she closed the door, leaning against it with a guilt-ridden sigh.

*

Holly Mount

A cluster of staff and residents was gathered around the notice board in reception. Beth walked over to find out what they were looking at:

'Elvid Preistly, "the best Elvis impersonator in the county", is performing live here at Holly Mount on Saturday 15th June at 2.00 p.m.

It promises to be an exciting and entertaining event which we hope you will all enjoy.

If you'd like to hear him singing all Elvis's number one hits, please give your name to Bethany at reception so that appropriate seating and refreshments will be provided.'

A warm glow seeped through her. She'd explained to Sandra how much Evelyn and Mae used to enjoy celebrating their birthdays together, and how much they'd loved Elvis. Sandra had taken it all on board, and, with Beth's help, she'd managed to find a tribute act willing to come to the home to perform on Evelyn's birthday.

For the next few hours, she was rushed off her feet. Sandra asked her to organise things so that they could get prepared for the show, including printing out all the invites for relatives and friends.

As she battled to print them off (the printer had seen better days), Evelyn shuffled up to reception, her eyes bright. 'Thank you so much, nurse.'

Beth smiled. No matter how many times she'd explained that she wasn't a nurse, so many of the ressies insisted on using the title.

'We'll be able to have a good old sing-song,' the old lady continued. 'It'll be like the good old days – and on my birthday too! How Mae would have loved it.'

Catching the bitter-sweet tone in her voice, Beth nodded. 'I'm sure Mae would have approved.'

Evelyn chuckled. 'Oh, yes, nurse. Mae would

have approved alright.'

'I think this Elvid thing is ridiculous,' Kate, a day carer, remarked during break time.

With a frown, Beth glanced up from the magazine she was reading. 'Why d'you say that?'

Kate shrugged. 'It's going to be far easier said than done, that's all I'm saying. We'll have to do bloody risk assessments and organise Zimmer frames and wheelchairs and all that paraphernalia.' Pausing, she helped herself to a custard cream from the biscuit tin before squashing her ample frame on the seat next to Beth. Hadn't she heard of personal space?

Kate chomped into her biscuit. 'I can't see the point,' she continued, spraying biscuit crumbs. 'It's a waste of time and resources, if you ask me.' She gave another dismissive shrug before shoving the remainder of the biscuit into her mouth.

'Well, I think it's a great idea – it'll give the ressies something to look forward to. Just because they can't get around like they used to doesn't mean they shouldn't enjoy life.'

'Hark at you! You're only a temporary receptionist – not a welfare officer!'

Jackie walked into the room before Beth could reply, and Beth did a double-take; her friend looked completely washed out. 'What are you doing here? I thought you were working tonight?'

Jackie flicked on the kettle. 'I'm doing an extra

shift as I need a day off next week.'

Kate looked up enquiringly. 'What do you need a day off for?'

'It's none of your business,' she replied cagily. Beth's mouth fell open. It wasn't like Jackie to be evasive and snappy, not even with the irritating Kate.

'Charming!' Kate huffed, placing a half-eaten biscuit down on the coffee table. 'You've been on a right one, lately.' She turned to face Beth. 'D'you know she turned down a date with Tom, the lift guy with the hot bod?'

Beth struggled to hide her surprise; she'd met Tom a few times now and he seemed a nice guy. She knew he liked Jackie, and Jackie seemed to like him too. 'What Jackie does or doesn't do is no one's business but her own,' she told Kate loyally.

Just then, Sandra bounced into the room clutching her "World's Greatest Boss" mug and wafting the fragrance of Estee Lauder "Beautiful". 'Come on – I want to know what you think about our Elvis concert.'

'I think it's a great idea,' Kate gushed, a faux smile splitting her face. 'Everyone's super-excited about it, and I'm sure if we work together as a team, it'll be very successful.'

Sandra beamed. 'We have Beth to thank. It was her idea.'

Beth's cheeks developed two high spots of colour.

'That's what we need here at Holly Mount,'

Sandra continued, seemingly unaware of Beth's embarrassment, 'Innovative thinkers. It's going to take a lot of sorting out, so we'll need all hands on deck.'

Kate nodded enthusiastically. 'Yes, of course.'

Beth tried to catch Jackie's eye, but she looked to be in a world of her own.

Sandra rubbed her chin thoughtfully. 'I know you're sorting out the invites for relatives and friends, Beth, but can you make sure they're worded to encourage people to come along and help out? As you know, some of the residents are going to need extra help and walking aids. Naturally, some won't be interested in coming at all. I know it's a tall order, but can I leave it to you to organise things?'

'Yes, of course,' she replied, with more confidence than she felt. She was, in fact, bricking it and she was also worried about her friend.

As soon as her break was over, Beth found several of the ressies queuing up at reception. Some wanted to add their names to the list of attendees, others wanted to ask questions about the show.

Bert gave her a gummy grin. 'Where 'ave you bin hidin', me ducks?'

She smiled at the old man of whom she'd grown so fond. 'I've been moving house, Bert.'

'Ah, I thought you'd deserted us! Things wasn't the same wivout you, ducks.'

She flushed with pleasure, realising things hadn't been the same without seeing the ressies either, *(well, at least some of them, anyway).*

She was busy adding Bert's name to the list when Fanny pushed in front of him. The old lady banged her walking stick on the desk. 'Service!'

Taking a deep breath, Beth concentrated on using her best soothing tones. 'I'm dealing with Bert at the moment, but I'll be with you in a minute.' Try as she might, she could never address the old woman as Fanny.

'You'd better get a move on, before I change my mind.'

(If she thought for one minute that was true, she'd really drag it out).

Fred Thompson, who was also in the queue, came forward. 'Don't you speak to her like that! She doesn't have to put up with bad manners, you know.'

Beth rose from her chair. 'It's alright, thank you, Fred; I can handle this.'

Jackie rattled past, pushing the drinks trolley. 'H-e-l-p!' Beth mouthed silently.

Abandoning the trolley, Jackie hurried over. Without any messing, she linked arms with Fanny. 'Come on, now,' she coaxed, with the calm yet authoritative air Beth so admired, 'don't go getting yourself in a tizzy. I'll get you a nice cup of tea and Beth can sort things out so you won't have to wait.'

Miraculously she shuffled off with Jackie, muttering expletives under her breath.

The rest of the afternoon was hectic. It took Beth

an age (and several failed attempts), before the printer churned out the last of the invites and she could finally let Sandra know that it was sorted.

As she left Sandra's office and walked along the corridor, Kate fell into step with her. 'So you're Sandra's right hand woman now, are you?'

Thinking she'd left pettiness behind now she didn't have to mingle with the wives and girlfriends of Paul's colleagues, Beth rolled her eyes. 'I'm just doing what I'm paid to do.'

Kate shrugged. 'Whatever. It strikes me you'd do anything to get noticed.'

'Oh, for goodness' sake, grow up!'

She walked away from the sullen Kate and out of the building into the late afternoon sunshine.

Jackie was about to get into her car, and Beth hurried over. 'What's up, Jacks – are you alright?'

'I'm OK; I've just got stuff on my mind, that's all.'

'Is it about Tom?'

Jackie's forehead creased into a frown.

'I think he seems like a nice guy,' Beth went on. 'He obviously thinks a lot of you and –'

Jackie shook her head crossly. 'You're as bad as Kate! Why can't everyone just mind their own blooming business for once?'

Beth felt as if she'd been slapped. 'I'm really sorry, Jacks. I didn't mean to upset you – I was only thinking –'

'Well, don't!' Jackie climbed into her car and turned her key in the ignition.

Beth stood open mouthed as, without a backward glance, her friend sped out of the car park.

Chapter Forty-Eight
Jackie

Jackie's throat constricted painfully; she'd just shunned her best friend.

On the drive home, she tried reasoning with herself that it was because she wasn't able to cope with Beth's concern and the questions she'd no doubt ask her. Right now, all she needed was to be left alone and not have to explain anything to anyone, or, at least, anyone she knew. If she saw a pitying look in someone's eyes, she knew she'd crumble. She was worried the floodgates would open. If they did, she was terrified they'd never close.

Jackie was the caregiver: that's just the way it had been since she'd left home. She was strong, capable and independent; she'd had to be. Yet, right now, she didn't have the strength to care for anyone else. As painful as it was to hurt her friend, she convinced herself she had had no choice. The strange thing to her was the aching need she had to offload to someone non-judgmental: someone who didn't know anything about her or her background and who wouldn't see her any differently.

She let herself in and picked up the rectangular card sitting next to the telephone. She turned it over and over, fingering the edges, before finally plucking up courage, and tapping the number into her phone, before she could bottle out – again.

Chapter Forty-Nine
A Dog Sitter and a Rural Existence

Beth fought back her tears. She'd never had a cross word with Jackie before, and she just couldn't understand her friend's reaction; they'd always shared everything. Surely Jackie would realise she wanted the best for her?

Rodney pounced on her the moment she walked in. 'Hello, boy.' She knelt down to kiss his furry head. 'I've missed you so much. Did Granddad come and take you for walkies?'

For the past week, Dad had made the twenty mile round trip just to spend time with Rodney. He'd told Beth he didn't mind. Today he'd had to make an even longer trip as he'd taken Lena to the bank. Aunt Lena had sold her house, and, following her recuperation at Beth's parents' home, she planned to move into a purpose-built retirement flat close to them.

At first, she'd felt sad about her aunt giving up her old home; she had such fond memories of it, but Lena was adamant it was what she wanted. The flat was on the ground floor with all mod cons, which, in itself, would be a novelty for her after her rather rural existence. It was also surrounded by well-tended communal gardens complete with benches and a water feature. Beth knew that Lena would feel more secure living close to Mum and Dad.

Beth was really grateful for her dad's help with Rodney, but she couldn't allow it to continue. Dad was getting too old for all that malarkey, although she wouldn't dare say that to his face. She knew it would be easier if Rodney lived with her parents full-time, but her heart twisted at the thought.

She pulled on her trainers and put Rodney on his lead. As she was about to close her front door, Ryan ran downstairs. He smiled in greeting. 'How are you doing?'

'I'm good, thanks.' Her face flushed at the thought of him witnessing the poo incident.

'I hate to bring this up, but Rodney was whining quite a lot while you were out.'

Beth frowned. 'Didn't my dad come over and let him out?'

'He took him for a walk, but he said he had to make it a quick one because your aunt had an appointment.'

'Oh, dear.' Beth sighed. 'I'm sorry if he disturbed you. I think I'll have to advertise for a dog-sitter for when I'm at work; it's not fair on Rodney.'

'I could help you out.'

'I couldn't trouble you to do that –'

'It wouldn't be any trouble. I normally pop home during the day if I'm working locally, which I am at the moment. I could spend some time with him and take him out for a walk, if you'd like?'

Beth considered this for a few moments. It would be a great help, there was no denying that, but was she relying on Ryan too much? That thought worried her more than words could say. She'd relied on a man before and look where that had got her.

Quickly summing up the facts, she decided she'd be cutting her nose off to spite her face if she refused. Ryan had already been kind enough to install a cat flap into the back door so Rodney could get in and out easily. In fact, her flat was ideal for him. She made sure he'd always got plenty of water, and she left the radio on for him for company, but that was no substitute for having a bona fide human being around, and she realised it would be difficult to find someone to help out with the dog now she lived out in the sticks.

Beth smiled sheepishly. 'To be honest, that would be a great help. If you're sure?'

He nodded eagerly, his face breaking into a grin. Beth couldn't help noticing how fanciable he was, in an unassuming, different kind of way. 'I'll go and get you my spare key, if you could hold Rodney?'

When she returned, key in hand, Ryan was kneeling down fussing the dog, whose tail was wagging nineteen to the dozen. 'I'd like to join you on your walk today, if that would be OK? Rodney can get to know me better.'

'I think that might be a good idea.'

They strolled along, tracing the path that ran around the perimeter, the late sun still giving off a gentle heat.

'This is really peaceful,' Ryan said.

'Yes, it is,' she agreed.

As they fell into a comfortable walking rhythm, he cleared his throat. 'I want to explain about the other night; I must've looked a total idiot, gawping at you like that.'

'You don't have to explain –' she began, but he felt he most certainly did.

'I really didn't mean to stare – in fact, I was going to come down, but my niece was staying the night. She's my brother Josh's four year old daughter.'

'Oh, I see,' Beth replied, understanding why he wouldn't leave a four year old girl alone.

'Josh and I don't get along too well,' he confessed. 'But he had a business meeting in Worcester and had arranged to stay overnight at the Fownes Hotel. His wife had to work late unexpectedly, so I agreed to have Louise. She's registered blind.'

Beth's heart twisted. 'I'm so sorry to hear that,' she trailed off, unsure what to say.

'I felt bad not coming out,' Ryan continued.

She shook her head. 'No, please don't feel bad. I totally understand. Does Louise come and see you often?'

'Not as often as I'd like.'

She caught a hint of sadness in his voice. 'What

does Josh do?' she asked.

'He's a computer whizz. He goes round to big companies, installs PCs and trains up their staff,' Ryan explained. 'Actually,' he added, 'I was wondering if Louise could meet you and Rodney one day when she visits? She loves dogs; well she loves all animals really, and she can't fail to love you too.'

Beth blushed. 'Of course she can. I'd like that very much.'

Chapter Fifty
Unrequited Love and Birthday Treats

Secretly, Beth hoped Ryan fancied her as much as she fancied him. She began to take her make-up bag to work each day, making an extra effort to look presentable after her shift when she'd see him.

A couple of weeks passed by, and although Ryan was always friendly towards her, she was disappointed he didn't mention the prospect of a date. She wondered whether to bite the bullet and ask him out, but that wasn't really her; she held onto the belief, as old fashioned as it may be to some, that the male should make the first move. Besides, what if he'd decided she was too old for him? Perhaps he saw her only as a friend? After all, she'd discovered he was only thirty and she was nearing forty. She'd come a long way, but she felt too vulnerable to risk a knockback. She also valued his friendship too much.

*

Holly Mount

'Crikey Ben! – Talk about jumping in at the deep end!

He winked. 'I know, but it's all good fun, eh?'

Beth rolled her eyes in an exaggerated fashion.

'I'm glad you think so!'

Jackie stood next to the stage, deep in conversation with Elvid, the Elvis impersonator. Beth caught her eye and smiled. Jackie gave a half smile in return before turning away. Beth's heart plummeted. For the hundredth time, she wondered what on earth she'd done for her friend to be like this. Yet if Jackie refused to talk to her, how could she possibly find out?

Vi spotted Beth and waved. 'We're going see Tom Jones!' she called.

'No, Mum,' her daughter, Janet, explained patiently. 'We're going to see the Elvis impersonator. I showed you the brochure, remember?'

She pursed her lips defiantly.

'But I'm sure we can get you an ice cream,' Janet added, knowing it was her favourite treat. 'Come on, let's find a comfy seat.'

With her short, dark hair and robust stature, she was a far cry from the delicate-looking Vi.

Beth looked around the room and smiled as she spotted Bert, his face plastered with his customary grin. He wore a Bay City Rollers' tartan cap, a white shirt and red braces.

Fanny away to her long-suffering grandson, Simon: 'I'm not going to listen to some rubbish for hours.'

He shook his head as he gently took her by the arm. 'Come on, Gran. You don't want to get thrown out, do you?'

She scowled up at him but shuffled off to find a seat.

Beth had to team up with Kate to do a room check before the show started.

'Mr. Morris isn't coming down,' Kate remarked tartly. 'He says it's a waste of time and resources and asked why you didn't organise a nice a game of bridge instead.'

Beth inhaled a deep, calming breath, determined not to let her rile her. 'I'm sure we can arrange a game of bridge sometime, but a lot of the residents are looking forward to this,' she said, giving Maud's door a loud knock before entering.

Kate pushed past Beth. 'Afternoon, Maud. Have you got your earplugs ready?'

Maud put her hand to her ear. 'Eh?'

'HAVE YOU GOT YOUR EARPLUGS READY?'

The old lady scowled. 'No need to shout! I ain't deaf!'

'Not a fan of Elvis, then, Maud?' Beth asked.

She pouted. 'I was going come down and have a look, but I didn't put my name on that list.'

'That won't be a problem; we've got enough staff to help, if you'd like to watch the show?'

'Will I get a cup o' tea?'

Beth smiled. 'As much tea as you can drink.'

'Aye, go on, then. I might as well.'

Kate stalked out of the room. Beth went off in search of Ben; she knew he'd be more than happy to help with Maud.

*

Beth felt a twinge of nervous anticipation as she gazed around the lounge where the residents and their friends and relatives had gathered.

Fanny nudged Simon. 'You'll tell them, won't you, lad?'

He frowned. 'Tell them what, Gran?'

She grasped the string of pearls at her throat. 'They're not to touch my things. They might go through my jewellery box when I'm not there.'

He heaved a sigh. 'No one's going to touch your stuff. Let us just try and enjoy the show.'

'Thank God she's compliant for her grandson,' Beth whispered to Ben.

It seemed to take forever to get everyone settled and seated. Wheelchairs stood in better vantage points; walking aids were safely stowed away so no one could trip over them and there was general confusion about who wanted to sit where. Beth decided that she should have put more thought into a seating plan and made a mental note that it would be top of her priority list when Holly Mount arranged another "do".

She beamed when she saw Evelyn seated in the

front row. Although she would be thinking of Mae, she looked happy.

Sandra sat at the front next to Jackie.

Beth manoeuvred her way along the third row and sat next to Fred, who grumbled that he wanted to sit next to Vi. Although hard of hearing, Vi heard what was going on and turned around to tell him, in no uncertain terms, that she was saving the seat next to her for Mr. Dervischi. Reluctantly, he settled for Beth.

Having received an invitation, Fred's son had phoned to say that both he and his wife were far too busy. Beth knew from his tone he simply couldn't be bothered. Poor Fred rarely had visitors, and she was sad when she'd see him sitting alone during visiting times, sometimes trying to muscle in on others' conversations. In the main, people would respond to him politely, but occasionally he was ignored or there was a detached inclusion, making him appear lonelier than ever. Then, of course, there was Violet, his unrequited love interest. She knew there wasn't much she could do about unrequited love, but she'd often pop along to have a natter with him once her shift came to an end.

*

As she observed the expectant faces, she reflected on each resident's individuality, the uniqueness that made them into the characters she knew and cared about. She understood how important it was to engage with them, getting to know them on a deeper level. It gave her genuine satisfaction to help bring some sunshine into their lives in whatever small way she could.

Sandra climbed the steps onto the improvised stage, clapping her hands to get everyone's attention. 'Ladies and Gentlemen – I would like to welcome Mr. Elvid Priestly, our very own "Elvis". There will be an interval for refreshments.' She looked over at Evelyn and smiled. 'But before he sings for us, let's wish Evelyn a very happy birthday.'

Led by Sandra, the room erupted into an out-of-tune rendition of "Happy Birthday".

Evelyn's face lit up. Beth knew she was actually enjoying being in the limelight.

'Has it finished?' Vi asked in a loud voice, once the singing subsided.

'No, it's just starting,' Janet whispered.

'Why's everyone clapping, then?'

Elvid strutted around the makeshift stage in his silver platform boots, the glitter on his white jump-suit twinkling. Despite his puckered lips and black quiffed wig, at five feet tall in his boots and with a roll of fat clearly visible around his midriff, he didn't exactly look the part. The ressies didn't seem to care. Some of them even began to clap and sing along.

'This first song's forrr the loverrly Everrlyn,' he drawled. 'Twenty-one today, Ladies and Genle'men.'

Evelyn beamed as Elvid crooned 'Love me t e n d e r r r r,' rolling his Rs in his Herefordshire burr.

Kate, who was sitting to Sandra's left, screwed up

her face in a '*what the hell?*' expression. Sandra noticed and gave her a hard stare. Kate shrank back into her seat.

The staff bustled around handing out drinks in the interval.

Beth glanced over at her son, who was helping Maud out of her seat. He'd taken to the job like a duck to water, she thought proudly. He looked happier than she'd seen him in a long time.

Once again thinking the show had ended, Vi tried to wander off, but Janet coaxed her back into her chair.

Beth finished handing out drinks and was about to take her seat for the second half when Vi called to her, but she was unable to catch what she'd said. 'Are you alright?' she mouthed.

Vi shook her head and pointed towards Janet. 'I need a wee, nurse, and she says I can't go.'

'You've only just been, Mum. Are you sure you need to go again?'

'I need a wee,' she repeated adamantly.

Heaving herself out of her chair, Janet linked her arm through her mother's and helped her to her feet.

'D'you need any help?' Beth offered.

'It's OK thanks. Come on, Mum, let's get you sorted,' she said patiently. We don't want to miss it.'

The spotlights beamed down on stage once more and Elvid sashayed on, his hips gyrating to the music.

'Who's he meant to be?' Fanny asked Simon. 'It's Elvis,' Simon whispered, his tone urgent.

'Elvis is dead!' Fanny pointed an accusing finger towards Elvid. 'He's that gay one – off the telly.'

A few seconds of calm ensued and Elvid crooned, '*Let Me Be Yourrr Teddy Bearrrrr,*' which seemed to be a definite favourite with Bert, who hooked his thumbs through his braces and jigged around in his seat.

Elvid sang '*Are You Lonesome Tonight?*'

When it ended, Sandra rose from her seat and squeezed along the row to join him on stage. Beth was elated and relieved it had gone well. Maybe Sandra would consider other events in the future, which would be a real plus for the ressies. She'd done some research and had a few ideas lined up: there was a local lady she'd read about on the internet that rescued ponies and took them to visit schools and care homes. People could interact with them, and one horse could actually kick a ball using his hooves! She felt sure some of the ressies at Holly Mount would love it.

Janet helped Vi from her seat. 'Have you enjoyed the show then, Mum?'

'I haven't had any dinner yet,' she grumbled. 'And I don't know where they've put my teeth.'

Janet rolled her eyes. 'You've got your teeth in, Mum – and you've already had your dinner.'

Linking his arm through Vi's free arm, Ben grinned. 'I can get you a nice ham and tomato sandwich, if you'd like.' he said, as he guided her towards the exit.

'What about Mr. Dervischi?'

Janet made wide eyes at him and Ben winked. 'We'll sort him out, too, don't you worry.'

'Guess what?' Fred asked Beth, rocking up and down on the balls of his feet in excitement, his ruddy complexion matching his red cravat.

'What is it, Fred?'

'Vi said I can sit by her tomorrow – and look what I've got for her...' He delved his hands deep inside the pockets of his brown corduroys and began foraging around. Beth held her breath. *What on earth had he got in there?* To her relief, he pulled out a fistful of unwrapped, gooey, striped humbugs. They stuck to his palm like super glue. He shook his hand violently, flinging the gooey mess onto the carpet. 'Oh, bother and damnation - they've gone all sticky!'

When Fred had gone off to the loos to wash his hands, Beth fetched a bowl of soapy water and got down on her hands and knees. Having managed to tear the offending humbugs from the nylon fibres, she scrubbed energetically to remove all traces of stickiness.

Sandra came over to her. 'The show was a great success – well done. You should be very proud of what you've achieved.'

She looked up and smiled at her boss. 'Thank you, but everyone had a hand in it.'

'Maybe,' Sandra said thoughtfully. 'But it wouldn't have happened in the first place if you hadn't spoken out. You know, Bethany Bishop, sometimes you should give yourself a bit more credit.'

'Careful!' she laughed to cover her embarrassment. 'I won't be able to get my head through the door at this rate!'

Chapter Fifty-One
Regrets and Disappointment

On her drive home, one thing cast a shadow on Beth's day. More than anything, she needed to understand why Jackie was avoiding her. Each time she'd try to talk to her, Jackie would be "too busy", or she'd be working a different shift. The whole thing was driving her mad.

She parked her car and headed inside. As she inserted her key in the lock, no urgent barking came from Rodney. Thinking that maybe he was upstairs with Ryan, she climbed the fifteen stairs to his flat, but there was no one at home.

Beth went back downstairs and stood gazing out of her window onto the field. She soon spotted Rodney contentedly trotting alongside Ryan.

Ryan was so refreshing, she thought, and then considered this was a stupid description – *but he was!* She felt a pang of disappointment. He still hadn't made any attempt to ask her out, and she guessed he must see her as a friend.

Moving away from the window, she pulled off her shoes, and rubbed her aching feet before shoving them gratefully into slippers.

As she made herself a cup of tea, there was a knock at the door.

Her eyes widened when she saw Greg Harrison. 'Hi, Beth, how are you?'

Although he was the last person she'd expected, Beth kept her tone light. 'Oh, hi! I'm good, thanks.

There was an awkward pause before Beth chivvied him up; she was gasping for that cuppa. 'So what brings you here?'

He flashed a smile. 'I was in the neighbourhood for a viewing, so I thought I'd call round and see how you're getting on.'

'I'm getting on fine, thanks. The place is really coming along – would you like to have a look?'

With a nod, he followed her inside, looking around approvingly. 'I like the red feature wall,' He pointed to Beth's electric stove housed in a wooden surround. 'Is that a real fire?'

She shook her head. 'No, but it's the next best thing.'

Greg sat on the sofa while she made tea for both of them.

'Look,' he said, as she handed him his cup. 'I wondered if you'd like to come out for a drink with me tomorrow night?'

Unsure how to react; she busied herself shuffling some magazines into a neat pile on the coffee table. He was more her age than Ryan was, and Ryan hadn't shown any sign of asking her out. Maybe it wouldn't hurt to go out for another drink? After all, Greg had helped her to find her flat, and there was no doubt that he was handsome. She'd become totally reliant on the residents for adult company, just lately.

Yet something unsettled her. She couldn't ignore her gut instinct; attractiveness soon faded if it didn't extend to the inside.

She looked at him before she answered; there was something about him that reminded her of Paul: his self-assured manner which seemed to err on the side of cockiness. 'I don't think that's a good idea.'

His face hardened. He put his unfinished drink down and got to his feet. 'If that's how you want it –'

She heaved a sigh of relief as she shut the door behind him. As she plumped up the cushions where he'd been sitting, she noticed a brown leather corner poking out between the seat pads. She gave it a tug and pulled out Greg's wallet. Damn! It must've fallen out of his jacket pocket. Snatching up her mobile, Beth scrolled through until she found his number, and then hurriedly pressed the call button. His answer-phone kicked in straightaway, so she left him a brief message telling him she'd drop the wallet into his office on her way to work next morning.

As she opened her handbag to put it in, it occurred to her that Greg's home details might be inside.

She opened it and a photograph of a red-haired woman holding a young baby stared out from behind the plastic window. The woman was smiling down at the sleeping baby, her wavy hair sitting prettily on her shoulders. She remembered Greg saying that his sister had a baby; perhaps it was them in the photo?

Lifting it out, Beth took a closer look and discovered a square of paper lying underneath it with. an address and phone number written on it.

After a moment's hesitation, she dialled the landline number. It rang out several times and then a woman answered.

'Hi - is that Marie?'

'Yes, it is,' answered a cautious female voice. 'Who's speaking?'

'My name's Beth Bishop. I'm – a friend of Greg's,' she explained. 'He left his wallet at my flat. I've tried calling him. Can you let him know it's safe? I'll drop it off at his office tomorrow on my way to work.'

There was silence at the other end of the line.

'Hello?' Beth repeated.

'He's just walked in,' Marie said, her tone curt. As Marie handed the phone to Greg, Beth heard snippets of a brief exchange between them.

'It's a client, darling,' he said, without hesitation. 'I did a valuation for her, that's all.'

Marie said something else she couldn't catch and

Greg came on the line. 'What do you think you're playing at, calling me on my home number?' he hissed.

She felt the blood rush to her face. 'Now hang on a minute – I didn't know this was *your* home. I only rang to say you'd dropped your wallet –'

'*Where does this client live?*' she heard Marie's voice again in the background. The poor woman, she thought, knowing that her own instinct had been spot on.

'She lives a few miles away, sweetheart,' Greg called to Marie. 'Now, go and get yourself ready for a night out. I've called your mum and arranged for her to babysit.'

Hearing Marie's retreating footsteps, Beth knew she'd bought into her husband's lies.

'I'll drop your wallet into your office before nine tomorrow morning,' she told him brusquely. Just make sure you're not around when I do.'

Chapter Fifty-Two
Raindrops and Paradise

Rain was dripping off the end of Ryan's nose as he reached the flats. He patted Rodney's bedraggled head. 'Come on, boy, let's go and get you dried off.'

As Beth let them in, Ryan noticed she seemed flustered. 'Are you OK?'

She was still fuming about Greg, but pulled herself together and smiled. 'I'm fine,' she said lightly, 'which is more than can be said for you two – you're soaked through!'

She ushered them through to the cosy sitting room and brought out a couple of towels from the airing cupboard. 'Here,' she said, handing one to Ryan, 'dry yourself off.'

He dried his hair while Beth rubbed at Rodney's fur.

'Do you want a cup of tea?' she offered.

'Thanks... but I think I'll jump in the shower and change out of these clothes.'

Desperate to pull off his wet clothes, Ryan took the stairs two at a time. He got to his front door and reached into his jacket pocket for his key. Strange, he thought, when his hand failed to make contact with metal. He patted his other pocket and then checked the pockets of his soggy jeans. *Shit! I must've dropped them somewhere,* he thought crossly. He groaned inwardly as he became aware that Alex, who kept his only spare, would be at work and it would be some time before he'd be able to drop it round.

Ryan texted Alex asking him to drop off his spare key when he'd finished, and then he went back downstairs and knocked on Beth's door.

'I've managed to lose my key and it'll be a while before my friend can drop off my spare. Is it OK if I wait here?'

She smiled. 'Of course it is.'

It dawned on her that Paul's old dressing gown was hanging in her wardrobe; it was the one thing he hadn't taken to Emily's. She'd meant to take it to a charity shop, but hadn't got round to it. Paul probably wore a silk kimono in its place now he'd come up in the world, she thought cynically.

'Why don't you use my shower?' she suggested. 'I've got a dressing gown you can use and I'll put your clothes into the tumble dryer.'

'That'd be great! Thanks, Beth.'

She busied herself fetching the dressing gown and a large bath sheet, and Ryan disappeared into the bathroom.

A couple of minutes later he stood at the kitchen door. Beth was waiting to put his wet clothes into the dryer. She felt him behind her, rather than saw him. As she turned to look at him, she swallowed. The bottom half of Ryan's body was wrapped in the bath sheet, but his chest was bare and tanned, toned. He wasn't a typical gym body muscle-man, but he was every inch a man. His bronzed skin colour, with his red-blond hair colouring, surprised her, but she guessed his tan was due to his outdoor work.

Noticing the way she was looking at him, Ryan gave her a cheeky grin.

She blushed furiously. 'If you give me your wet things, I'll pop them in the dryer,' she said hurriedly

With Ryan showered and wearing Paul's dressing gown, they sat on the settee, each with a steaming cup of hot chocolate. Beth'd selected Coldplay tracks on her iPod; *Paradise* was playing softly in the background.

'I love Coldplay,' he told her. 'This one's my favourite.'

Beth smiled. 'Mine, too. I'd love to go and see them on tour.'

Ryan agreed it was something he would love to do too.

They chatted for ages, and she was amazed at how much they had in common: their love of animals, music, books and films.

Taking a tissue from a box on the table, Ryan gently wiped above Beth's top lip where the hot chocolate had left her with a frothy moustache. Her heart pounded at his proximity; she fancied him like mad. She looked up at him, shyly at first, and their eyes met.

In an instant, his lips were on hers, firm, warm, and inviting. His tongue probed hers and she clung to him, savouring his strong arms as he held her tightly, responding with a passion and longing that surprised and overwhelmed her.

As the doorbell rang, they sprang apart. Ryan's eyes still held an intensity of longing and tenderness.

Alex grinned when he saw Beth's flushed cheeks. Ryan tried hard to swallow his disappointment.

Chapter Fifty-Three
Chamomile Tea and Russian Dolls

At work the following day, all Beth could think about was Ryan. She marveled at the passion he'd aroused in her and the tender way he'd looked at her.

As soon as she got home, she jumped in the shower, using Herbal Essences to wash her hair. Regrettably, it didn't make her orgasmic like the woman on the TV ad, but at least it smelt nice, she thought.

Rodney gave a loud bark, his paws skittering down the hallway at the sound of the doorbell.

Was she fated, she wondered? Why now, when she had no make-up on and a towel turban wrapped around her head? She slipped on her dressing gown and went off to answer it.

Penelope's eyes travelled from Beth's turban to her slippers.

Beth blinked in surprise. 'What are you doing here?'

'Can I come in, Beth?' Penelope said hesitantly, 'I won't keep you long.'

Beth? Penelope never called her Beth!

Beth nodded. After fending off Rodney, she

showed her mother-in-law through to the sitting room.

Penelope slung her Louis Vuitton handbag onto the sofa. Rodney made another lunge at her. She reached out and patted his head. 'Good boy, don't jump up at Granny Penny,' she cooed.

Beth did a double take. *Granny Penny?*

Exhaling deeply, Penelope held Beth's astonished gaze. 'I've got a few things I need to get off my chest, dear. I want us to clear the air.' She sat down next to her Louis Vuitton and crossed one trouser clad leg over the other.

Beth sat in the chair opposite, holding her breath in anticipation.

'The thing is –' Penelope began, steepling her fingers. 'I want to – no, *I need* – to apologise.'

'*Apologise?*' Beth echoed.

Her mother-in-law nodded in reply. 'I've been very unfair. I only realise that now.' She lowered her gaze before continuing. 'You have always made me welcome in your home, dear, which is more than can be said for Emily and my son.'

Beth let out an audible gasp. 'But I thought you were happy there?'

'I was - at first,' Penelope replied, her shoulders drooping. 'But let's just say I've outstayed my welcome.'

'Are you staying there now?'

She shook her head. 'I'm living back at the house. Of course, the place is far too big for me – Clive wants us to sell up. At least now I'm back in my own four walls, I'm not being criticised for everything I do.'

Beth could certainly empathise with that. She wracked her brain to find something positive to say; it was against her nature to kick someone when they were down.

'I'm sure they didn't mean to criticise you,' she managed.

Penelope shrugged. 'That may be true of Paul, dear. However, unfortunately the same can't be said for Emily.'

They sat in silence for a few moments. 'I thought Emily was the sort of person Paul needed in his life, but, I was wrong, dear – I was very wrong.'

Beth shook her head. 'I don't know what to say –'

'You don't need to say anything. I'm the one who should apologise. It's no secret that I thought Paul married far too young. And I thought –'

'You thought I wasn't good enough for your son,' Beth volunteered.

Penelope sighed. 'Yes, I'll admit it. I thought he should marry someone, who was, well – more of his intellectual calibre. I believed someone like Emily could help him succeed – and maybe she can, but she's totally self-centred with no consideration for others. You may not have been an A star student, dear, but you did make the grade as far as being a decent wife and mother is concerned.'

'So what's happened to make you feel like this?'

Beth asked.

Penelope chewed her bottom lip thoughtfully. 'Paul's changed since he moved in with Emily. He's lost his sense of family values; he sides with her over every little thing. That dreadful cat was the last straw – it got into my room and clawed my silk duvet cover. I was so angry; that cover cost a small fortune. Emily told me, in no uncertain terms, that Celine came first and *I* had to fit around *him* – can you imagine?'

Beth took a deep breath; she could imagine it well, although Emily certainly hadn't taken that approach with Paul: she'd completely disregarded the fact *Beth* was there first.

She knew that Emily had done her a favour. The life she'd been living with Paul had been a shallow one, and she'd tried desperately hard to be something she wasn't for years, simply to fit into her husband's world.

Penelope sank back against a cushion. 'Paul never calls to see me. He doesn't even bother to phone to check I'm alright.'

'He's probably busy,' Beth offered.

Penelope looked at her, her eyes narrowing.

'He wasn't too busy to shag his PA, though, was he?'

Beth's eyes widened.

' The only time he contacts me is if he needs a favour,' Penelope continued, ignoring her daughter-in-law's astonished gaze, 'such as when he wants me to feed the wretched cat.'

A tear slid down her mother- in-law's cheek and, grabbing a box of tissues, Beth rammed several into her hand. 'Don't upset yourself,' she said. 'I'll go and make you a cup of tea. I think I've still got some chamomile teabags somewhere.'

'Thank you dear,' Penelope dabbed at her eyes with the balled up tissue.

Beth rose from her chair, and Rodney, who'd finally settled at her feet, leapt onto Penelope's lap, attempting to lick her face. Beth tugged at his collar. 'Get down, Rodney!'

Penelope rubbed the dog's ears. 'He's not doing any harm, are you, you silly boy?'

On her way out, Penelope took hold of Beth's hand. 'Don't be a stranger, dear.'

Beth watched, aghast, as she climbed into her BMW. With a cursory backward glance, Penelope drove off.

The different sides to her mother-in-law were stacked up like Russian dolls, she thought. Just when she thought she'd seen them all, yet another one was revealed. Despite everything that had happened, she couldn't help feeling sad for her mother-in-law, who now seemed totally lost.

Chapter Fifty-Four
Paul

Paul gave an exasperated sigh as he tooted his horn.

Emily had made them late yet again - the third time in a row. What the hell could she possibly be doing? She'd been pampered and preened to within an inch of her life at that ludicrously priced salon. Surely she should be ready now.

At least his wife had had the good grace to be on time whenever they'd gone out for dinner. And she'd been low maintenance too. Ironically, he considered she was somewhat too low maintenance. Why couldn't women strike the happy medium? It wasn't rocket science.

As if Emily wasn't enough to contend with, he had his mother to worry about too. He simply couldn't understand why Emily hadn't made her more welcome. She'd been happy enough with the arrangement at first; in fact it had been her idea to invite his mother to live with them in the first place. He should've known it would all end badly. Put two women in the same kitchen and you'll end up with fireworks every time. He knew the cat incident hadn't helped matters; Celine shredding his mother's pure silk quilt cover had certainly put the cat amongst the pigeons, so to speak. It had been the last straw, and he secretly wished he'd sided with his mother on that one.

Infuriated now, he glanced once more at the dashboard clock, his hand hovering again over the car horn.

Finally, Emily tottered out on skyscraper Jimmy Choos and headed towards the car. It was a wonder the silly cow didn't break her neck, Paul thought, irritably. One of her heels appeared to be wedged in a gap between the paving slabs. Her thin arms flailed around and her rose tinted lips silently mouthed, 'Help!'

Hellfire and damnation! They'd be later than ever now.

Expelling a long breath, he climbed out of the car and went to her rescue.

Chapter Fifty-Five
Ryan

On his way to meet Alex, Ryan shoved his hands deep into the pockets of his leather jacket and breathed out a sigh. He wasn't in the mood for socialising tonight; his mind was too preoccupied with thoughts of Beth.

How should he tackle the situation with her, he wondered, then immediately chastised himself for trying to plan things out as he would a landscaping job. His face cracked a wry smile. In a way, he supposed that was what it was like – getting rid of the rubble in his life before trying to create something new and beautiful. And Beth was lovely, both inside and out, although she was too modest and understated to realise it. Her qualities were a rare find in this day and age. He liked modesty in a person, but he'd sensed there was more to it with Beth. *Vulnerability,* he thought to himself. Yes, that's what it was. She was vulnerable and still raw over her broken marriage. He shouldn't have kissed her last night. He'd wanted her urgently, but it wasn't fair to her. He swallowed hard as he remembered her passionate response. He must give her some space, though. A broken marriage was akin to bereavement, and the last thing he wanted to do was to go in all guns blazing and push her into something she might regret.

In just a few weeks' time he'd be leaving for Canada to work for six months. This thought, the one that used to fill him with excited anticipation, now caused his heart to catapult into his stomach.

Chapter Fifty-Six
Agendas and Regrets

Having lost her appetite, Beth pushed the food around the plate with her fork. She was still fuming about Greg, mixed up about her feelings for Ryan, and in shock over her encounter with Penelope. She also missed Jackie more than ever – not being able to talk to her friend was like a physical ache. She would love to tell her about Ryan. She'd been shaken up by her response to his kiss, and she knew they'd have made love if they hadn't been interrupted.

She'd left Jackie countless messages that had gone un- replied, but she felt determination swelling inside her not to give up. On top of everything else, she fretted there was something wrong with her best friend and resolved to get to the bottom of it.

Beth's thoughts were interrupted by a knock at the door. She abandoned her meal and went to answer it.

She reeled at the smell of whisky on Paul's breath. 'Can I come in?' he said, his voice slurred.

With a sigh, Beth nodded and moved aside for him to enter.

Pushing back his hair, he sat down heavily on the

sofa.

She sighed. 'What do you want, Paul?'

He reached out to her, taking her small hand in his larger, smooth one. 'Look -' he began weakly. 'This isn't easy for me to admit, but I know I'd taken you for granted when we were together – and – I want us to give things another go.'

'It's just the drink talking –' she stopped short as the doorbell rang a second time.

'Leave it,' he urged, gripping her shoulder. 'They'll go away.'

Rodney barked, and shrugging Paul off, Beth went to answer it.

Emily stood in the aperture, her face all red and blotchy. 'Is Paul here?' she asked hesitantly.

On cue, Paul appeared behind Beth. He frowned when he saw his girlfriend. 'What on earth are you doing here?'

Reaching out and tentatively placing her hand on his arm, Emily hiccupped back a sob. 'I'm so sorry, Paul, I ... oh, dahling -'

Not wanting to treat the neighbours to a free show, Beth ushered them inside. 'Would one of you like to tell me what's going on?'

Emily looked at her with bloodshot eyes. 'I ... I'm pregnant. I didn't mean it to happen – it just did.'

Paul shifted from one foot to the other and Beth realised he already knew.

'Say something – please, dahling –' Emily

implored him. He glared at her, his face now a shade of magenta. 'You *know* how I feel - you were on the pill! How can you be bloody pregnant?'

'These things happen,' she whimpered. 'I'm so sorry – '

Paul started pacing around the small room, his arms behind his back, in the manner Beth used to find endearing. He stopped suddenly and turned accusing eyes once more towards Emily. You didn't tell me until it was too late. You've no right deciding to keep it!'

'I'm sorry,' she repeated brokenly.

'You knew children were never on the agenda!'

'I didn't do it intentionally. I was so busy with everything; I must've forgotten to take my pill –'

His eyes seemed to bulge from their sockets. 'You *forgot?'* he cried. 'What sort of an excuse is that? You don't forget your salon appointments or lunch dates. How could you forget to take a bloody pill?'

Tears squeezed through Emily's lashes and she dashed them away with the back of her hand.

Beth felt a surprising sense of calm, like the night Harold had died. She placed a comforting hand on Emily's shoulder and looked at Paul. 'Not everything is based on an agenda,' she said.' I think you both need to go home and discuss this. And *you* need to sober up. Leave your car here and go home with Emily.'

He looked sheepish, but gave a curt nod of acceptance.

For an awkward moment, Beth thought Emily

was about to hug her, but Emily seemed to have second thoughts and scurried out to her car.

Paul hovered in the doorway. 'This doesn't have to be the end for us,' he whispered.

Beth shook her head with disbelief as he continued. 'I'll help her out financially, of course; I've no choice – but, well, we still have a bond – and we kind of worked, didn't we?'

Balling her hands into fists, she pressed her nails into her palms in an effort not to explode. 'Our bond was well and truly broken the minute you slept with someone else.'

He threw her a wounded look. 'Look – I'll call you when you've had time to think things through. We've both made mistakes, but I believe we can put them behind us. This doesn't have to be goodbye.'

Chapter Fifty-Seven
Buses and Edward VIII

Beth and Ryan strolled along the river bank. Rodney trotted contentedly alongside them, sniffing at all the different smells enthusiastically. He was obviously enjoying this change in his routine.

Ryan had suggested a drive out to the small town of Upton-upon-Severn, roughly ten miles from Worcester, and, although Beth had accepted, she felt anxious wondering what she'd do if he kissed her again. Would she go all the way? And if not, why not? She couldn't figure it out; here was a lovely guy who wanted her, yet, in the cold light of day, she wasn't sure if she was ready for another relationship, and she didn't want to lead him on. She definitely didn't want casual sex either.

He'd knocked on her door just after breakfast to see if she fancied the idea of a trip to Upton. He'd got the day off, too, he'd told her, and it would be a shame to waste it.

Beth had planned on painting the kitchen pale grey, but as it was a glorious June day and she'd decided that the painting could wait.

Her thoughts flicked once more to Jackie and what she'd say if she knew about the past couple of days. Knowing her friend it would be something along the lines of: *men are like buses, they all turn up at once.*

Sometimes her sadness at Jackie's silence gave way to anger; how dare she treat her this way? But she missed her friend and wondered what she could do to put things right between them. She wished her thoughts about the upset with Jackie didn't continuously play on her mind like a stuck record.

*

Beth had always loved Upton-on-Severn, with its distinctive tower and copper-clad cupola (known locally as the "Pepper Pot" due to its shape). It was the only surviving remnant of a former church. The town also comprised a jumble of quaint black and white cottages and an eclectic mix of shops.

Passengers on the larger tour vessels sailing on the Severn waved to them as they walked along the river bank, and they waved back.

Ryan noticed Beth was less chatty than usual and his brow creased with concern. 'Are you sure you're OK?'

'Yes, I'm fine,' she replied lightly.

'You seem quiet today.'

'I'm sorry – I am really enjoying the day.'

He sensed something was troubling her. 'Why don't we go and have a drink? They do good food at the

Swan; we can sit outside and watch the world go by.'

Beth agreed and they made their way back along the path, walking along until they reached the Swan. They chose a table facing the river. Beth took a plastic container and bowl from her bag and poured out some water for Rodney. He took a few laps and settled underneath her chair for a snooze.

Ryan grinned. 'The fresh air's worn him out.'

'It certainly has,' Beth said.

They ordered from the extensive menu, Ryan opting for Chilli Con Carne with rice and Beth choosing a simple cod, chips and garden peas. Whilst they waited for their food, she leaned back in her chair, feeling the warmth of the sun on her bare arms. Ryan's face softened as he watched her.

When they'd eaten, they gathered up their things and walked along the High Street, mingling with tourists, browsing around the numerous antique and second-hand shops.

Jackie would love it here; Beth thought, lifting the price tag on an Edward VIII sterling silver jewellery box and examining it; nine hundred and fifty pounds!

'Aren't you going to treat yourself?' Ryan quipped.

'I might.' Beth replied nonchalantly as she pointed to a beautiful Victorian cast iron fireplace and hearth. 'I think you should treat yourself, too. That would look rather fetching in your sitting room.'

'That's a good idea.' He grinned as he checked the contents of his wallet. 'I may just have to nip to the cash-point first, see if my lottery win's come through.'

Beth laughed out loud. They left the shop and Ryan took hold of her hand, and they made their way down cobbled side streets, exploring the quaint shops nestled between rows of neat terraced cottages.

Chapter Fifty-Eight
Zumba and Complementary Therapies

Holly Mount

Hearing someone knock on her desk, Beth glanced up from her filing.

Bert propped his walking stick against the desk and grinned. 'You look nice today, ducks.'

She gave the old man a warm smile. 'Thanks, Bert, that's nice of you to say so.'

'I like to see a woman taking pride in her appearance. By the way, Vi seems a bit upset.'

'D'you know why?'

'She said Mr. Dervischi ain't real,' he told her solemnly. 'I didn't say anything, but Fred Thompson did.'

'Well, Mr. D's real to her. Don't worry, I'll go and have a word with her as soon as I finish.'

'Ah, ta, me ducks. You can tell her I'm real, though.' Bert chuckled.

'I will, Bert. I promise.'

When Beth's shift ended, she went to see Vi, who was sitting alone at the far end of the communal lounge.

'Are you alright?' Beth asked gently.

Vi shook her head. 'Mr. Dervischi doesn't come to see me anymore.'

Beth took hold of the old lady's hand. 'You're a very special lady,' she told her. 'And I'm sure there are plenty of people who'd be glad to be your friend.'

'Do you think so?'

Beth nodded. 'Indeed I do. Tomorrow afternoon we're having a meeting to find out what activities you might like – why don't you come along with Bert?'

Vi frowned suspiciously. 'I'm not doing any of that zumba malarkey.'

'You won't have to,' Beth reassured her. 'We want to find out what you all like doing, and I'm going to see if we can arrange different activities for everyone to enjoy.'

'Could we plant some hanging baskets? I used to love my garden when I could bend my knees.'

'I'm sure we can sort something out. I'll come up to your room tomorrow and bring you down if you want to come.'

'Can Bert come too?'

'He'll be there.'

'And Mr. Dervischi?'

'Of course.'

She had no idea if Vi would recall their conversation the following day, but at least she seemed more settled.

Beth collected up her things and was on her way out of the door when Sandra caught her up. 'Have you got a few minutes to spare?' she asked.

Beth groaned inwardly as she followed her through to her office - today had felt like a long day.

Sandra gestured for her to sit down before settling herself into the chair opposite. 'I've been to a meeting with Rasheed, the owner of Holly Mount,' she said, her voice rising with excitement. 'He's proposing to extend the building to provide more bedrooms and better facilities for the residents.'

'That sounds good,' Beth agreed.

'It's great news – it means we'll need to attract more people who'll want to stay. Rasheed wants us to shine, to be the best in the area. He wants families to feel confident their loved ones are in safe and caring hands with their needs, both practical and emotional, being fully met.'

Beth nodded her understanding as Sandra continued. 'Instead of simply classing them as elderly people, he wants them to be valued as the individuals they are, people with enquiring minds, which is wonderful news for the future of Holly Mount,' she gushed. 'Obviously, we'd need to hire more staff. We'll need professional health care workers on board as well as occupational therapists and the like.' She paused and Beth wondered where she might fit into Rasheed's vision.

'The reason I'm telling you now rather than waiting until the staff meeting,' Sandra explained, 'is because I know Rasheed's really keen to employ an activities co-ordinator and a complementary therapist, both on a part-time basis.'

Beth felt a tingle of excited anticipation.

Sandra poured them both a tumbler of water before continuing. 'In addition to both physiotherapy and occupational therapy, we'd offer a comprehensive care package to include a range of complementary treatments. This would be something unique.'

Beth swallowed her drink, struggling to absorb the enormity of the changes that were going to happen.

Sensing her trepidation, Sandra smiled reassuringly. 'I saw you giving Liz a massage, remember?' 'When she came into work the next day, she said how much better she felt, and that you were a natural; she'd never felt so relaxed and she'd slept like a baby.'

'I'm really pleased to hear that.'

Placing the tumbler onto her desk, Sandra looked at her thoughtfully. 'I wondered if you'd be interested in going back to college to finish your training.'

Beth took a deep breath. 'I've wanted to go back to college for a while now,' she said uncertainly, 'but I'm worried about doing all the academic stuff; especially at my age.'

Sandra's eyebrows disappeared under her thick

fringe. 'Nonsense! Of course you'd cope; you're a mere spring chicken! Why not finish what you started? You've got great potential, Beth; your organisational skills are excellent and you have a "can do" attitude. Most importantly, you really care about people.'

Beth's cheeks flushed with a mixture of embarrassment and pride. She'd always dreamed of becoming a therapist. Although it may have been a small dream to some, it felt huge to her. 'What would happen if I qualify?'

Sandra tutted good-humouredly. 'You mean *when* you qualify! Well, there wouldn't be enough work to employ you in that capacity full-time, so we'd like you to work as a therapist during a couple of set afternoons each week and as activities co-ordinator for the remainder of the week, if you'd be happy with that?'

Too overwhelmed to speak, Beth stared at her wide-eyed.

'I know it's a lot to take in,' Sandra told her, 'so have a think about it and let me know. Of course, your pay would be commensurate with your duties. You can continue working shifts here while you study part-time.'

Beth felt like she was walking on air as she thanked Sandra and left her office.

Sandra had wasted no time in putting out feelers. She'd told Beth that the next complementary therapy course started in September, which was just three months away. If Beth decided to go for it, she realised, she'd be starting college at the same time as her son!

During the drive home, Beth reached a decision. She turned her Ka around and took the road leading to Jackie's. She was going to hammer at her friend's door until she couldn't ignore her any longer.

As she pulled up by the Old Mill, Beth did a double-take to see Ryan's work truck parked outside. He must be working on the gardens, she thought.

Most of the tenants were home from work, so parking was tight, but eventually Beth managed to park up. She couldn't see Jackie's car, but decided that if her friend was out, she was prepared to wait until she returned. They'd been friends for too long. She couldn't and wouldn't let this weird situation continue any longer.

She froze; her hand midway to the door handle. Ryan had pushed open the entrance door and was walking out of the building. Beth saw that he was standing aside holding it open for someone else. Her face paled as Jackie walked out into the sunshine to join him.

Beth's heart began to pound in her chest. She watched, as if in slow motion, they walked over to his van. Ryan opened the passenger door and Jackie slid into the seat. He climbed in the driver's side and started the engine.

Chapter Fifty-Nine
Man Trouble and Awkward Moments

After tossing and turning all night, Beth drove to work with a heavy heart.

She knew from the rota that Jackie was working days. She didn't have a clue what she was going to say to her when she did bump into her.

As it happened, she didn't have long to wait. As soon as she stepped through the door, she spotted Jackie in the corridor, pushing Bert in a wheelchair. In true Bert style, it had a Union Jack strapped to the handle.

Taking a deep breath, she walked over to meet them, and knelt down next to the wheelchair, her face creasing with concern as she saw his usual jolly face looked gaunt. 'What on earth have you done?'

'I was trying to get a moth out of me room, ducks. Being a silly old codger, I tripped over me chest of drawers.'

'Oh, no. Poor you,' she sympathised. 'You should've rung your buzzer, not tried to do it yourself.'

'I ain't gonna trouble someone over a bloomin' moth, ducks.'

Shaking her head, she smiled at him affectionately. 'Well, no more acrobatics,' she said in a mock-stern tone. 'Just ring that buzzer if you need anything.'

'I could do with one of them massages I've been hearing about, if you're offerin', ducks.'

'Of course, Bert,' she promised.

Looking up, her eyes locked with Jackie's.

Jackie looked away and busied herself straightening the pole of the Union Jack.

*

During break time, Beth joined the ressies for a drink and a natter.

'What's the matter, dear?' Vi asked, as soon as she saw her.

Blimey, Beth thought to herself. There she was, trying her best to look normal. Was she really so transparent?

She painted on a smile. 'Nothing's the matter, Vi. I'm fine.'

Vi leaned forward in her chair. 'Don't you worry, I know all about it.'

Beth's forehead creased into a puzzled frown.

'You've got man trouble,' Vi whispered conspiratorially. 'I can tell a mile off. They're all trouble, if you ask me.'

She'd get no argument from her on that one.

Chapter Sixty
Distress and Revelations

Beth's thoughts were in turmoil as she drove home. Was it possible Jackie didn't know Ryan was her neighbour? she wondered. Yet if that was the case, it didn't explain her being so furtive, and it certainly didn't explain why she'd been ignoring her.

Another thought squeezed into her brain, one she wished she could ignore, but it was both persistent and important. She had feelings for Ryan. They were good friends. They'd shared a kiss that she knew would have led to more. Yet she wasn't actually "seeing" him in the romantic sense, was she? OK, she fancied the pants off him if she was honest with herself, and sometimes they'd walk Rodney together. There was no doubt they enjoyed each other's company, but he'd never suggested a proper date. Perhaps he considered the kiss to be a mistake? She thought again about that passionate kiss, and how he'd held her hand when they'd visited Upton. They'd shared a lovely day, but he hadn't made any attempt to kiss her again, had he?

She felt stupid and angry with herself. Why had she been so naive? Was she really that desperate? Ryan was a kind person, a good friend. He was also a free agent.

Before she could change her mind, she turned the car around and headed to the Old Mill.

She couldn't let this situation with Jackie continue; they'd been best friends for years. She'd only known Ryan Morgan for five minutes.

Swallowing hard to quell her nervousness, she walked towards the building. She'd always been close to Jackie – they were like sisters. Now she felt as though she was meeting a stranger.

To her surprise, Ryan burst through the entrance door. She was glad she'd applied a fresh coat of lipstick and blusher before leaving work, and hoped the turmoil in her mind wasn't mirrored in her face. Ryan spotted her instantly and walked up to meet her. As he got nearer, she spotted Jackie hovering in the doorway.

'Hi, Beth,' he said tentatively.

Her heart was pounding so hard she thought he must be able to hear it.

Before she could respond, Jackie came out of the building and walked over to join them.

Beth stared from one to the other.

Jackie sighed. 'I think we've got some explaining to do...'

'I think that might be a good idea,' Beth said solemnly.

'Can you give us a minute, please, Ry?' Jackie asked him.

So its Ry now, is it? Beth thought crossly.

'I'll wait in the van.' he said, giving Beth a small smile as he left them to it.

She hitched her bag up on her shoulder; her stride dignified and self-assured as she followed Jackie towards the entrance. Well, at least, it would've been dignified if she hadn't tripped over the kerb. With a yelp, she automatically put out her hands to save herself.

Leaving his van door open, Ryan dashed to her aid. 'Beth! Are you alright?'

'I'm fine.' She scrambled to her feet and gathered up the contents of her bag.

'Here, let me help you.' He knelt down beside her, and, to her horror, he swooped over and picked up her lipstick and a tampon tube. She grabbed them from him, humiliation stinging along with her grazed knees.

Jackie led the way through the familiar hallway and into her sitting room, gesturing for Beth to sit. 'Your poor knees – shall I get you some TCP?'

Beth shook her head, biting back tears. 'All I want to know is: what's going on?'

Jackie fingered the charms on her silver Pandora bracelet and heaved out a sigh. 'I don't know where to start,' she said. 'I should've told you before –'

Knowing what was coming, Beth drew a deep breath. 'Look, Jacks,' she interrupted. 'It's fine. Ryan's a free agent and so are you. You're my dearest friend. I just wish you'd told me you were seeing him. There was no need for all this secrecy and bad feeling.'

Jackie flopped onto the sofa in a daze. 'You think I'm seeing Ryan?'

Beth sighed. 'As I said, it's fine.'

'Oh, God! – It really isn't like that –' Jackie hesitated for a long moment. 'The thing is, I've – '

Beth fidgeted uncomfortably. 'You've what?'

As the words left her lips, she saw that Jackie was trembling.

'There's no easy way to tell you this.' Jackie begun, her voice cracked with emotion. 'That's why I've been putting it off for so long. When I was fifteen, I was abused by my stepdad.'

Beth felt the blood drain from her face as she grappled to comprehend the enormity of what she was hearing. Her legs shook as she rose from her chair and sat next to Jackie, covering her hand with her own. 'I'm so sorry, Jacks,' she said softly.

They sat in silence, both occupied with their own haunted thoughts.

'There was a piece in the newspaper saying he'd died in a road accident,' Jackie explained. 'When I saw it, all the feelings of shame and disgust came flooding back. I couldn't face telling anyone – not even you. I wanted – *needed* - to feel normal –'

Beth squeezed her friend's hand in silent understanding: *She did see.* She just wished Jackie could've confided in her.

'You know me better than anyone,' Jackie ploughed on bravely. 'If I'd tried to be normal, you'd have seen straight through it. I haven't been able to acknowledge what happened for years. When I was fifteen, I plucked up the courage to tell my mother. She didn't, or wouldn't, believe me. After being with Bret for a year, I finally managed to tell him what had happened. He repaid me by sleeping with someone else. After that, I didn't think I could ever face telling anyone again.'

'That must've been so terrible. Don't continue if you don't –'

Jackie cut her off. 'I need to tell you, now,' she said determinedly. 'It was late night Christmas shopping and Mum was working on the cosmetics counter at Boots. Billy, my stepdad, came into my bedroom. He said it was *"our little secret, and I mustn't tell Mum because she'd be angry".* He told me no one would believe me and I'd end up in a care home away from my Mum and my friends. I couldn't sleep for worrying. Every day I'd pray Mum wouldn't have to work late – but she often did.'

Feeling sick to the pit of her stomach, Beth squeezed Jackie's hand. She knew she had to keep it together for her friend's sake.

'I tried to handle things my own way,' Jackie continued. 'He made me feel like it was my fault. He was so *normal* whenever Mum or anyone else was around. Sometimes I thought it must be me, that somehow I'd imagined the whole nightmare. It was like I was living two different lives - the normal family one and the shameful secret one.'

Beth fought back the tears of rage and sadness that threatened to spill down her cheeks. 'He was a predator, Jacks,' she said. 'He preyed on the vulnerability of a child.''

Jackie bit her bottom lip. 'I'd somehow managed to blank it out completely, pretend it had never happened, but, after reading about his death, I realised I needed to face it – secrets gnaw away at your mind. I knew I needed help.'

'You do know it was never your fault, don't you?' Beth asked softly.

She nodded. 'The reason I needed that day off work is because I was due to meet with my support worker,' she continued. 'And that turned out to be Ryan.' She was unaware of Beth's eyes widening.

'He's been helping me deal with the disgust and confusion I've lived with all these years,' she explained.

She told Beth that one night stands had become her default mode; she'd used men in the way she herself had felt used, but this way, she'd been the one in control of the situation. If anyone got too close to her, she'd instantly close ranks. She'd vowed to herself when Bret cheated that no one would ever make her feel worthless again.

Eventually, Jackie beckoned Ryan back inside. Beth felt an overwhelming sense of wanting to care for her dearest friend, and to make everything better, although, of course, she knew this wasn't possible. She also felt affection and admiration for Ryan, as a caring, kind and empathetic man.

Jackie also told her how she'd been pretty freaked out at first when she'd realised Ryan knew Beth, and Beth wondered how she'd found out.

As if sensing her friend's thoughts, Jackie glanced over at Ryan, whose cheeks were tinged pink. 'I'd told Ryan my car had been MOT'd and he offered to take me to collect it. We talked, and I asked him what he was up to for the rest of the day. He said he was dog walking for someone special. There aren't many dogs around called Rodney, are there?'

*

Beth stayed with her long after Ryan had gone. 'I'll never be able to forget what happened,' Jackie said. 'But I won't let him ruin my life.'

Beth hugged her. 'Too right, you won't,' she said, struggling to keep her emotions at bay. 'You're Jackie Clarke, the strongest, kindest person I know.'

Jackie managed a weak smile. 'I can't change the past, but I can take control of my future.'

Beth was humbled by her friend's courage. 'Would you like me to stay over?' she asked.

'I'd like that very much, but what about Rodney?'

'I won't disturb Ryan again; he'll probably be asleep by now. I'll ask Dad if he'd mind picking Rodney up and I'll collect him tomorrow.'

Chapter Sixty-One
Soul Searching and Excitable Humans

When Beth walked into her parents' sitting room, Dad glanced up at her and folded up his copy of the Daily Mirror. 'Hello, love.'

'Hi, Dad – where's Mum and Aunt Lena?' 'They're out choosing some curtains for Lena's flat. 'Come to take the boy home, have you?'

'Yes - he'd better come back home to guard the flat and earn his keep.'

'Rodney's a lovely dog with many qualities, but guard dog's certainly not one of them!'

Beth laughed for the first time in the past couple of days.

Dad looked at her and sighed. 'Your Mum's told me about Jackie,' he said gravely. 'What an absolutely dreadful business. I wish I could have got my hands on the evil bastard before he'd had that car crash – but she's a strong woman, Beth. She's got you looking out for her. It's time for you both to look to the future now, my girl. It goes without saying that your mum and I are always here for you both.'

Swallowing down a lump of emotion, she gave Dad a hug.

When she got home, she pulled on her wellies and put Rodney onto his lead and then headed into the field.

*

The sun's rays bathed everything in a warm, golden glow; people walked their dogs and threw balls and Frisbees. Everything went on as normal, yet things had changed more than she ever could have imagined.

As she strolled along with Rodney, she did some soul searching. Completely unknown to her, her best friend had been to hell and back, yet she was bravely looking to her future.

Beth decided it was time she faced her future with such bravery and determination too.

Sometimes, she realised, she lost sight of how lucky she was. She'd had a carefree childhood with a family who supported her through everything. She also had Jackie, her wonderful friend.

'I'm going to do it, boy!' she cried, much to the amazement of passers-by. 'I'm going to college!'

Rodney looked up at her, his expression seeming to say, 'Humans! You're all so over-excitable.'

Beth spotted Ryan heading across the field towards her. He waved in acknowledgement and quickened his pace. She waited nervously for him to catch up. As lovely as she thought Ryan was, she wondered if it was too soon to go headlong into another relationship when there was still so much about herself she had yet to learn.

Catching them up, he knelt down, and fondled the dog's ears. 'I'm sorry things have been difficult between you and Jackie,' he told her.

'Don't apologise. I understand about confidentiality. Jackie's told me what a help you've been.'

Ryan shook his head. 'It took a great deal of courage for her to ask for help,' he said as he fell into step with her.

'What made you become a volunteer?' Beth asked.

'It's a long story,' he replied quietly. 'Although I trust you enough to share it with you, if that's OK.'

Looking up at his anxious face, she placed her fingers lightly on his hand. 'Only tell me if you want to.'

He nodded and drew in a deep breath before he spoke again. 'When I was eleven, I was abused by a neighbour.'

Beth gave an involuntary gasp. 'Oh, God, Ryan – that's awful – I'm so sorry -'

He put up his hand to stop her. 'I became a volunteer because I understand what people who've suffered at the hands of an abuser are going through. I don't know what I'd have done without the support I had. My sister Meg persuaded me to get help, but I couldn't face telling anyone what had happened for a long time.'

Beth shook her head. 'I can't even begin to imagine how you must feel,' she said sadly.

He heaved a sigh. 'I buried it deep inside me. In my teens, I guess I was what you'd call a wild child; I know I caused my parents no end of grief. Then, when I was nineteen, I had a nightmare. Meg found me curled up and crying like a baby. I found myself pouring it all out, how a neighbour, a man we'd known for years, asked if I'd go and help him find his missing dog. I was eleven years old, and I'd gone willingly.'

'You were a child,' Beth reiterated, '...you trusted him. I can't find words to say how angry I feel.'

'Sometimes there are no words. Just being able to open up and talk to someone who assures you it wasn't your fault; that what happened to you doesn't define you as a person, is priceless.'

Chapter Sixty-Two
Something Money Just Can't Buy

Consumed with anger and horrified by what had happened to both Jackie and Ryan, Beth wished she could change the past, yet she knew that was impossible. All she could do was be there and support them in whatever way she could.

On her way to work, she parked her car and called into the Co-op to buy a box of Quality Street, Bert's favourites, hoping to cheer him up after his accident. He hadn't been the same chirpy chap since it happened.

Taking her place in the queue, she couldn't help noticing the lady in front looked as though she was in for a treat. Her basket was crammed with goodies: chocolate bars and cream cakes, together with a couple of family sized bags of crisps.

The woman unceremoniously heaved her wire mesh basket onto the counter and fished around in her Prada handbag. After much rummaging, she produced a fifty pound note.

The counter assistant totalled up her goods – eighteen pounds forty's worth. She took the woman's money. 'Haven't you got anything smaller, love?' she said, scrutinising the note.

'No, I haven't!'

Beth's eyes widened; she'd know that voice anywhere.

Emily heaved up her full carriers and turned around.

Beth struggled to hide her shock; Emily's huge pregnancy bump looked so strange on someone normally so petite.

Emily blushed furiously, struggling to stuff some of her junk food further down inside her bag.

Beth smiled awkwardly. 'Hello, Emily.'

'Oh– err – hello,' Emily muttered. 'I'm just doing some shopping – for a friend.'

'Have you got the day off?'

Emily shook her head. 'Paul's such a worrier - he's insisted I finish before my maternity leave starts.' She shoved her change into her purse. 'Look, I must dash – he'll be wondering where I am.'

She hurried out of the shop before Beth could say goodbye.

Never in a million years would she have believed anyone if they'd told her she'd feel sorry for Emily, but right now, she did. It was ironic to think that she'd considered her to be everything she was not: clever, successful and independent. She thought back to what Sandra had said at her interview at Holly Mount, which now felt like a lifetime ago, but in reality it was only several months: *"We can teach you everything about practical care, but what we can't teach you is compassion and empathy"*. She was hit by the realisation that she had something precious, something money couldn't buy.

Chapter Sixty-Three
Paul

Emily sat stuffing her face, yet again, with pickled onion Monster Munch. Jesus! What was wrong with her? Paul knew about pregnant women eating for two, but Emily seemed to be eating for twenty-two. He slammed his keys down on the kitchen counter.

Emily gave him a tentative smile as she scrunched up the empty packet. 'Can you pick up some more of these when you do the shopping, dahling? They didn't have any at the local shop.'

He gave a vague nod in response. The bloody weekly shop! How he hated trawling round pushing a trolley with the obligatory wonky wheel. He could always guarantee some toddler would be screaming or barging a trolley into his ankles.

Paul's memory skimmed back to his old life, a previous existence which now felt a million light years away. Beth had never expected him to do the supermarket shop, not even when she'd been pregnant.

Emily heaved herself up from the kitchen stool, her face brightening. 'You'll never guess what –' she said, her voice high-pitched with excitement. 'Jules Russell-Smythe's expecting! Isn't it wonderful?'

Expecting what? Paul wondered vaguely. His heart dipped as the penny dropped. He was aware that Emily's mouth was still moving, but he only took in a fraction of what she said.

'Just think, we can hold a joint baby shower and our children can start pre-school together,' she gabbled, gathering momentum. 'We could go on holidays, too. Our little Hermione will always have a playmate.'

Paul envisaged his nappy-filled future with Emily and her pal and their two "mini-me's" dressed in tots' designer gear, throwing tantrums about who was the better dressed, who was the first to be potty trained and so on. The list of competitiveness was endless.

He thought of his grown-up children and the quiet life he and Beth could be living.

How the hell was he going to cope? To make matters worse, if that was possible; with the way his luck was going he felt certain that Charles Mortimer would outlive them all.

He made his excuses to Emily and went out to his car.

*

Beth picked up her phone on the third ring.

'Beth,' Paul blurted. 'Please hear me out – I really think we can make this – us –work. All I'm asking is that you give things another try.'

She gasped. 'The answer's "no", Paul. I can't

believe you'd think I'd even consider it. You've got responsibilities – a life with Emily and a new baby on the way. Believe it or not, it's not all about you! I've got my life to live, too – one I'm working hard to build.'

'Look – just give me a chance, I'll explain everything – '

'It's OK,' Beth told him, her voice devoid of emotion. 'I don't need an explanation. It's simple: you wanted a new life and that's what you've got.'

'Now wait a minute –'

'Press three for goodbye, Paul.'

'*W h a t?*' What on earth are you talking about?'

'It doesn't matter. Goodbye, Paul.'

Chapter Sixty-Four
Made for Sharing

Beth smiled to herself as she walked into the residents' lounge. Bert's wheelchair stood folded against the wall; he said he'd soon be back on his feet.

She looked around at the handful of residents. Some were simply gazing into space, Maud was knitting a never-ending scarf and Vi was seated in her usual chair in the far corner. The old lady rocked to and fro, muttering to herself. Beth realized she was having one of her bad days when she became agitated at the slightest thing.

Vi's daughter, Janet, scurried into the room. 'You're an early bird this morning,' Beth remarked.

She stopped in her tracks. 'You don't know, do you?'

Beth frowned. 'Know what?'

'I'm very sorry to tell you that Bert died last night.'

Beth's mouth dropped open. Janet took her by the arm, and led her to a chair.

'*How?*'

'He had a heart attack. Mum keeps asking for him. Sandra called me in to sit with her for a while.'

Beth took a few minutes to regain her composure. She rose from the chair, walked over to Vi and took her frail hand in her own. The old lady stared up at her with red-rimmed eyes. 'They said Bert's gone away, but Mr. Dervischi will look after him now, won't he?'

Beth gave her a wobbly smile. 'I'm sure he will.' She handed her the Quality Street. And Violet put the box in her lap. 'I'll save some for Bert and Mr. Dervischi.'

Fred Thompson, dapper as always in a white cotton shirt and navy silk cravat, walked into the room. 'Ooh, chocolates!'

Vi hugged the box protectively to her chest.

'Don't be a spoilsport, my dear. Surely you can spare one?'

'You can have *one*,' she said reluctantly. 'Don't take the strawberry creams. They're Bert's favourite.'

Beth walked out of the lounge, glancing once more at Bert's folded up wheelchair and realising that the Union Jack now hung forlornly.

*

Alone in the staffroom, she closed her eyes, imagining Bert's reaction if he'd seen Vi giving away the chocolates to his love rival. At first he'd act all cross. She smiled to herself at the thought. But after enjoying a bit of drama, he'd have said something in true Bert style: 'Go on, then. They're made for sharing – it says so on the telly.'

*

Driving away from Holly Mount, tears burned at the back of her eyes. Why did bad things happen to good people?

She decided to call in on Jackie – knowing how much her friend thought of Bert, she didn't want her to hear the sad news from anyone else.

One look at her friend's blotchy face told Beth that Jackie already knew. 'Sandra rang,' Jackie told her. 'It's hard to believe Bert's gone.'

She asked Beth to stay for tea, saying she could do with some company. Feeling the need for some company herself, she readily agreed.

'I know you're gutted about Bert, but how are you feeling in yourself?' Beth asked, as they ate beans on toast.

Jackie pushed the beans around her plate with a fork. 'I understand that being young and vulnerable was a valid reason why I didn't tell anyone.'

Beth put down her knife and fork; she didn't have much of an appetite either. 'People like Bill Parsons's prey on vulnerability, Jacks. Think about what you'd say to a child who'd been through what you have; you'd tell them they weren't the grown-ups – they weren't responsible.'

*

When she left Jackie's, she didn't head home. She wanted to see her parents, so she called Ryan to check it was OK for him to take Rodney up to his flat for a while.

As soon as Mum saw her tear-stained face, she gave her a hug.

Beth told her all about Bert. 'I couldn't let Jackie know that I'm this upset. She's got so much to cope with. I can't get my head around such bad things happening to good people; life's so unfair.'

Mum slipped her arm around her daughter's shoulders. 'Life's bittersweet, love; yet without sadness, we'd never know happiness. Wicked things like what happened to Jackie should never, ever happen, but you've both got the rest of your lives to live and you should try and make the most of them.'

Beth had a little cry on Mum's shoulder.

As she drove home, she reflected on what Mum had said. Perhaps her mum wasn't so different to Aunt Lena after all.

Chapter Sixty-Five
Unwelcome Communication

Before she'd knocked on Ryan's door, with the absence of any barking, Beth guessed Ryan was walking Rodney. She went back downstairs, glad of the time alone to compose herself.

Ryan had collected up her post and propped it up by the kettle. She picked it up, absently flicking through the junk mail before coming upon a formal brown envelope. She tore it open. Her eyes widened in disbelief as she read the letter. The landlord was selling up; his wife was ill and needed to go into a care home. He needed the money from the sale of the house to cover the fees.

She'd barely had time to register all this when Ryan arrived with Rodney, who gave her his usual enthusiastic greeting.

Ryan's forehead creased into a frown. He inclined his head towards the letter. 'I wanted to warn you,' he said, 'but I'm obviously too late. What are you going to do?'

She shrugged. 'I've no idea ... I guess I'll have to look for somewhere that'll accept Rodney and me. It's ironic; I never thought I'd settle here and now I can't imagine living anywhere else. What will you do?'

Ryan sighed. 'I'm off to Canada next week. Meg will store my furniture and I can stay with her when I get back until I can find somewhere. I'm more worried about you.'

Chapter Sixty-Six
Karma and Wobbly Eyes

Beth asked Mum if she and Rodney could stay with them while she looked for another place to live.

'Of course you can, love. You know you're always welcome. Aunt Lena's moving into her new flat soon, so there'll be plenty of space.'

She bit back her disappointment and frustration. She was lucky and she knew it; having a family who cared meant more than anything, yet, at the same time, she couldn't help feeling down-hearted. She was fast approaching her forties and having to rely on her parents yet again.

'Thanks, Mum, I don't know what I'd do without you and Dad.'

To take her mind off things, Beth asked Ryan if he'd look after Rodney and she and Jackie headed into town. She needed to buy stationery for college; there was just over a month before her course started.

They wandered around WH Smith, looking at what she might need.

Jackie tapped Beth's shoulder. 'Look!' She held up a pink furry pencil case with a pair of wobbly eyes. 'Isn't it cute?'

Beth grinned. 'It is, but I'll look like I'm about six years old if I take that!'

Jackie put the pencil case back on the shelf. 'I loved choosing a new pencil case when I was a kid,' she said wistfully. 'Before term started, Mum would take me to get my school uniform and stationery – and he never came.'

Beth's heart lurched for her friend.

'I always had my feet measured for a new pair of Clark's school shoes, too.' Jackie continued, with a faint smile at the memory.

'Yes, me too, although I never wanted the ones that Mum chose for me. I'd want patent strappy ones with heels and bows, not horrible dog poo brown ones with fiddly laces!'

'D'you fancy a coffee and a cake?' Beth suggested, a while later.

'That sounds like a plan.'

Beth paid for her purchases: a selection of brightly coloured A4 folders, reams of lined paper, assorted pens and pencils, the obligatory pencil sharpener, rubber, ruler and – of course – a pencil case. Much to Jackie's disappointment, she'd opted for a clear plastic one and not the pink furry case.

They headed into the café in Marks & Spencer's on the High Street. Beth ordered a latté and a large slice of carrot cake. Jackie ordered a toasted tea cake with butter and blackcurrant jam.

They both reasoned the food would give them

one of their five a day - it would just taste better.

As Beth drained the last of her coffee, Jackie dipped her hand into her bag and produced a small package. It was wrapped in cream coloured paper embellished with pink roses.

She raised her eyebrows. 'What's this?'

'Just open it and see!'

Beth ran her thumbnail along the sellotaped seam and carefully lifted out a small gold box. She read the copperplate script printed on the attached card. It was called a "Karma" card, explaining the concept of Karma. She read aloud, *'An ancient Indian notion that suggests a person can change their fate based on an ongoing cycle of their own conduct.'*

Intrigued, she lifted the lid to reveal a necklace made up of five solid silver rings suspended on a fine chain. 'It's beautiful, Jacks,' she whispered. 'Thank you so much.'

*

Taking a packet of minced meat from the fridge, Beth mixed it together with tomatoes and red, yellow and green peppers, garlic paste and onions. She set about preparing spaghetti bolognaise. She'd invited Ryan to dinner; a thank you for him looking after Rodney.

Mixed emotions bore down on her about the evening ahead; Ryan was great company and she felt comfortable and happy whenever they were together, but so much was happening in her life right now– she wondered once again about zooming headlong into a relationship.

Her eyes smarted as she sliced through the raw onions. What she definitely didn't want was not to have him in her life at all, but was she being selfish to want him there for her, yet not to feel ready to offer him anything more than friendship – at least for the time being?

Hearing a knock on the door, she put down the onion and dabbed at her eyes with a tea towel as she walked along the hallway to answer it.

Her "hello" died on her lips when she saw her parents and Aunt Lena; they hadn't mentioned they might call over. Beth was concerned that something might be wrong.

Mum smiled and she breathed a sigh of relief, though Mum's smile faded rapidly. 'Have you been crying, love?'

'Oh, no!' Beth laughed for good measure as she ushered them inside. 'I'm peeling wretched onions! How are you doing, Aunt Lena?'

'I'm feeling so much better, thank you, Beth. I asked your dad if we could drive out to see you. I wanted to tell you in person how pleased and proud I am to hear you're going back to college.'

Beth smiled, happy her aunt was pleased.

Aunt Lena cleared her throat. 'I also thought you'd be keen to meet your new landlord.'

Beth's mouth fell open as realisation slowly

dawned. 'What? – OMG! It's you! You've bought the building!'

Her aunt beamed. 'I got a good price for my house and I've got my nice little place sorted. I've decided to invest the remainder of the equity – in this place!'

'I can't believe it!' Beth enveloped her in a hug.

'I haven't got children of my own, but you've been like a daughter to me, Beth. I can't think of any better use for my money than seeing you happy.' She thrust an envelope into Beth's hand. 'I've popped a cheque in here for you, a treat for you to use as you wish. Book yourself and Jackie a holiday or something before you get on with your studies.

She shook her head. 'Oh, gosh, this is just too much! I don't know how I can ever thank you.'

'No thanks are needed,' she insisted. 'It's my money and I want to see you have some enjoyment while I'm alive. I've got more than enough to keep me comfortable.'

Beth expelled a long breath as she looked at her parents and aunt. 'Thank you.' 'Thank you all so much for everything.'

She popped the envelope behind the floral tea caddy. 'Why don't you stay for dinner? Ryan will back with Rodney soon, so he'll join us.'

'You don't want us all here, love,' Dad said. 'We only came round as your aunt wanted to surprise you.'

'It's a surprise alright - the biggest surprise I've

ever had! Please stay and have dinner so you can break the good news to Ryan.'

'We don't want you to go to any trouble,' Mum protested. 'We'll pick something up from the chippie on our way home.'

'It's no trouble,' Beth told her firmly. 'I've made enough spag bol to feed a small army!'

Ryan and Rodney arrived, and soon the flat was buzzing with easy, pleasant conversation. Everyone enjoyed the tasty meal accompanied with garlic bread and a bottle of Sauvignon Blanc.

Ryan was over the moon about the news and promised Lena he'd sort out all the handyman jobs around the place, as well as tending the garden, once he got back from Canada. If only the worry about losing his friendship wasn't nagging at her, Beth would have thoroughly enjoyed the evening.

She knew her parents and her aunt thought a lot of Ryan. They might think she was being silly, but clichéd as it sounded, it was time for her to be true to herself.

Circumstances tonight had prevented her from having a heart to heart with him, but she'd have to face it sooner rather than later.

Chapter Sixty-Seven
Padlocks and Commitment

'It's a lovely day – how d'you fancy taking Rodney for a walk along the river?' Ryan suggested.

'That would be great,' Beth said, although her stomach twisted with nerves. There was no more putting it off; she needed to clear the air. If she lost his friendship she'd be hurt and disappointed, but, at the end of the day, she couldn't commit to something or lead him on when she didn't know how she felt about things herself.

They strolled together over the Diglis Bridge, breathing in the fresh air and enjoying the feel of the sun on their backs. Ryan reached into the back pocket of his jeans. 'I've got a surprise for you.'

As he produced a heart-shaped padlock and key, Beth's heart sank. Oh, God, what was she going to do if he declared his undying love for her and fastened the padlock onto the bridge?

Ryan grinned as Beth lifted up the label attached and read the message written on it in marker pen: "*Beth & Rodney. 2017*".

Her face broke into a wide smile. 'That's brilliant! Thank you!' She laughed with relief as they chose a spot for it and fastened it securely.

As they reached the other side of the river they strolled along the pathway. Beth's tummy churned when she thought of their impending conversation; what if she'd got it all wrong and Ryan didn't want to be with her? Surely though, after what Jackie had told her and her own intuition, she couldn't have read too much into it, could she?

Ryan raised a speculative brow. 'Is everything OK, Beth?'

'I just wanted to talk – about us,' she said, in a small voice. 'I don't know how to put this, and perhaps I'm being too presumptuous, but I value your friendship and I don't want to lose it.'

He stopped walking and took hold of Beth's hands in his. He gazed intently into her emerald eyes. 'For a minute I thought we were going to have the "It's not you, it's me" conversation.'

'No – it's not like that at all... I really like you; I think you know that. It's just I don't think I'm ready to be *with* someone.'

Ryan studied her worried face, a smile playing on his lips. 'You've been worried about telling me this because you think I'll want nothing to do with you if I can't take you to bed?'

She blushed and dropped her gaze.

'I do have feelings for you, Beth: strong ones.' He put his arm around her shoulders. 'But the fact is I don't know where we go from here. We've both been through so much and the last thing I want to do is rush you into anything. Anyway,' he said, with a grin, 'patience is my middle name.'

'And I don't want to let you down,' Beth said sincerely. 'I know it's a cliché, but I want to find myself. I want to settle into my new life before I can consider anything else.'

He nodded slowly. 'I do understand,' he said softly. 'When my ex-fiancée slept with my brother, Josh, and fell pregnant with Louise, it knocked me for six. It's taken me a long time to feel anything for a woman.'

'Oh God, Ryan, I didn't know. I'm so sorry –'

He put his finger to her lips. 'I'm happy to be your friend, Beth. As you know, I'm in Canada for six months; then maybe we can see how things go when I get back. No pressure.'

Knowing she was going to miss him, Beth swallowed a lump of sadness. 'That's a deal,' she replied over-brightly.

He kissed her cheek. 'You bet it is. Although don't forget, Louise still wants to meet Rodney.'

Chapter Sixty-Eight
Ryan

Ryan took some flour and a bag of mixed fruit out of the cupboard.

What had happened still hurt. After his childhood experience, he'd put his trust in Sarah and she'd let him down badly. But he'd done enough soul searching to last him a lifetime.

As he weighed out the ingredients, he reflected on things. He was glad Josh had married Sarah. It would have all felt so pointless if it had been a one night stand. He loved Louise dearly; she was the good thing to come out of it. The depression he'd gone through after two heartbreaking ordeals was something he wouldn't wish on anyone.

It wasn't totally selfless when Ryan had become a volunteer; he'd realised that sometimes you have to experience heartache and healing before you can help someone else do the same. He spooned the mixture into his loaf tin. This would be the last cake he'd be baking for a while.

Chapter Sixty-Nine
Good Friends and Pharaohs

When Beth told Jackie about her conversation with Ryan, her friend understood her need for space, yet she felt sad at the same time. 'He'll be back,' Jackie said. 'For what it's worth, I think you're made for each other.'

'I hope so, Jacks, I really do, but as you've said to me before, we've got a lot of life to live, missus!' She handed Jackie a pale blue envelope. 'We can start with this.'

Jackie frowned. 'What is it?'

'Open it and see,' Beth said, mimicking her friend's words to her.

Tearing open the envelope, her blue eyes widened as she read the e-mail Beth had printed out. '*OMG*!' she squealed. 'You've booked us a holiday in Egypt!'

'We go a week tomorrow!'

Jackie pinched herself to make sure she wasn't dreaming. 'Ooh, that's fantastic – I can't believe it!'

Beth was surprised when Jackie's face fell.

'How can I get Sandra to agree to my taking more time off?' she asked worriedly.

'You don't have to! I've already cleared it with

her and Mum and Dad are going to look after Rodney for me, so it's all sorted.'

Jackie gasped. 'Blimey – I'm speechless…'

'That'll make a change – '

'You cheeky mare!'

Chapter Seventy
The Magic of New Beginnings

Beth crammed her third pair of high heels into her suitcase. 'What else do you think I should take?'

Jackie laughed. 'Well, you've packed everything but the kitchen sink, but you should definitely take out that old granny cossie and put this in instead.' She dangled Beth's long-forgotten bikini top on her fingers.

Beth frowned. 'D'you really think so?'

'Definitely!' she insisted. 'You've got a great figure and I'm sure you'll get plenty of opportunities to show it off.'

Taking the bikini from her, Beth held it against her body. It was pretty and feminine in shocking pink with tiny silver flowers. 'Paul never liked me wearing it,' she said. 'He said it made me look cheap – and showed every lump and bump.'

Jackie grabbed it and shoved it into the case. 'And you care because? –'

'That's the point, Jacks,' she said breezily. 'I really don't give a monkey's!'

'Good! Now, are you absolutely sure you've got everything? Passport? Tickets?'

'Yep. They're all here.'

Dad was dropping them off at Birmingham Airport. Before he arrived, Beth scanned her bedroom, doing a final check to make sure she'd got everything she needed.

*

'D'you think there's a chance you and Ryan might get together when he's back from Canada?' Jackie asked as they settled back in their seats and jetted off for the sun.

Beth sighed wistfully. 'I honestly don't know, Jacks. I'm glad to have him in my life, but it's as Aunt Lena says: if it's meant to be, it'll happen. None of us knows what the future holds, but I do know one thing for sure.'

'What's that?'

'Whatever happens and wherever we end up, you'll always be my dearest friend.'

Jackie raised her plastic tumbler of wine. 'I'll drink to that.'

Author Bio

Diane was born in the West Midlands. She has a background in counselling and voluntary work and a great passion for writing fiction and poetry. She has three grown-up children; Amanda, Stephanie and Christopher, and a grandson, Oliver. She now lives in Worcester, with her Jack Russell cross Ruby. This is her first novel.

Facebook: Diane Need - Author Page
Twitter: @DianeNeed

Made in the USA
Middletown, DE
24 April 2017